"Do you have a girlfriend?" Layla asked, wincing slightly.

Hunter tossed a kernel of popcorn ~~~~~~~~~~~ as she neatly caught it, before an~~~~~~~~~~~~~~~~~~~~~~~~~~

Heaven help her, ~~~~~~~~~~~~~~~~

Then, because she ~~~~~~~~~~~~~~~~~~~~~~~~~~~h get ahead of her co~~~~~~~~~~~~~~~~~~~~~~~~~e an attractive man with a ~~~~~~~~~~~~~~~~own home."

He laughed. "If I didn~~~~~~~~~~er, I'd ask you if you're applying for the positi~~~~

Though she knew he was only teasing, heat suffused her. Embarrassment mingled with desire and a kind of nervous anticipation that made her go dry in the mouth.

"Maybe I am." She batted her eyelashes at him. Though she'd never been good at flirting, ever, something about this man and the way he teased made her feel comfortable and safe. And wanted.

His gaze zeroed in on her mouth. He scooted closer, dislodging a disgruntled Goose. The basset jumped to the floor and headed off toward the kitchen, probably in search of water.

"You've got a bit of popcorn there," he said, his voice husky. He reached out with one finger to brush it off. Enthralled despite herself, she opened her mouth, her heart hammering in her chest.

"Layla," he groaned. And then he kissed her.

* * *

The Coltons of Red Ridge: A killer's on the loose and love is on the line

* * *

If you're on Twitter, tell us what you think of Harlequin Romantic Suspense! #harlequinromsuspense

Dear Reader,

I love dogs. I volunteer for a dog rescue. I've trained and obedience shown dogs. So imagine my delight when I got to write about a dog as amazing as Goose! My editor for this particular book had done her research, which she kindly shared with me. I had no idea dogs could be trained to detect computer storage drives! Fun and fascinating, to say the least. And give me a hero who partners with a police dog like this, and I'm in love.

This story was so enjoyable to write. Layla Colton is a many-faceted, successful career woman, yet she'd never felt able to earn her father's approval. And Hunter Black is her opposite in many ways. Sexy, confident and capable, he stands by her when she's falsely accused of a crime she didn't commit.

Add in a serial killer, a town on edge and many obstacles to their love, and you have quite the entertaining ride, I hope you enjoy reading about Layla and Hunter's love story—and Goose—as much as I enjoyed writing it.

Karen Whiddon

COLTON'S CHRISTMAS COP

Karen Whiddon

HARLEQUIN®ROMANTIC SUSPENSE

Special thanks and acknowledgment are given to
Karen Whiddon for her contribution to
The Coltons of Red Ridge miniseries.

ISBN-13: 978-1-335-45662-5

Colton's Christmas Cop

Copyright © 2018 by Harlequin Books S.A.

Recycling programs
for this product may
not exist in your area.

Printed in U.S.A.

Karen Whiddon started weaving fanciful tales for her younger brothers at the age of eleven. Amid the gorgeous Catskill Mountains, then the majestic Rocky Mountains, she fueled her imagination with the natural beauty surrounding her. Karen now lives in north Texas, writes full-time and volunteers for a boxer dog rescue. She shares her life with her hero of a husband and four to five dogs, depending on if she is fostering. You can email Karen at kwhiddon1@aol.com. Fans can also check out her website, karenwhiddon.com.

Books by Karen Whiddon

Harlequin Romantic Suspense

The Coltons of Red Ridge

Colton's Christmas Cop

The CEO's Secret Baby
The Cop's Missing Child
The Millionaire Cowboy's Secret
Texas Secrets, Lovers' Lies
The Rancher's Return
The Texan's Return
Wyoming Undercover
The Texas Soldier's Son

The Coltons of Texas

Runaway Colton

The Coltons of Oklahoma

The Temptation of Dr. Colton

The Coltons: Return to Wyoming

A Secret Colton Baby

Visit the Author Profile page at Harlequin.com for more titles.

To all the dedicated dog rescuers everywhere.
It's hard to see what mankind is capable of,
but so rewarding to have a small part in helping
an animal heal and find love again.

Chapter 1

Layla Colton ran the numbers one final time. No doubt about it—this sale would send Colton Energy's stock through the roof, which would definitely help their sagging bottom line.

It was well after midnight, and the November dark outside carried the chill of winter. Everyone else in the building had gone home hours ago, but Layla considered her office her sanctuary, while the lavish condo where she actually lived felt more like an impersonal hotel room than anything else. She only went there to sleep, shower and eat, preferring to spend as much time as possible here, in her corner office on the executive floor of her father's company.

Stifling a yawn, she rubbed the back of her aching neck. She needed to straighten up her desk and head home to catch a few hours' sleep before coming back in the morning.

As she tidied up, her private line rang, the single, long buzz that indicated an internal call. She pressed the button for Speaker, curiosity warring with impatience. "Yes?"

"Security here, ma'am. I have a couple officers from Red Ridge Police Department asking to see you."

To see *her*? At nearly one o'clock in the morning? Had something happened to one of her cousins, many of whom worked at the RRPD as K9 officers? Layla's stomach twisted, and she took a deep gulp of air to help her stay calm.

"Send them up," she ordered, careful that her cool tone betrayed none of her trepidation. She'd learned the hard way what a mistake it could be to display the tiniest bit of weakness. There would always be someone watching and waiting for the chance to take her down.

Two uniformed officers appeared in her doorway a few minutes later. A third stood a few feet behind them. "Come in," she said, her gaze searching first one face and then the others.

"Layla Colton?" the taller of the two asked.

Words failed her, so she simply nodded.

"You're under arrest for stalking, threatening and harassing Mark Hatton."

"What?" Flabbergasted, she briefly lost her tenuous grip on her refusal to be ruffled. "Have you lost your mind?" Mark Hatton worked for her, first as a junior analyst and then as a salesman. She'd regretted hiring him due to his sloppy work and questionable ethics and had begun keeping detailed documentation as a prelude to letting him go.

"I'm afraid not, ma'am." The second officer stepped forward with handcuffs. "We have evidence. Emails in your name, texts from your phone number making sexual advances and threatening him when he turned you down." The disgust in his voice would have made a lesser woman cringe.

"That's impossible," she began.

"Is it?" he cut her off. "Tell it to the judge. It's not only women who are victims, you know. You rich people always think you can get away with anything. Well, not this time."

A silent scream formed in the back of her throat. *No.* This couldn't be happening. Not to her, not now. She'd never threatened anyone a day in her life. And as for making sexual advances to a man like Mark, even the thought made bile rise in her throat. Lies. They were all lies. "I need to call my lawyer," she said.

"You'll be afforded the opportunity to do that later."

She barely listened as they read her rights and stood wooden while they cuffed her like a criminal, the metal cold and hard around her wrists. Still numb, she kept her chin up and her shoulders back as she allowed them to hustle her from her office, down the marble hall, through the lobby and out into the frigid night air to the waiting patrol car. The security officer stood at his desk and watched it all, wide-eyed and clearly stunned.

This would all be on video. There were cameras mounted both inside the building and out. Her father would see. Anyone could see, including Hamlin, her fiancé. He might even decide to make the temporary hiatus they'd placed on their business deal of an engagement a permanent thing. She wouldn't mind personally, but her father would. They needed Hamlin Harrington's money to shore up Colton Energy.

What a mess. Her blood felt as icy as the northern

wind. She wasn't a fool—one couldn't be a female executive in a mostly male industry without making a few enemies. But this? Trumped-up charges that would sound ridiculous to anyone who knew her?

She could only hope word of this wasn't leaked to the press. She'd be crucified before she even had a chance to defend herself. Tears stung the backs of her eyes, and she furiously blinked them away. Once again, she felt like that little girl who, no matter what she did, couldn't manage to make her father proud. Even at age thirty-one, she never could seem to make herself stop trying. She'd even agreed to marry a man she didn't love, just because her father wanted her to.

She'd worked so hard to stay above reproach, and now this insanity. While she had no doubt she'd get this straightened out, it would take time. During which her reputation would be trashed and the multiple deals she had in the works as executive vice president of Colton Energy could fail. She needed those deals—*they* needed them and their stock to rise. Why would Mark Hatton make false accusations that could jeopardize the company he worked for? If Colton Energy went under, he'd lose his job along with all the others. As would she.

To Layla, working for the family business was more than just employment. Her job, the company, was her entire life. Without it, she had no idea what she'd do.

The drive to the Red Ridge police station seemed to take forever. She ran over a hundred different scenarios in her mind, discarding each one. She had to get this straightened out before her father learned of it.

Finally, they pulled up to the back of the building. The place where she suspected they brought people in to book them. Embarrassment flooded her, even though she'd done nothing to be ashamed about.

"Come with me," the tall officer said, helping her from the back of the car. He took her arm and led her, still handcuffed, inside.

Due to the lateness of the hour, the squad room seemed deserted. Only a skeleton crew worked these hours, apparently. Lucky for her, as that meant fewer people to stare. She wasn't particularly close with any of her cousins on the force, even the chief of the K9 unit.

"I'd like my phone call now," she announced, trying to keep her tone cheery and optimistic.

The officer barely even glanced at her. "Not yet. I'll let you know when."

"Layla? Layla Colton?"

She froze. She knew that voice. Hunter Black. He'd been a VP at Colton Energy—and one of her father's favorites—when he'd abruptly quit to attend the police academy so he could work in law enforcement. Though at least eighteen months had passed since Hunter's departure, her father still occasionally mentioned him, mocking his decision as unwise. Police officers only made a third of the salary Hunter had pulled in as an executive.

"Hunter." Slowly she turned, keeping her face expressionless. As before, a buzz of awareness skittered across her skin at the sight of him. He still wore his reddish-brown hair the same way, kind of spiky. And his bright blue eyes still crinkled at the corners.

Of course his gaze immediately went to her bound wrists. "Why are you in cuffs? Are you under arrest?"

He glared at the officer still holding her arm. "What the hell is going on?"

Though she kept her shoulders back as the two officers filled Hunter in, she braced herself for Hunter's reaction. He'd made no secret of his distaste for everyone and everything to do with Colton Energy before he'd left. The other executives had joked about how he certainly knew how to burn his bridges.

To her shock, after hearing her charges, Hunter looked pissed. Not at her. He glared at his coworkers. "Why was I kept in the dark about this?" he demanded. "Is it because I used to work with her?"

One of the men shrugged. The other nodded. "We couldn't take a chance on you trying to influence our investigation."

Judging from the rigid set of Hunter's jaw, he didn't appreciate that statement at all.

"Now if you don't mind, we need to book her."

"Knock yourself out," Hunter replied. To Layla's disappointment, he turned and started to walk away. But he'd barely taken a few steps when he spun back around. "Let me see your evidence."

The first officer jerked his chin toward the other. "Show him."

Handing Hunter a manila folder, the second guy grinned. "I'll need that back when you're finished with it."

Grim faced, Hunter walked away, folder in hand.

After she'd been fingerprinted and booked, Layla was finally allowed to call her lawyer. Luckily, since she dealt with legal matters constantly as part of her job, she had his number memorized.

Once he'd answered—sounding groggy since she'd

no doubt woken him—she filled him in as succinctly as possible. He promised to head to the police station right away, and she ended the call.

"Now what?" she asked the officer standing guard.

"Now you go to the holding cell with all the other women we've brought in tonight," he said.

"And then what?"

"You wait."

Hunter hadn't been prepared for his reaction at seeing Layla Colton again. In the time since he'd left Colton Energy, he'd gone out of his way to avoid her, and not only because she'd reminded him of all the things one could do to sell their soul for personal gain.

She was beautiful, in a remote, detached sort of way. He'd constantly fought the urge to see if he could make her smile, mainly because the few times she had, she went from beautiful to stunning. But she'd smiled less and less, probably because her father had never let up on his constant badgering of her.

Hunter didn't understand it. Layla worked harder than anyone else in the company, including the old man himself. Yet as far as Fenwick Colton was concerned, she was borderline incompetent, incapable of doing anything right, probably because she was his daughter rather than his son. Anyone else would have left a long time ago. But not Layla. Like the proverbial hamster on the never-ending wheel, she kept at it, determined to succeed at an impossible task.

By the time Hunter had quit, he actually felt sorry for her. Didn't like her, but pitied her.

Thumbing through the pages, Hunter rapidly reached the conclusion that this case was 99 percent bogus. Mark Hatton, the former analyst and now junior salesman, claimed Layla Colton had sexually harassed and threatened him. There was no way. No way in hell.

He read the text messages purported to be from Layla to Mark in disbelief. Supposedly, she'd gone from flirty to threatening. There were several suggestive photos Mark claimed she'd texted him at midnight. Layla posed in lingerie, looking sexy as hell. Privately, Hunter thought no red-blooded male could fail to react to these. But he found the idea ludicrous that Layla, who not only was known around the office as the ice princess, but also was engaged to one of the richest men in the state, would have sent these to a junior staffer.

No matter was else she might be, Layla Colton wasn't stupid. Far from it. And any woman who looked like her knew there were a hundred other ways to find a man willing to be your bed partner.

Though Hunter hadn't been a police officer for long, he'd learned years ago to trust his gut instinct. And right now, everything within him said Layla was being set up. Why, he didn't know.

Yet.

He watched as they marched her off to the holding cell, wondering how she'd do in there with the drunks and the prostitutes. Judging from what he'd seen in the time he'd worked with her, she'd survive.

Still, for whatever reason, he didn't like the idea of her being arrested.

Instead of trying to figure out why Layla's arrest affected him so strongly, he read the report again. Objectively, it seemed like a strong case. Rather than he said / she said, Mark Hatton had backed it up with compelling evidence. He had not only the text messages, but numerous emails sent from her company computer. He even had security camera footage from his home, showing Layla standing on his doorstep, ringing the bell. When he hadn't answered, Layla left a large envelope on the porch, tucked behind a potted plant, and walked away.

If Hunter didn't know Layla the way one does from working with her for three years, he would have closed the file and walked away. After all, she had money and connections and would most likely settle out of court, her reputation untarnished.

Then the station phones started ringing. Someone had leaked the story.

By the time Layla's attorney arrived, two news vans were parked in front of the police station. Both had come from Sioux Falls. Whoever had tipped them off had wasted no time. Hunter had a hunch it had been Mark Hatton.

Checking his watch, Hunter swore. Time to go home and let his dog out, plus catch a few hours of shut-eye. But he didn't want to leave until he saw what happened with Layla. While he thought she was the epitome of everything wrong with the corporate world, she'd always been kind to him. She didn't deserve this, especially since he felt positive she'd done nothing wrong.

"What's going on?" he asked Tim Lakely, one of the officers who'd brought her in. Though Lakely wasn't on the K9 team, Hunter knew him well.

"She's still in with her attorney," Lakely replied, his expression disgusted. "And they must have called in Judge Kugen, because he just showed up. And he doesn't look happy. Of course she gets special treatment since she's a rich Colton."

Hunter followed the direction of the other man's gaze. Judge Roy Kugen sat in one of the uncomfortable metal chairs that dotted the room. Suspect chairs, though occasionally they were used by citizens wishing to file a report. The judge had clearly been roused from bed, at least if his disheveled gray hair was any indication. He also appeared to be wearing plaid pajama pants under his heavy coat, though he'd had enough foresight to put on a pair of boots.

The lawyer appeared, some hotshot corporate attorney from Sioux Falls, and asked the judge if he'd mind coming with him. Roy pushed to his feet and they vanished inside the conference room.

Lakely shook his head. "One more example of how rich people get away with everything. If Layla Colton was just a regular person, she'd be spending the night here and be arraigned in the morning. But no, she got Judge Kugen to come to her so she could go home tonight."

"I can't say I blame her," Hunter said, in the interest of fairness. "You know if you were in the same position, you'd do the same thing."

Rolling his eyes, Lakely muttered under his breath and stomped away.

A few minutes later, Judge Kugen appeared again. He glanced around the virtually empty squad room until his gaze landed on Hunter. "Here," the judge said, thrusting a sheaf of papers at him. "I've waived bail and we're letting Ms. Colton go on her own recognizance. These will be filed with the court in the morning. Those are your copies."

Accepting the papers, Hunter nodded. "I'll make sure the officers working this case get these."

"You do that." Judge Kugen narrowed his eyes. "I sure as hell hope you've got an airtight case. People like the Colton family don't take kindly to being arrested under false accusations."

Since he privately agreed, Hunter simply nodded.

Once the judge had left, the attorney stuck his head out the door. "Are you Hunter Black?"

"I am."

"Ms. Colton would like a word with you," the guy said.

Summoned. Just like she thought he still worked for her. Hunter briefly debated declining, but in the end, he headed for the conference room. Call it curiosity or call it compassion, but he truly wanted to hear what Layla Colton had to say.

When he entered the room, she raised her gaze to his, her long-lashed blue eyes troubled. Her platinum blond hair swung, settling back into place.

"I'll leave you two alone," the attorney said, grabbing his briefcase from the table. "Ms. Colton, do you need anything else from me?"

"No, I don't think so," she said, her normally cool voice sounding a bit shaky. "Thank you, Anthony."

With a brusque nod, the lawyer left, closing the door behind him.

She tucked a strand of her silky hair behind her ear, clearly waiting for Hunter to speak first. Instead, he studied her. Her tailored suit and silk blouse meant she'd most likely been arrested at work. At this hour of the morning? He'd heard she was a workaholic, but still.

Suffering his perusal in silence, she finally sighed. "Won't you please sit down?"

Instead, he jammed his hands in his pockets. "What's going on, Layla? It's late and I really need to get home."

At his words, her icy composure crumbled. She covered her face with her hands so he wouldn't see her weep.

Damn. He seriously went to pieces when a woman cried.

"Hey, now," he said, awkwardly patting her shoulder. "It's going to be okay."

"Is it?" When she raised her face, her perfectly applied mascara had run, sending black streaks down her face. She angrily tried to wipe them away and only succeeded in smearing sooty color all over her face. She looked, he thought, like a bedraggled raccoon. He actually liked this Layla better than the icy tycoon.

Resigned now, he pulled out a chair. "Tell me exactly what's going on."

She did, replaying what she'd been told—basically what Lakely had told him earlier. "I just don't understand how anyone could honestly believe I'd sexually harass someone like Mark Hatton." She shuddered. "Or anyone, for that matter. You know me. You worked with me. I took care to keep my conduct businesslike, above reproach."

"Yes, you did." He leaned forward. "But what about the text messages? The photos?"

Though she blushed, she didn't look away. "I never sent them. Those two cops who arrested me confiscated my phone or I'd show you. I'm being set up, though I have no idea why."

"Someone with a grudge against Colton Energy?" he gently pointed out. After all, it wasn't like the company didn't have enemies.

Again, her expression went from glum to miserable. "I... I don't know."

He wasn't sure if she was telling the truth or not. But then, he wasn't surprised. The entire time he'd worked there, everyone had known Colton Energy was Layla's life. Whether she turned a blind eye or just didn't know about her father's shady business deals, he had no idea. Certainly, few in town even suspected the true nature of Fenwick Colton. After all, they'd elected the man their mayor.

The uncomfortable thought hit him. If she'd lie about this, then who knew what else she'd do? "Layla," he asked gently. "Did you proposition and then threaten Mark Hatton? I know it can get lonely at the top."

She recoiled, her expression aghast. "No. I most certainly did not. I swear to you on the lives of my family that I didn't send those texts, emails or photos. I'm being set up."

Unimpressed, he continued to study her. "Swear to me on your job, on Colton Energy." In other words, what truly was the most important thing to her.

Hurt flashed across her face, but she lifted her chin and swore again, exactly how he'd asked.

He nodded, satisfied. "Now I know you're telling the truth."

"Why did you quit, Hunter?" she asked, surprising him. "You were well regarded and performed your job duties well. And we paid you an excellent salary. Yet you gave notice without even the prospect of another job offer. When we heard you'd signed up for the police academy, we were surprised, to say the least."

How to tell someone that the life they'd chosen for herself was one he found abhorrent? Corporate greed and lies, constantly wondering if the things he was asked to do skirted the border of legality...

"Working in law enforcement had been a longtime dream of mine," he said. Then, deciding the time had come to change the subject and wrap things up, he checked his watch. "Do you want to call someone, maybe your fiancé, to come and get you?"

"No. My engagement is currently on hold, like everyone else's in this town," she replied. She had a point. With some crazed serial killer going around murdering grooms right before their wedding day, just about every scheduled wedding had been postponed.

"And to tell you the truth," she continued, "I'm afraid if Hamlin finds out about these charges, he'll end the engagement for good."

She looked so miserable at the prospect, his heart went out to her.

"Come on, then," he said, making an instant decision. "Let me run you home. It's on my way, so it won't be any trouble."

"What about the news vans?" She pointed toward the front of the police station. "Is there any way we can avoid them?"

Eyeing her, in her tailored suit and heels, he considered. "We'll go out the back and take my squad car, but I wouldn't be surprised if they don't have someone watching that exit, too. It'd be better if you had a disguise."

"I don't."

"I might be able to come up with something," he replied.

"Please tell me you're not planning on raiding the police lost and found." She shuddered. "No one knows where those things have been."

He couldn't help but laugh. "I wasn't, but that's an idea. No, I keep a clean change of clothes here in case I have to spend the night. These uniforms aren't the most comfortable to sleep in."

To his astonishment, she blushed. "Oh. But I don't think your clothes will fit me. At all."

"We'll figure out a way to make do. Come on, follow me." He led the way down the hall, toward an area marked Employees Only. They went through the double doors and into a large room filled with lockers. From his locker, he retrieved a flannel shirt, a pair of sweatpants and socks. He'd even stuffed back a pair of old snow boots. "Here." He handed everything to her. "The bathroom is right there. Put these on."

Eyeing the folded bundle dubiously, nevertheless, she did as he asked. When she emerged a few moments later, he felt like he'd just been punched in the stomach. His plaid flannel shirt hung down to her knees. She'd gotten creative and rolled his sweatpants up so they didn't drag on the floor. She'd gathered the excess waistband to one side and held it in her small hand. And she struggled to walk in snow boots that were clearly several sizes too large for her.

She looked like misfortune had guided her clothing choice, as if she were a homeless vagabond wearing whatever she could find in order to stay warm.

And she looked, he thought, while struggling to catch his breath, sexy as hell.

Dizzy with a sudden rush of desire, he tried to regain his equilibrium.

This Layla Colton spelled trouble. Not just for him, he figured, not wanting to make of it any more than he had to. Hell, the intriguing contrast between super-sleek, buttoned-up Layla the executive and this one would catch the attention of any man with a lick of sense. He couldn't gather his scattered thoughts enough to speak a single coherent word. It took every ounce of his willpower to keep from focusing on her lush lips and how badly he wanted to kiss them.

Luckily, he wasn't likely to ever see her looking like this ever again.

"Here." He handed her a baseball cap and his down parka. "Put these on and we'll head out. I don't think anyone would recognize you now."

He was right. If there were reporters stationed at the back of the building, he couldn't tell. Which meant he could get her out of there without any undue attention. She got in his patrol car and they drove away unnoticed.

Chapter 2

Sinking down in the passenger seat, Layla started laughing as soon as they exited the police station parking lot. She couldn't help it, even though she realized her inexplicable mirth bordered on hysteria.

She laughed until tears ran down her cheeks, until exhaustion made her catch her breath. As she wound down, Hunter handed her a box of tissues. "Here," he said. "I keep them in the car just in case. You never know when you'll need them."

Grateful, she accepted. After wiping her eyes and what little mascara remained, she blew her nose and took a deep breath. "Sorry about that," she told him, meaning it. "I really don't know what came over me."

"It's okay." He glanced sideways at her. "People do strange things when under stress."

Grateful for his easy acceptance, she settled more

comfortably in her seat as she rattled off her address. "Though I guess I should have you take me back to Colton Energy to get my car."

"I think you're too upset to drive," he said.

After a moment, she agreed. "It's been pretty crazy lately, even before this," she admitted. "I mean, who would have thought our town would have a serial killer? And what a strange one, singling out men about to get married."

"Yeah. It is bizarre. And in addition to the grim reality of murder, there's damage to the local economy. With all the weddings that have been placed on hold, lots of our local small businesses are suffering. Your sister's bridal salon is in danger of going out of business. I've heard that returns and outright cancellations have destroyed Bea's cash flow. And of course the wedding planners and caterers, like Good Eats, are struggling to pay their bills."

They reached the downtown area. Due to the hour, the streets were deserted. A light snow had fallen earlier, just enough to dust everything with white, so the sidewalks appeared pristine and untouched. When she'd been younger, Layla had loved to leave the first set of footprints in fresh snow. She knew even now, when they reached her town house, she'd take a private delight in walking from the parking lot to her front door.

"It would be a shame if all those mom-and-pop stores went under," he continued. "They're hardworking people, good folks, and I hate to see that happen to them."

Again, her stomach twisted. Though she tried to keep everything bottled up inside, her stress level had her feeling as if something might blow at any moment. "It's crazy," she agreed. "We're so close to Thanksgiving, and we've got some murderer running around killing off grooms. Everyone is scared."

"Are you?"

Without hesitation, she nodded. "I am. Colton Energy is in trouble, too." What had caused her to blurt this truth out, she wasn't sure. But she felt better having actually said it out loud. "That's why I agreed to marry Hamlin Harrington. He's promised my father a fresh influx of money."

"An arranged marriage?" He sounded so shocked.

"He's wanted me for years." As if that justified it. While she knew how it appeared, she didn't see where she had a choice.

"Layla, he's twice your age."

With a nervous laugh, she discounted that statement. "Not really. He is quite a bit older, though. But it'll be fine. I'll do anything to save the family business. Marrying Hamlin will do that, as long as the wedding goes off without a hitch by the end of the year."

He signaled a right turn onto her street and shot her a curious glance. "Why the time constraint?"

Taking a deep breath before answering, she considered swearing him to secrecy. If she told him the truth, she'd be letting him in on something only very few people knew. "Will you keep this between us?" she asked.

"Of course."

For whatever reason, she trusted him to keep his word.

"If Colton Energy doesn't get that cash by the end of the year, there's no help for us. We'll have to file bankruptcy and most likely close our doors." She bit her lip before continuing. "Not only will many people be out of work, but we won't be able to continue to help fund my pet project, the police K9 unit and training center." All of her father's wives had been strong supporters of the K9 unit and training center, including Layla's late mother. Trusts had been left by her and her half sisters' mothers to keep the unit and center going, and when those trusts ran out, Fenwick had stepped up. Now, unless her marriage to Hamlin went on, the K9 unit and training center would be in as much jeopardy as Colton Energy.

Her words hung there in the air between them as Hunter pulled into her parking lot and up next to the curb in front of her town house. Turning in his seat to face her, he scratched his head. "Layla, the K9 training center is now completely self-sufficient, thanks to K9 chief Finn Colton, who came up with a plan. Once the center started training dogs for police departments all over the country, they quickly got out of the red. A fully trained police dog goes for over ten thousand dollars."

Stunned, she wasn't sure how to respond. With the truth, she supposed. "I didn't know. That entire thing is under my father's control. He never told me about that." In fact, he'd led her to believe the opposite. He talked about the K9 training center as if it was a money pit, draining Colton Energy dry. This made her wonder what else he might have misdirected her on.

"You were the VP of finance and accounting," she said. "I know it's been a while since you left, but what—in your opinion—was the biggest drain on Colton Energy's finances?"

He only stared at her. "You should already know that. You're executive VP of everything."

Of course, he had no way of knowing how empty her title truly was. "Not really, though that's a general misconception. While I am in charge of several departments, my primary duties are more in sales and marketing," she said. "I oversee our sales force and step in when necessary to help get corporate contracts for companies that want to break away from traditional energy and do something more earth friendly and renewable." She managed her normal professional smile as she recited the spiel she knew by heart. "I also oversee the payroll department and human resources. My father still oversees the accounting department and has the final say on any big decisions."

"But you have access to the books, right?"

Put that way… "No," she admitted. "I haven't seen the books. I'm thinking I should take a look."

His sideways glance was telling. "Since you're head of HR, were you the one who hired Mark Hatton?"

Right to the gut, that question. Her smile slipped. "I was. I regretted that decision within a month. Mark cuts corners and makes sloppy deals, and I have to wonder at his ethics. I'd begun keeping a detailed accounting of his mistakes so I'd have backup when I fired him."

"You really were going to let him go?"

"Yes. And I promise you, it had nothing to do with him refusing to go out with me." Her stomach churned. "I don't understand why he's saying that."

For one breathtaking second, as her gaze locked with Hunter's, she thought he might kiss her. Her heart raced and she felt dizzy, but in the end, he looked away first.

Suddenly, she realized they'd been sitting in front of her town house for several minutes. "Thanks for the ride," she said, her voice too bright. "I'll have someone pick me up and take me into the office tomorrow." Opening her door, she practically jumped out, sliding a little in the fresh snow.

Watching Layla rush into her town house, Colton tried to analyze what had almost just happened.

He'd almost kissed her. Layla Colton, the woman who epitomized everything he'd despised about the corporate world.

Except she didn't.

He'd never really talked to her, one on one, until tonight. Her devotion to her job, to her father's company, had always been legendary, and she clearly didn't appear to see the irony of working her fingers to the bone for a man who barely acknowledged her existence.

Not his business, he reminded himself. The only situation he needed to concern himself with was the case against her. His gut told him she'd been charged with a crime she hadn't committed.

Shaking his head at his own foolishness, he put the car in Drive and headed home. Unlike Layla, who lived in trendy North Red Ridge, his small house sat in an older part of town. Which suited him fine.

He loved his small frame house. He had a large, fenced yard and lots of trees. Pulling into his driveway, he hit the remote garage door opener and then parked in the garage.

As he stepped into his kitchen, Hunter immediately crouched down. Goose, his basset hound, launched herself at him as she always did, wiggling and doing her best to lick every inch of his face.

This was his absolute favorite part of the day.

He let Goose outside, standing on the back porch to watch her, a habit he'd continued from when she'd been a tiny puppy and he'd worried an eagle would swoop down and carry her off. Since she hated the cold, she took care of her business quickly and then rushed at him to be let back inside.

He'd stopped by earlier during his dinner break to feed her, so he only gave her a dog biscuit as a reward. "Such a good girl," he crooned. As she gazed up at him, he could swear she grinned.

No one could tell it by looking at her, but Goose was only one of four dogs in the entire county trained for electronic storage detection.

When Hunter had brought in the young dog, who looked more like a mixed breed than a pure-bred basset hound, everyone had assumed he was joking when he'd announced his intention to train her in the highly specialized field. Then, as he'd begun working with her, their amusement had turned to incredulity. No one had ever seen a dog who could detect electronics. None of the other trainers had even known such a thing was possible. Hunter hadn't, either, until he'd happened on an article about one of the dogs on the East Coast. He'd made it his mission to learn everything about it, even making a trip out to the training facility so he could learn in person how it was done.

As with any other kind of detection work, electronic storage detection training was done through scent. It turned out that thumb drives, micro-SD cards and external hard drives all contained two different chemical compounds, both of which dogs could be trained to locate.

Goose had proved an apt pupil. Even though Labrador retrievers were considered the best breed for this type of work, Hunter had known his Goose was a natural. As she grew, she looked less and less like a typical basset hound. She had longer legs and a leaner body, and she was slightly taller and more agile. In other words, as far as Hunter was concerned, she was just perfect.

Soon, she'd proved herself to all the other K9 officers in the unit. Goose and her nose had provided the crucial evidence to take down a large child pornography ring out of Sioux Falls. She'd been able to locate hidden computer evidence that might not otherwise have been found.

And she belonged to Hunter, not to the K9 department. She'd been his from the beginning and he'd trained her on his own time, without costing them a cent.

He adored her, and she him.

"Come on, girl," he told her, heading into the bedroom to change out of his uniform. Goose followed, her toenails clicking on the wood floor. He hummed as he changed, even though exhaustion made him want silence. He hummed because Goose liked it and she'd been alone with the quiet since he'd popped in earlier.

Once he had on his comfortable sweatpants and a flannel shirt, he padded into the kitchen to make a quick snack. He turned on the TV, popped a beer and put together a bologna sandwich. The rest of the world might be sleeping, but this was the end of his workday and it would be several hours before he'd wind down enough to hit the sack.

To his chagrin, he couldn't stop thinking about Layla Colton. He'd known her for years, distantly. Even so, he couldn't understand how anyone could legitimately believe she'd done what Mark Hatton accused her of doing. True, as law enforcement officers, they were trained to look only at the evidence, but what evidence they had seemed sketchy. The video might have been doctored. No doubt a competent computer analyst could make that determination. He'd have thought there would have to be more in order for charges to be brought against her.

Clearly, she'd been stunned and shocked by it all. He'd been a cop long enough to know when someone was faking it. Layla's bewilderment seemed all too real.

At this time of the night, he didn't much care what he watched, though if he found himself still up at 5:00 a.m. he tried to catch the local morning news. Stifling a yawn, he realized it was doubtful he'd be awake then, so he let the DVR record it just in case they ran a story on Layla.

As often happened, he dozed off in his chair, Goose snuggled up next to him. When he opened his eyes again, the morning news program was in full swing. He started it over and wasn't surprised to see news footage of the front of the Red Ridge police station. A perky reporter stood in front, bundled up in her parka, and laid out the charges that had been brought against one of the town's wealthiest and most influential citizens, Layla Colton. Toward the end of the segment, she mentioned that they hoped to be able to interview others close to the case for later airing.

Shaking his head, Hunter clicked the TV off. He stretched, let Goose out once more and stood on the back patio until she came in. Though the cold air usually provided enough of a shock to his system to wake him, his weariness felt bone deep. Stifling another yawn, once Goose ran inside, he followed, extinguishing lights as he went.

When he climbed into his bed, Goose leaped up and curled at his feet. He covered her with her own soft blanket, scratched her behind her ears and then burrowed under his own covers.

The sound of his cell phone ringing woke him. Whether he'd slept hours or merely minutes, he wasn't sure. He sat up, rubbed his bleary eyes and fumbled around on his nightstand, trying to locate his phone.

"Hello?" he rasped, wondering why he felt like he'd been run over by a truck.

"Sorry to wake you," Chief Finn Colton said. "But I need to talk to you about Layla Colton's case. Since news of her arrest was plastered all over the news, I'm going to play it safe and recuse myself from the investigation, since she's not only family but the mayor's daughter."

"I understand." Hunter struggled to clear his foggy head. Glancing at the nightstand clock, he saw it was nearly nine, which meant he'd been in his bed four hours. "Sorry, I got in late."

"I understand, and I apologize for waking you. But we've got media up here wanting statements, the mayor demanding answers, of course, and Mark Hatton's attorney threatening to sue if we release his client's information. It's a cluster."

"Okay." Though Hunter didn't get what any of that had to do with him, he knew the chief would fill him in soon enough.

"I'm putting you on the case."

"Me?" Flabbergasted, Hunter rubbed the back of his neck with one hand.

"Yes. All of the evidence in this is based on electronics—text messages, emails, etc. I think with Goose's skill set, you might get to the bottom of this fairly quickly. While there apparently was enough evidence to bring charges, I took a look, and it's on the light side. We need more. There must be hidden data storage drives or something."

"I have my doubts," Hunter confessed. "Remember, I worked at Colton Energy. While I can't say that I know Layla Colton well, I can tell you she never acted in any way other than professional."

"Good to hear," Chief Colton said. "To be honest, I'm not buying Mark Hatton's story, either. While I'm not sure of his motive, my gut tells me he's lying."

"I agree."

"Pay him a visit and bring Goose. See what she can uncover."

Of course after that, there was no way Hunter could go back to bed. After letting Goose out and feeding her, he took a hot shower. Once dressed, he grabbed a pod and made a cup of strong coffee to go with his instant oatmeal. Thus fortified, he checked the weather forecast on his phone and suited up in his uniform.

The instant he put that on, Goose started her happy, hopeful dance. She loved to work and didn't understand why she didn't get to every single day.

"That's right, Goose girl," he told her. "I need your help today."

When she heard that, the little basset hound could barely contain her glee. She wiggled her entire body, swinging her head as she twirled and sending her long, floppy ears flying. She let out a low woo-woo-woo sound—her way of expressing her joy.

As he grabbed his car keys, she stuck so close to him that he almost tripped on her. She kept her liquid brown gaze fixed on him, not letting him out of her sight in case he managed to somehow leave without her.

Once he opened the door heading into the garage, he scooped her up and loaded her into his squad car. Even though her legs were significantly longer than a typical basset's, she often had difficulty jumping into the back seat, even with a running start.

Turning into the police station parking lot, he grinned when Goose let out a low bark—she knew exactly where they were.

As soon as they entered the squad room, everyone rushed over to make a fuss over Goose. Panting and grinning, she accepted this as her due. While Red Ridge PD had a larger than usual K9 unit, Goose was the smallest dog on the force, and in Hunter's opinion, the cutest. Of course, he knew he might be biased.

He glanced around, noting that none of the officers who'd been working graveyard last night were in yet. Hunter could sympathize. He was glad he rarely had to work nights.

Heading to his cubicle, he whistled for Goose. Immediately, she left her fan club and hurried after him, long ears flying as she ran. She caught up with him and they entered his work area together. Goose headed to the bed he kept for her in the corner, turning several circles before lying down with a contented huff.

Once he'd logged in to the computer, he accessed all the files they had on Layla Colton's case. As he read through everything, he shook his head. The chief was right. This was an extremely sensitive case, and he hoped it wouldn't stand up in court.

Next, Hunter decided to pay Mark Hatton a visit. He wanted to sound the guy out, see if he'd give anything away.

Stepping into the lobby at Colton Energy brought back conflicting emotions. Hunter remembered entering this very building the first day of his new job, how excited he'd been, how he'd felt positive that he'd take the world by storm. How he'd make a difference. He'd believed wholeheartedly in the work Colton Energy did. Sustainable, alternative energy. The first step in saving the earth.

It hadn't taken long before he'd learned that his job had nothing to do with that. Lofty ideals and hopeful dreams had zero to do with corporate machinations and greed. Fenwick Colton was all about the profit, and he spent it as fast as it came in. Layla's comment about the company being in trouble didn't surprise Hunter. If anything, he wondered why it hadn't happened sooner.

The receptionist greeted him with a sweet smile. She hadn't been there during his employment, so she had no idea who he was other than a uniformed police officer with a cute, goofy dog. Very few people outside the K9 unit knew what Goose could do, and Hunter preferred it stay that way.

"I'd like to see Mark Hatton," he said, keeping his tone pleasant.

Instantly, her smile vanished. "One moment, sir. Let me call and tell him you're here."

Since he knew how fast gossip raced through this place, he thought it safe to guess the receptionist was not on Hatton's side. He wondered if anyone actually believed the junior salesman's story. While he understood that sexual harassment could go both ways, in this case he doubted any of it had ever happened.

A moment later, the young woman hung up the phone and told him he could go right up. "Second floor. He'll send someone to greet you."

Thanking her, Hunter headed toward the elevator, Goose close on his heels. When they exited on the second floor, Mark Hatton himself waited.

"What can I help you with, Officer?" he asked, after shaking Hunter's hand. "I hate to say, it's strange seeing you in uniform rather than a suit and tie."

"Do you mind if we go to your office?" Hunter asked, resisting the urge to wipe his hand on his pants. The other man's grip, while firm, had been damp.

"Of course not." He eyed Goose. "Cute dog," he said, though the tight set of his mouth indicated otherwise.

The office was small, only slightly larger than Hunter's cubicle. With a pristine, uncluttered desk, a computer monitor on top and a printer/scanner/fax, nothing about the space gave a clue as to the occupant's personality. Turning slowly, Hunter eyed the modern artwork on the walls. "Did you choose those?" he asked, even though he figured he already knew the answer.

"Nope." Mark's voice sounded completely uninterested. "They were left over from the guy who was here before me."

The fact that there were no framed photos of family or friends, no knickknacks or mementos, not even a plant told Hunter that Mark spent as little time as possible in this space. The room completely lacked personality.

"Did you just move in here?" Hunter asked, genuinely curious. Maybe Hatton simply hadn't had time to spruce the place up.

Mark eyed him over the rims of his oversize glasses. "No. I mean, I moved here after my last promotion, which would be after you quit. But it's been a few months."

"Okay." Deciding he'd wasted enough time dwelling on Mark's lack of office decorating skills, Hunter eyed the chair across from the desk. "Mind if I sit?"

"Is this going to take long?"

"Depends. I've been brought in on your case and the chief asked me to bring myself up to snuff. I've read the file, of course, but I wanted to come talk to you and get it straight from the horse's mouth."

Just like that, Mark's uptight posture relaxed. "Oh. You should have said so. Go ahead and take a seat."

Amused, Hunter did. He watched as Mark made a show of settling himself into the oversize leather executive chair behind his desk. No doubt if there'd been papers on the desk, he would have squared them up, too.

Mark then launched into a story about how Layla had started flirting with him long before he'd moved into this office. "When I turned her down the first time, she gave me a bad review," he said. "She knew not only would that mess up me getting promoted but would affect my holiday bonus. I'm the top salesperson in the company," he boasted. "Fenwick recognized me in front of the entire sales department. He gave me a cash bonus and took me to dinner personally."

Hunter nodded, listening carefully.

"Layla seemed to find my success intoxicating," Mark continued. "She's four years older than me, but that didn't seem to bother her. I think she liked the idea of me having a young guy's stamina."

It took every ounce of willpower for Hunter to keep from laughing. Instead, he nodded.

"She didn't like the fact that her father gave me this promotion and she tried to stop it. When he overrode her, she made her first threat." Mark pulled out his cell phone, scrolled to something and then handed it across the desk. "Take a look for yourself. Those texts came from her."

Accepting the phone, Hunter scrolled through the entire conversation. The earlier texts were flirty and light, complimenting Mark on his looks, his education—hell, virtually everything about him. She'd invited him to her town house twice and he'd declined. Then the threats had started. If you don't make love with me tonight, I'll make sure you not only lose your bonus, but your office and your job, the last one said. In fact, if you don't take care of my needs, you might even lose your life.

Chapter 3

Once upon a time, Layla Colton had believed in fairy tales. She'd thought if she worked hard enough she could make her father notice her, something he never seemed to do. Though it felt disloyal, she'd long suspected he was skimming money off the top of the company's profits, but until Hunter Black had mentioned the accounting department, it hadn't occurred to her to take a look at the books.

Now she had. In her office since the crack of dawn, she'd taken a good, hard look at the bookkeeping files. Saving the file to her Dropbox, she clicked out of it, feeling queasy. And disappointed. No wonder Colton Energy was in trouble. As she'd thought, the sales department was rocking and rolling, getting lots of new contracts and extending old ones. With numbers like the ones she'd seen, they should have been expanding.

But instead, Fenwick Colton dipped into and spent the profits like there was no tomorrow.

Of course, this wasn't illegal. He owned the company and could do whatever he wished with the profits, as long as he met all his corporate obligations. The vendors were still being paid, payroll still met and all the taxes were handled on time, so technically he was meeting them. But the advertising budget had been sliced in half, and lately whenever an employee quit, they were not replaced. Other employees were asked to tighten their belts and double down to help the company get through this crisis.

Crisis. The word sent a knife edge of worry through those who depended on their jobs to provide for their family. After all, Red Ridge wasn't exactly a mecca of jobs. So, of course, everyone pitched in, worked longer hours and did what they had to do in order to help Colton Energy survive. She'd done the same thing herself, determined to do her part to keep the company afloat.

Except after reading these reports, she could clearly see there would be no problem if her father weren't running through money like crazy. He'd always liked five-star restaurants, expensive cars and high-maintenance women. She'd assumed his salary was adequate to cover that lifestyle, since he made almost twice as much as she did, but apparently it wasn't. Not by a long shot.

Damn.

How many people were aware of what her father was doing to the company, she wondered. Surely the VP of accounting knew, and probably Fenwick's assistant, at the very least.

Her phone pinged. Another text. Her siblings had all made contact, via text or phone messages, offering their support.

As she stood up and stretched, another realization struck her. Not only had her father lied to his employees, but he'd lied to her. He'd actually convinced her of the necessity of her marrying Hamlin Harrington, a man she didn't love—or even like, for that matter. He'd claimed this would be the only way to save Colton Energy, as Hamlin had promised a fresh influx of cash. Millions, to be specific.

But would the money even go to the company, or would it end up in Fenwick's personal accounts? Would he then spend it all on lavish vacations, exotic cars and his model girlfriends?

Except…even a lifestyle as lavish as her father's couldn't burn through this much money so fast, could it? There had to be something else, something she'd missed.

No matter what the truth was, Layla had been played for a fool. Closing the file, she sat back in her chair and took a deep breath. While she prided herself on being a team player, on giving her job her all, the time had come to speak to her father. She needed answers, and most of all, she needed his assurances that he'd stop hurting his own company. Too many employees, herself included, would be destroyed if Colton Energy went under.

Pacing the confines of her corner office, she eyed the windy outdoors. Not in the mood to walk outside in the chilly air, she decided to go for a walk around the office to clear her head. Since her third-floor office was right next to her father's executive suite, she elected to head down to the second floor, where the bulk of the sales force worked. Privately, she often thought the busy sales department was the hub of the company. Noisy and boisterous, with constantly ringing phones, salespeople pitching their product, she always felt upbeat whenever she visited. The positive energy simply hummed from every desk. Corny, but true.

In contrast, the executive floor—her floor—felt somber and too quiet. As if the weight of the company sat like a heavy quilt over everything.

Striding toward the elevators, she pressed the button for the lobby. The doors opened almost immediately and she stepped inside, please to see she had this elevator alone. Perfect, since she wasn't in the mood for speaking with anyone after the startling revelations of a moment ago. She'd come in super early, as was her normal habit, though this time doing so also helped her avoid anyone staring, whispering or sharing gossip about her.

The elevator stopped on the second floor. As the doors opened, she was surprised to see Hunter Black heading toward her. She frowned, guessing he'd come from the Mark Hatton's office. But then she caught sight of the adorable little dog padding alongside him, and all apprehension vanished.

"Oh my goodness," she said, dropping to her knees on the elevator floor, heedless of her expensive suit. "What a cutie. Who is this? What's her name?"

Hunter grinned, startling her with how devastatingly handsome he was. "This is Goose. She's my little partner."

"Goose?" she asked, startled. "I bet there's an interesting story behind that name."

Clearly pleased by the question, Hunter shrugged. "She was a silly puppy when she was young. A silly goose. So the name stuck."

"Too cute." Charmed, Layla held the doors open while Hunter and the dog settled into the back. With her brown, tan and white coloring, Goose looked like a cross between a beagle and a basset hound. A mutt, as one of her uncles used to like to say, even though Goose was purebred.

Goose, apparently knowing an adoring fan when she saw one, wiggled her entire long body and worked her way as close to Layla as she could get.

"Hey, there," Layla crooned, leaning in and scratching behind the floppiest set of dog ears she'd ever seen. They felt like velvet and smelled like corn chips, oddly enough. While she'd never had a dog of her own, she'd always wanted one. Only the long hours her job required kept her from getting her own.

That might soon change.

Goose woofed, a low sound of pleasure as she closed her ridiculously cute brown eyes and leaned into Layla's hand, clearly enjoying the petting.

"She likes you," Hunter said, his husky voice radiating approval.

"I like her, too." Layla grinned up at him. "I didn't know you had a dog." The instant she'd finished speaking, she blushed. "Sorry. I know I don't know you all that well. I didn't mean…"

"It's all right," he said, still grinning as he waved away any awkwardness. "Goose is my K9 partner."

"Really?" Rocking back on her heels, Layla looked from him to the odd-looking Goose and back again. "I thought all police dogs were shepherds or labs."

"Most are. Goose is a unique dog."

"Yes, she is. If I had to guess her breed, I'd say a cross between—"

"She's a purebred basset hound."

"No." The denial slipped out before she had time to think. While she might not own a dog, she'd spent countless hours learning about each breed so that when she was finally ready, she'd know which one was for her. "Goose looks like a cross between a basset hound and a—"

"Beagle," he finished for her. "Yes, I know."

Belatedly, she realized she might have just offended him. "I'm sorry." She kissed the top of his dog's head before climbing to her feet and dusting off her slacks. "Whatever she is, she's adorable."

He frowned, letting her know she had inadvertently said the wrong thing. "Again, she's purebred. I bought her from a breeder. I have papers. I chose this particular breeder because they don't breed to AKC standards."

Nodding, she smiled at the cute little dog. "Is she good at her job?"

"Yes. She's the best." He pointed. "The elevator is on hold. We're not moving."

Blushing, she released the doors and again pressed the button for the lobby. "Sorry, sometimes it sticks."

He nodded, but didn't reply.

"Were you here to talk to Mark?" she asked, unable to help herself.

"Yes." His cool blue gaze slid over her. "I've been assigned to the case."

Relief flooded her, though she made sure to keep that from showing. "I'm glad," she said softly.

"Why?" The elevator reached the ground floor and

he exited, bending down to clip a leash on his dog. Even though she'd meant to go up, toward her own floor, she followed.

"Because you at least see me as a person," she said softly. "Those other two officers didn't. To them, I was just another rich person."

"I'm going to be fair," he told her, his gaze locking with hers. "And I'll do my job and uphold the law. But…"

She tensed. These days, it seemed there always was a *but*.

"To be honest, I don't believe you did it."

Gratefulness flooded her, so strongly she almost reached out and grabbed his arm. But that would have seemed weird or pushy or something, so she didn't. "Thank you," she said, her voice quiet. "I appreciate that."

They'd walked past the reception desk and were nearly at the front door. Instead of heading out, Hunter went to one of the ornate benches situated around the lobby and gestured, indicating she should sit.

Glad she didn't have to follow him outside since she didn't have her coat with her, she took a seat on the edge of the bench. The instant she did, Goose trotted over and rested her head on Layla's knee.

Hunter watched his dog with an indulgent smile before turning his attention back to Layla. "Do you have any idea why Mark Hatton would make these claims against you? I can't figure out his motive."

She shrugged. "I hired him and his performance has been…subpar. I've been doing quite a bit of documentation. As a matter of fact, next week I'd planned to place him on warning."

"Would that affect his bonus?"

"Yes." She frowned. "Do you think that's why he's doing this?"

"Anything is possible." Again he studied her. Though she couldn't read his expression, she thought she saw compassion in his gaze.

"It just seems a bit...excessive. This is business, nothing more. It's not personal, but he's making it that way." She swallowed hard. "To be honest, I don't think he has the technical skills to pull off something like this. Fake texts, an old video that he would have had to hack and doctor... There's no way."

"Interesting. Maybe he had a partner. Who else would have reason to want to ruin your life besides him?"

At first, the turn of phrase stunned her. But then she realized Hunter was right. This did feel like an attempt to absolutely ruin her life. "I don't know," she finally admitted. "I'm pretty focused on my job. I don't have much of a social life."

"What about enemies inside the company? Surely someone in your position has to have made a few."

She shrugged, refusing to allow herself to feel embarrassed. "If I have enemies, I don't know about them. Again, I tend to concentrate on work. I deal with the employees in a professional, businesslike manner. No one should have any reason at all to be antagonistic toward me."

"Unless they're wanting warm and fuzzy," he said with a wry smile.

Straightening her spine, she eyed him. "I'm their employer, not their mother or friend. I learned the hard way there are some lines that should never be crossed."

"Intriguing." Clearly, he was waiting to hear more. But she'd already said more than enough.

When it became apparent she wasn't going to elaborate, he sighed. "What about your upcoming wedding? Is there anyone who might want to stop you from marrying Hamlin Harrington?"

His question made her laugh, though quietly. "Well, I did once overhear Hamlin's son Devlin arguing with his father about marrying me. He seemed to think I wanted to wrest control of Harrington Inc., and destroy his entire future."

Hunter didn't blink. "And would you?"

"Of course not. I have enough responsibilities with my own company. Why on earth anyone would think I'd want to take on another is beyond me."

"I see." Still, he watched her closely. "How did Hamlin respond to his son's accusations?"

"He brushed them aside, exactly as I would have done." She allowed herself a slight smile. "He said I was gold."

"Gold," Hunter repeated. "As in a commodity rather than a person."

"Or," she interjected, refusing to frown, "something precious. I prefer to think of it that way."

One corner of his sensual mouth quirked. "All right. I'll keep looking into this."

"Thank you." As he turned to go, she grabbed his arm. "I really appreciate your help. This came out of left field and I'm still a bit shell-shocked."

He looked from her to her hand on his arm. "No promises, Layla Colton. I'm not on anyone's side. All I care about is finding out the truth. Here." He dug in his pocket and extracted a business card, which he handed her. "If you think of anything else that might help, give me a call."

Accepting, she slipped the card into her purse and thanked him.

Once more, he flashed a quick smile. "You're welcome." With that, he whistled to his dog. Ears cocked, Goose immediately went to Hunter's left side. Even though he held the leash loosely, the basset stayed smartly in the heeling position as they went through the door and out into the parking lot.

Once they'd disappeared from view, Layla turned to head back upstairs. Right now, she felt like she couldn't trust anyone. She wasn't even sure she trusted Hunter. When he'd quit Colton Energy, he'd made no secret of how he felt about the company and what he'd called their greedy ways. He'd claimed the demands they placed on their staff came with a high emotional cost.

Interesting that Hunter had asked her if she had any enemies. It wasn't until he'd gone that she'd realized she might actually consider him one.

Driving back to the station after leaving Colton Energy, Hunter considered the new information Layla had given him. While her wedding to Hamlin Harrington might be on hold—along with everyone else's in town—the fact that a large sum of cash was involved was definitely news. If Fenwick Colton needed the money as badly as Layla claimed, he must be extremely riled up that this Groom Killer had halted the wedding.

Everyone on the police force, as well as most of the citizens of Red Ridge, had their own opinions about who might be the Groom Killer. Hunter also had his personal number one suspect, though he'd yet to voice his suspicions out loud. Maybe the time had come to do exactly that. What Layla had revealed provided yet another possible motive for Devlin Harrington to want all weddings stopped. Even if Devlin didn't fit the profile 100 percent, Hunter still felt certain he had a strong motive.

Unfortunately, Hunter knew he might be the only one who suspected Devlin. Most cops instinctively trusted the criminal profile they'd been given by the professionals.

As well they should. Last month, RRPD officer West Brand had finished working on the profile of the killer. A ex-FBI agent who'd been undercover on the force until recently, West, along with his former colleagues at the bureau, had developed the profile, which indicated that the Groom Killer was male, white and single. Probably middle to upper class. Stocky build, not particularly attractive and a loner.

Unfortunately, there were a lot of men in Red Ridge who fit that profile. Devlin Harrington wasn't one of them. Sure, he was male, white and single, and definitely upper class. And yes, he still lived in one of his father's mansions. But there the similarities ended. Tall, muscular and golden, Devlin surrounded himself with his admirers. Everyone wanted to be with him, probably due to his money and his good looks, as Hunter knew without a doubt it wasn't his personality.

Pompous, arrogant and sneering, Devlin looked down his aristocratic nose at those he considered beneath him. Which seemed to be just about everyone who wasn't in his inner circle. Hunter himself had had several run-ins with the guy and personally couldn't stand him. Which was yet another reason he'd kept his suspicions about Devlin to himself.

After all, there already was an official suspect— Demi Colton's name had been spelled out in blood next to the first victim. That man, Bo Gage, had been her fiancé before he'd broken up with her in order to propose to another woman. It hadn't helped that Bo and the Gage family had long been feuding with the Coltons. But the investigation had had unexpected results: Gages and Coltons falling in love. Bo Gage's brother Detective Carson Gage had fallen for Serena Colton, whom he'd suspected of harboring Demi early on in the case. Now, a few other Coltons and Gages were keeping their romances on the down low until it was safe to announce their engagements. But some on the force still believed Demi could be the guilty party. She'd fled town. There was circumstantial evidence. There were witnesses.

And Layla's father, Mayor Fenwick Colton, wanted Demi Colton brought to swift and immediate justice, maybe more than anyone—so that Layla could marry Hamlin for his money.

Hunter had long doubted Demi's guilt, and he didn't blame her for going on the run. His gut told him she was being framed.

Much of the town remained convinced she was the murderer, but the majority of the police force didn't believe it. Yes, she was a rough-around-the-edges bounty hunter with a temper. But the witness who claimed to have seen her running away from the crime scene at the time of Bo Gage's murder was a drug dealer with a rap sheet. Demi wasn't a killer. Even if she had up and disappeared.

Several of the other guys in the K9 unit had set up a betting pool. Pay twenty bucks, write down your best guess and put it into the pot. When the Groom Killer was finally apprehended—and no one doubted he or she would be—whoever had guessed correctly would get the cash. If no one even came close, the money would be donated to the Red Ridge animal shelter. So far as he could tell, Hunter was the only one in the unit who hadn't participated.

Today he planned to pony up his Andrew Jackson and put his own guess in the pool. After he talked to the chief, that was.

Once he'd parked in the lot between the police station and training center, Hunter helped Goose down from the vehicle and they headed inside. Goose could scarcely contain her excitement. Her cute little tail twirled circles as she bounced up the sidewalk. This was her favorite place next to home. She'd trained here since she was three months old and knew all the other K9 officers and their dogs.

Before heading to the squad room, Hunter dropped Goose off with one of the assistant trainers, a young woman named Callie who lit up when she caught sight of the basset. Hunter left them to their mutual admiration lovefest and headed back to his desk.

Once there, he glanced toward Chief Finn Colton's office. Now would be as good a time as any. The chief's secretary, Lorelei Wong, was in charge of the betting pool. Hunter jotted Devlin Harrington's name on a slip of paper, folded it in half and slipped it into an envelope, which he sealed. He dug a twenty from his wallet, put it with the envelope and passed both to Lorelei with a wink before proceeding around the corner.

Since Chief Colton kept an open-door policy, Hunter simply knocked on the door frame twice before poking his head in. "You got a minute?"

Finn glanced up from the report he'd been reading. "Of course," he said, gesturing to one of the chairs across from his desk. "Have a seat."

"Mind if I close the door?" Without waiting for an answer, Hunter did. "I wanted to talk to you about the Groom Killer case."

Finn's brows rose. "Do you have a new lead?"

"Not exactly. But I'd like to investigate Devlin Harrington's tech—his phone, laptop, work computer, etc." Hunter sat, leaning forward earnestly. "I got some information today that gives him a motive. Sort of," he amended. He filled the chief in on what Layla Colton had told him.

"So you think Devlin has a problem with his father getting married? To the point that he'd go around killing grooms?"

Put that way, Hunter had to admit it did sound farfetched. "It's possible. Maybe he hates that Hamlin has found a younger, beautiful woman to marry him. Or maybe he's against Dad putting a huge amount of money into Colton Energy and squandering his inheritance. We also know that Nash was suspicious of Devlin when he discovered Devlin asked out Hayley Patton and she rejected him."

Last month, Nash, one of the K9 officers, had spotted Devlin ogling a photo of Hayley on his laptop. Hayley had been engaged to the first victim of the Groom Killer—Bo Gage—after Bo broke his engagement to Demi Colton.

Coincidence? Not likely.

"That's still not enough evidence to justify a warrant," Chief Colton said, his tone a bit chiding.

"Well, if you also consider that Layla Colton feels someone's framing her with the sexual harassment charge against her, that would be two attempts to stop the marriage. And who would want to stop the marriage more than anyone? Devlin Harrington."

"Again, only speculation. You know better than that, Hunter."

Maybe he did, but Hunter was prepared to continue with speculation that might stick.

The chief shook his head before Hunter got a chance to speak. "Look, I want to exonerate Demi as much as anyone. While having another viable suspect would certainly go a long way toward doing that, you know as well as I do that's nothing. Haley's photo on Devlin's laptop could simply mean he likes looking at her, as do a lot of guys."

"But—"

The chief held up his hand. "Enough. Devlin's being watched. If you truly believe he's behind anything, you'll have to find more evidence, legally."

Hunter nodded, careful to mask his disappointment. "Then that's what I'll do," he said. "Thank you for your time."

Back at his desk, he took a seat and began making notes on a pad. Writing things out always helped him clear his head.

But all he could think of was Layla Colton and the hurt and pain he'd seen in her beautiful blue eyes. When he'd worked at Colton Energy, he'd actively avoided her since he'd figured she was tied—at the

deepest levels—to the corporate greed and indiffer-
ence perpetrated by her father.

He should have known it wasn't so simple. There
were always two sides to everything. And after talking with Layla, he had the distinct possibility that she
might be less involved than he'd believed. And a hell
of a lot more naive. He still struggled with the concept
of her agreeing to allow her father to marry her off to
a man she didn't love, just for an infusion of money.

That situation wasn't his problem, he reminded
himself. He had two active cases—more than enough
to consume his time. Arresting the Groom Killer remained his number one priority. Second would be finding out the truth about the charges Mark Hatton had
filed against Layla. He'd do his job there, too, whether
she turned out to be innocent or guilty.

And he'd do his damnedest to ensure her sky-blue
eyes didn't make frequent appearances in his dreams
at night.

Chapter 4

As Layla pressed the elevator button, her phone pinged. A text from her father. I need to see you in my office, now. Your fiancé is here and he's upset as hell.

Perfect. How one day could go from crappy to decent and then right back into the toilet, she had no idea. But she figured she was about to find out. Her stomach, already upset from stress, churned. She thought longingly of the roll of antacids she kept in her desk drawer but decided not to make a quick detour to get them. Fenwick Colton despised being kept waiting.

As soon as she reached the third floor, she headed directly to her father's office suite. His assistant, a sullen young woman named Brielle who always seemed to be on her cell phone, waved her through without even glancing up.

After rapping softly on the door, she opened it and

went inside. Her heels immediately sank into the plush carpet.

Both her father and Hamlin went silent at the sight of her. They were sitting side by side on the ridiculously expensive lambskin couch Fenwick had hired a specialty design store to make.

Hamlin jumped to his feet when she entered, though he didn't smile. Her father did not rise or smile either.

"There you are," Hamlin said, reaching for her to pull her into his customary, stiff, full-body hug. Pretending not to notice, Layla managed to avoid him. Today, his silver-white hair frizzed around his head like a foggy halo, reminding her of photos she'd seen of Albert Einstein. In stark contrast to her father, who wore a three-thousand-dollar custom-made suit, Hamlin wore his "ranch suit"—a diamond-studded denim jacket and dark jeans—with thousand-dollar cowboy boots. He kept an office at his green energy company, Harrington Inc., but he loved his ranch, even if he barely bothered to oversee the people he'd hired to run it. She spotted his pricey Stetson, one of his affectations, on the back of the sofa.

"Explain yourself," Fenwick barked, making her jump. "What is all this nonsense about you sexually harassing Mark Hatton?"

Though she lifted her chin, Layla felt the heat of a blush spreading over her face. "It's not true," she replied. "At all."

Hamlin's bushy gray brows rose. "Are you saying you're being framed, my dear?"

"Yes."

Though Hamlin frowned, her father's hard expression didn't change at all. "You need to clean that up, run damage control. Settle if you have to, but do whatever you must to make that go away."

"Settle?" She stared in disbelief. Of all the things her father had asked of her, this ranked as one of the worst. "I'm innocent, so, no, there won't be any settling. Of any kind. The police are investigating and I feel confident they'll unearth the truth."

"The truth doesn't matter," Fenwick insisted. "What matters is the damage to your public persona and to our company. If people believe you actually did—"

"Enough already," Hamlin interrupted. "Personally, I don't really care if Layla has the hots for some twenty-two-year-old underling. But this is also, as you say, very embarrassing. Even if the police were to catch the Groom Killer today, the wedding will have to continue to be postponed until Layla is cleared of all charges."

"But—" Fenwick started to protest.

"No debate." Hamlin's implacable tone matched his steely expression. "Matter closed."

Hating how the two men carried on as if she wasn't even there, Layla cleared her throat, and once she had both their attention, she made a show of checking her watch. "I have work to do. Is there anything else?"

The scorn in her father's gaze cut her to the bone, though she took care not to show it. "Just get your mess cleaned up. Use my attorney if you have to."

Since she already had, she simply nodded. Her fiancé watched her, looking her up and down as if she was nothing more to him than livestock up for auction. As always, lust sparked in his eyes, but nothing more.

Distaste filled her. Now that she knew the reason for Colton Energy's money problems—and that they were fixable—she felt a lot less inclined to offer herself as a sort of sacrificial lamb.

"We'll see how this plays out," Hamlin drawled. She couldn't help but notice not only did he not offer to help, but he expressed no concern for her emotions. He didn't even bother to ask if she was all right after being arrested and dragged off to jail.

Of course, what had she expected? He'd never claimed to love her, just to want her in his bed. He'd made it clear from the beginning that he saw her as a trophy wife, a pretty younger woman he could flaunt on his arm. Never mind that she was a person in her own right, a successful businesswoman with a brain.

She sighed.

As he watched her, Fenwick's gaze sharpened. "Might I remind you, the fate of your favorite charity depends on this wedding going off without a hitch."

Subtle—not. She'd worked tirelessly to ensure Colton Energy's charitable contributions went toward dog rescue. Specifically, rescues that rehabilitated dogs and trained them as service animals or police dogs. Part of the donations went to the Red Ridge PD's K9 training unit. Except according to Hunter, they now made enough to operate without accepting charity.

Clearly her father didn't know this, even though as mayor he had access to all the bookkeeping for all town agencies, including the police department. She doubted he'd even care, except for the loss of one more thing he could hold over her head in order to make her do his bidding.

She felt as if blinders had been removed from her eyes and she could suddenly see. Disconcerting, to say the least.

Not trusting herself to speak, she turned on her heel and left without another word.

Back in her office, she closed the door and went to stand at her floor-to-ceiling window. Fuming, she realized she needed not only to have a long talk with her father, but a separate conversation with Hamlin. Eventually. Not today. Her head had started to ache.

Again she found herself thinking of Hunter Black and the way his eyes had crinkled at the corners when he'd smiled at her. She'd definitely felt a tug of attraction.

Impulsively, she pulled his card from her purse and dialed the number. He answered on the third ring.

"Officer Black."

"Hunter, it's Layla Colton," she said. "I was wondering if you'd like to have coffee or a drink with me later."

Silence. An awkward, uncomfortable silence that stretched out for way too long.

"I'm sorry, but I can't date the subject of an ongoing investigation," he finally said. "That'd be unethical, not to mention against the rules."

"Not as a date," she rushed to explain, horrified. "I just thought we could go over a few things pertaining to my case." Swallowing hard, she hoped she didn't sound too pathetic. After the meeting with her father and her so-called fiancé, she needed some quiet companionship. Why she'd thought of Hunter first, she wasn't sure. "Perhaps you're forgetting I'm engaged to Hamlin Harrington?"

"Ah, right. You know what, that actually sounds great, then," he said. "Coffee, though, as I can't drink while on duty."

On the verge of asking him to go when he was off duty, she bit her tongue. She *was* engaged, wedding postponed or not. Plus, she really just needed a friend right now.

"When?"

Again, he took a moment to consider. "I work graveyard this week. What time are you thinking?"

"Lately, I've been working long into the night," she said. "But it's been a really long day, so I'm going home at five. Maybe sooner." Except the last thing she wanted was caffeine in the evening. From personal experience, she knew she'd be up all night. She explained this, feeling rather sheepish since she'd been the one to throw the idea out there.

"All right. I get that. How about we grab a bite to eat instead?"

She froze. "Okay," she finally agreed, telling herself that this was *not* a date. "Where?" So help her if he said Peretti's. The cozy Italian restaurant was well-known as the most romantic place in town to take a date.

"Pizza Heaven?" He sounded as if he was smiling. "I could use a good slice of Canadian bacon and pineapple."

"That's my favorite, too," she said, surprised and also relieved. "And Pizza Heaven will be perfect."

They agreed on a time to meet—six thirty. With a quiet sigh of relief, she ended the call.

Leaning back in her chair, she smiled. Odd how just hearing the husky bass of his voice made her feel better. It had been a long time since she'd let herself be attracted to someone. It just figured that when she finally did, he'd only want to be friends.

Oh, well. Though her half sister Patience, as well

as her other siblings, had called and left several messages expressing their worry about her arrest, she'd been avoiding returning them. Mainly because they always tried to talk her out of marrying Hamlin. She didn't have many friends, either. Right now, she'd take any offers of friendship she could get.

After hanging up the phone, Hunter wondered why he felt so jazzed at the idea of going for pizza with Layla Colton. Okay, she was gorgeous, true. And much more warm and personable than he remembered. Of course, they'd barely spoken to each other back when he'd worked at Colton Energy. He'd been guilty of basing his impression of her on what he'd heard around the office. Monikers like Ice Princess and Daddy's Hatchet hadn't gone a long way toward making her seem kind and fuzzy.

Chief Colton walked out into the main room and whistled, the sharp sound cutting through the chatter and background noise. Officers hurriedly concluded their phone calls, and the room became eerily silent.

"We've got another murder," he announced, his voice as grim as his expression. "One more groom has been killed. This time, the victim was Xavier Wesley. His body has been transported to the coroner."

"How long ago?" someone asked.

"Time of death has yet to be established." The chief cleared his throat. "However, Demi Colton's bracelet was found near the body."

Immediately, the chatter started back up. Chief Colton waited a moment before whistling again. "What's more, we have a witness who claims to have seen Demi pull the trigger. If he's credible, we might just have solved the case."

With that pronouncement, the chief went back to his office and closed the door.

The squad room erupted in noise. The Groom Killer was all anyone ever talked about these days. At the police station, even while dealing with the normal routine of routine crime—shoplifters, a hot-check writer and the occasional drunk driving or drug possession arrest—every single officer wanted to be the one to solve the Groom Killer case.

Even in town, whether at the breakfast café, the tire shop or the pizza parlor, the first thing everyone asked Hunter was if they'd caught the Groom Killer yet.

The first murder had been a shock and everyone in law enforcement had considered it an aberration. Things like that didn't happen in Red Ridge. But then another groom had been killed, and another, and a clear pattern had emerged.

Apprehending the murderer was the RRPD's number one priority.

And now it appeared the case might have been solved.

Except Hunter didn't believe it had. Too cut-and-dried. First up, Demi Colton might be a lot of things, but she wasn't stupid. Even if she'd lost her mind and decided to become a serial killer, she wouldn't go around leaving personal belongings at the scene. Or witnesses.

And lastly, she didn't fit the profile. At all. West Brand and his former colleagues at the FBI had mentioned that very few women were serial killers. West didn't believe Demi was the Groom Killer.

Hunter got up and made his way to the chief's office. He tapped on the closed door and then opened it a crack to peer in. With the phone to his ear, Chief Colton held up one finger to indicate Hunter should wait.

Since the door had been closed, Hunter started to step back out of the office. But the chief shook his head and gestured toward the chair, phone still up against his ear.

Apparently, whoever was on the other end had a lot to say, because Chief Colton didn't say much, other than the occasional *uh-huh* and *I see*. Finally, he placed the phone back in its cradle and shook his head. "That was one of West's former colleagues at the bureau. He insists there's no way Demi can be the Groom Killer. She doesn't match the profile."

Relieved, Hunter nodded. "That's exactly what I was coming to talk to you about. My gut is telling me it's not her."

The chief rubbed his eyes. "We just need a break, you know? Between the Groom Killer, the Larson twins and their criminal activity that we haven't been able to get a decent lead on, and now the Layla Colton case, it's looking like we're going to have our hands full right through the holidays."

"No breaks on the Larsons, either?" Hunter asked, surprised. Though he wasn't assigned to that particular case, he'd listened with interest when it had come up during their weekly briefings. Everyone knew the Larsons were involved in crimes ranging from manufacturing and dealing drugs to illegal weapon sales to theft. The DEA had paid numerous visits to Red Ridge, even setting up an undercover sting operation. Thus far, they had been completely unsuccessful in garnering any concrete evidence on the Larsons. They were never seen dealing, and thus far any stash of drugs or weapons had not been located. Not only were those particular criminals well organized, but they appeared to be widening their distribution area, expanding throughout the entire county.

"Nothing." The chief's glum tone matched his expression. "That's why we really need a win. Finally catching the Groom Killer would really help. Not only for our officers' morale, but to help rebuild the town's confidence in us."

Hunter nodded. "I get that. But if we arrest the wrong person, that means the real killer will still be out there."

"I'm aware of that." Dragging his hands through his short hair, Chief Colton grimaced. "Just keep digging, all right? As long as Demi is on the run, we can't arrest her. However, if the actual murderer *thinks* we've stopped looking, he'll get careless."

"We can only hope." Excusing himself, Hunter went back to his desk. His stomach growled, reminding him it was nearly dinnertime.

After collecting Goose, Hunter took her home. She went out into the backyard to take care of business, and he filled her food bowl with her usual dry kibble. With a grateful sigh, she dug in.

"I'll be back to let you out again before I go back to work," he told her. Like most of the other K9 officers, he'd gotten into the habit of talking to Goose as if she was a person rather than a dog. Sometimes he even felt quite certain she understood every word he said.

Knowing she'd climb up on the couch for an after-meal nap, he locked up and got back into his squad car.

Usually on his dinner break, he ate either a sandwich or a TV dinner at home. Occasionally, he picked up fast food. He couldn't remember the last time he'd sat down in a restaurant.

Everyone in town loved Pizza Heaven. Even on weeknights, the place was usually packed. He couldn't wait. Ever since that phone conversation with Layla, he'd been alternating thinking about pizza fresh from the oven and Layla's clear blue eyes.

A problem, considering she was engaged to another man.

When he pulled up to the restaurant, the parking lot was already nearly full. He lucked out and nabbed a spot close to the front, since another car had just backed out.

Trying to contain his eagerness, he strolled inside, dodging various small children, looking for Layla's shining cap of blond hair.

He didn't see her. As he surveyed the crowded, chaotic pizza parlor, he realized maybe Layla Colton would feel out of place here. He couldn't actually picture her, in one of her tailored suits and heels, moving between the kids chasing each other and their frazzled parents trying to corral them.

Again, she managed to surprise him. When she walked through the front doors, he saw she'd changed to a pair of jeans and boots, along with a button-down cotton shirt and a fuzzy vest.

The sight of her like this nearly brought him to his knees. Beautiful didn't even begin to describe her. Sexy and self-assured and gorgeous and sweet, all rolled into one. Lust mingled with awe as he watched her saunter toward him.

"Hey," she said, smiling. "Have you been waiting long?"

It took him a second or two to force the words from his throat. "Nope, not at all. Let's see if we can find a table."

They lucked out and got one in the back, as far from the arcade area as it could be.

Once they were seated, he couldn't keep from staring.

"Why do you keep looking at me like I've grown a second head?" she asked, her smile making her blue eyes sparkle.

He started to shrug, but then decided what the hell. "Because you look totally different."

Her smile widened. "I don't wear business clothes all the time, you know."

And of course, that comment had him flashing back to the pic he'd seen of her in lingerie, reclining on a bed with a come-hither look on her beautiful face. Since now would be the absolute worst possible time to bring that up, he didn't. But he resolved to ask her later who had taken that picture and how Mark Hatton might have gotten a hold of it.

The waitress came over, asking if they were ready. Though the menus were kept on the table, they hadn't looked at them.

"Are you good with Canadian bacon and pineapple?" he asked. When she nodded, he grinned. "Just making sure you didn't have a change of heart. One large," he told the waitress. They also both wanted iced tea to drink.

"You two sure are simpatico," the waitress commented, giving the thumbs-up sign. "I can't tell you how many couples fight over what kind of pizza to get."

Couples. Neither he nor Layla corrected her, which Hunter found amusing for whatever reason. It had been a long time since he'd been part of a couple.

Layla grimaced. "Sorry, but I refuse to explain myself any more. It's been a long, long day."

The waitress returned bearing two tall glasses of iced tea, both with lemon wedges stuck on the edge of the glass. Layla put one packet of artificial sweetener in hers, stirred and then took a small sip. "Perfect," she said with a sigh. "Though I really do deserve a glass of wine. Too bad they don't sell alcohol here."

Curious, he decided to go ahead and ask what had happened. Not only was he genuinely interested, but he figured she might need someone to talk to.

Turned out, she did. He listened, resisting the urge to comment, while she told him about the meeting with her father and her fiancé. But when she reached the part where Hamlin had said he didn't care if she had the hots for a twenty-two-year-old underling, he nearly choked on his iced tea. "He really said that?"

Slowly, she nodded. "I confess to being a bit shocked myself."

He waited for her to say more, maybe something along the lines of how she now realized she couldn't possibly marry a man like that. But when she didn't, he figured it might be safer to change the subject.

Luckily, the waitress arrived with their pizza and two plates. "Here you go," she said, setting it down. "Hot from the oven. Enjoy."

Hunter couldn't contain his glee. "It's been a long

time since I've had this," he said, rubbing his hands together.

Eyeing the pizza, Layla helped herself to a slice, which meant he could, too. He inhaled the fragrant scent before taking a bite, chewing slowly so he could savor his mouthful. Once he'd swallowed, he made a sound of pleasure low in his throat. "That's so good," he exclaimed.

When he looked up, he realized she hadn't touched hers. Instead, she watched him, wide-eyed. "You really enjoy your food," she commented.

About to take another bite, he grinned. "It's amazing. Go ahead and taste it. I promise, you'll see what I mean."

Without taking her eyes from him, she lifted up her pizza and took a slow bite, the way she did making it clear she intended to savor the taste.

Sensual as all get-out. Damn. Layla Colton. Who would have thought it? Arousal thrummed in his blood, though he tried to ignore it. This wasn't a date, and he definitely shouldn't be fantasizing about how he'd like to taste those lips of hers.

Instead, he focused on devouring his slice of pizza. He went back for a second and ate that, too, all before she'd finished her first one.

"Do you not like it?" he asked.

"Oh, I do. But I have to be careful eating stuff like this," she replied, unable to keep from eyeing the rest of the pizza with a wistful expression.

"Go for it. You deserve it."

Though she shook her head, she took another slice.

Once they'd demolished the pizza—well, once mostly *he'd* demolished the pizza—they sat back and sipped on their iced tea. The waitress returned to ask if they wanted dessert, and when they said no, she left the check.

Both Layla and Hunter reached for it at the same time.

"My treat," she insisted. "After all, I'm the one who invited you."

"For coffee. Not pizza. This was my idea."

When she still hesitated, he gently slid the check out from under her hand. "How about I get it this time and you can get it the next?"

One perfectly arched brow rose. "Oh, is there going to be a next time?"

His answer came easily. "Of course. How can there not? You're the only other person I know who likes this pizza."

"You're really into food," she observed. "You must have a fast metabolism."

"I am and I do. In fact, I'm looking forward to Thanksgiving," Hunter said. "It's my favorite holiday. So much food. I can't wait."

Instead of replying, she only smiled and shook her head.

After he left a generous tip on the table, they headed to the cashier so he could pay.

"Where'd you park?" he asked. Darkness had already fallen, and the breeze carried a hint of the winter yet to come.

She pointed. "I'm in the overflow lot across the street. There weren't any spots left close up."

Glancing across the street, he saw one of the tall streetlights had gone out. But the rest of the lot appeared well lit. And this was a safe part of town.

But still...

"I'll walk you to your car."

"You don't have to," she started to say, but she stopped when he shook his head.

"I know," he told her. "But I'm going to anyway."

Though she shrugged, he could tell by the slight curve of her lips that she was pleased.

He wanted to take her hand. Instead, he settled on taking her arm. She flashed a startled look his way but didn't comment.

Looking both ways, they started to cross the street.

The sound of an engine gunning and tires squealing alerted him seconds before the car came roaring around the corner. Layla froze. Hunter's survival instincts kicked in and he shoved her hard, sending them both flying out of harm's way.

Adrenaline pumping, he pushed to his feet, rounding to try to see the car. He fully intended to chew the driver out for his or her careless behavior.

The car had reached the end of the short street. To Hunter's disbelief, it swung around, pulling a U-turn and once again heading straight for them.

"Run," he shouted, snagging Layla's arm and hauling her along with him. They leaped for the curb, over the sidewalk and into the relative safety of the crowded parking lot just as the car raced past.

"Die, bitch," someone—a man—shouted as the car went by. Hunter tried to make out the license plate but couldn't.

With a flash of brake lights, the vehicle disappeared around the corner.

Breathing fast, Layla swayed. "That was deliberate," she said, closing her eyes. "Someone just tried to kill me."

Chapter 5

Once she'd voiced the truth out loud, Layla started trembling. She tried, oh, how she tried, to get that under control, but once the shakes began, she couldn't make them stop. She folded her arms around herself and clenched, trying. She was strong, she was tough, so why couldn't she seem to handle this?

At first, Hunter didn't appear to notice. From his fighting stance, she honestly thought he might go chasing after the car on foot.

Jaw tight, when he finally turned to face her, she realized he wasn't frightened, he was furious. "I'm calling that in," he began. The anger in his eyes disappeared when he got a good look at her.

"You're in shock," he said an instant later. "Come here." Without waiting for her to respond, he wrapped his arms around her and pulled her close. "It's going to be all right."

The sound of his deep voice rumbling from his chest reassured her. So did the warmth and strength of his muscular body. Though Layla had never been the type to rely on anyone but herself, maybe just this once it wouldn't hurt. Especially since she still couldn't stop the trembling.

"I'm not letting you go home," he announced. "You're coming with me."

Again, under usual circumstances a declaration like that would have had her digging in her heels and outright refusing. But these weren't ordinary circumstances.

"Okay," she said, in a very small—completely unlike her—voice.

"One step at a time." He kept his arm around her shoulders, turning her back toward Pizza Heaven. "This way. My car is in their lot."

As they approached, she realized he was in a marked police car. Of course, that made sense, as he wore his uniform. "Are we going to the police station?" she asked, hoping against hope that he'd say no.

He unlocked the car and opened the passenger-side door for her before going around to the driver's side. Once she'd buckled in, he started the engine. "I thought you might like to make a report," he said.

"Is that necessary? You were there, too. Can't you make the report?" She sighed. "To be honest, my last experience at the police station wasn't that great. I'd prefer to avoid going there again anytime soon."

Backing out of the parking spot, he shifted into Drive. "I didn't think of that. I'll take you to my house and drop you off."

"Your house?" She eyed him, realizing he'd so

shocked her that she'd finally stopped shaking. "What do you mean?"

"It's either there or the police station. I do have to go back to work and I can't let you go home. Not now. It's not safe."

Again, once upon a very recent time, had anyone told her they couldn't let her do something, she would have argued about her right to do exactly as she wished. But deep down inside, she suspected Hunter might be right. Alone in her townhome might not be the safest place for her.

"Unless you have somewhere else you'd like to stay," he offered helpfully. "Your fiancé's place? Or your father's?"

"I'd rather go home than go to my father's or Hamlin's." She didn't tell Hunter, but she knew if she showed up at her father's house, Fenwick would most likely send her away.

"Okay." He shrugged. "Then it looks like you can stay at my place. I have a guest bedroom. Plus Goose will definitely enjoy the company while I finish my shift."

The thought of getting to play with his dog made her feel better.

They pulled up in front of a small ranch-style house. The property appeared neatly kept and gave off a homey vibe.

"Here we are," he said cheerfully. "I know this might not be the kind of accommodations you're used to, but it's all mine."

"It looks lovely." She meant it, too. While she might live in a high-end town house, it had always felt sterile and cold to her. "I can't wait to see the inside."

His grin brought those sexy crinkles back to the corners of his eyes. "You're about to. Come on."

The second Hunter opened the door, Goose launched herself on him, spinning and wiggling in a frenzy of joy. He dropped down to his knees, gathering the dog close, crooning to her with such unabashed love that Layla's chest felt tight.

"She always greets me like this," he told her over Goose's head. "Even if I'm only gone a few minutes, she's over the moon to see me again."

A flash of longing hit her. "You're making me seriously consider getting a dog." A large one, who'd be able to protect her and keep her safe, as well as love her.

"You should." He didn't even hesitate. "They're the greatest."

Goose, who'd finally noticed Layla once she'd spoken, bounced on over, putting all her energy into another equally enthusiastic greeting.

Touched and gratified, Layla mimicked Hunter's movements, dropping to the floor and making a fuss over the adorable dog.

"She's so sweet," she told him. "I remember being so amazed when I learned about her particular skill set."

Her words brought out another grin. Briefly, she thought she could get used to seeing that smile every day.

"Thanks. No one believed me when I said I could train her to locate electronics. I'd been doing some reading on a facility that did that. When I contacted them, they were gracious enough to let me visit so I could soak up some tips. Goose is an expert at it. And, since she doesn't look anything like what most people consider a police dog, no one ever suspects her."

He reached down and ruffled Goose's head. "She's a smart girl. I'm proud of her. Goose, do you need to go outside?"

To Layla's surprise, Goose jumped up at his question and ran to the back door. He let her out, standing at the door to watch her. Once she'd come back inside, he locked the door and checked his watch.

"I've got to get back to the station," he said. "Help yourself to the fridge. I have lots to drink and snack on." He pointed to the television remote on the coffee table. "I've got cable, so watch whatever you want."

Suddenly tongue-tied, she nodded. "Will you be taking me home once you finish your shift?"

"Nope. I think it's best if you spend the night. I keep the guest bed made up with clean sheets and blankets. Follow me and I'll show you where it is."

He led her down a short hallway, past a bedroom he'd made into a combination exercise room and office. "Here you go."

To her surprise, she liked the decorating. A thick quilt that looked handmade brought a warmth to the room. Framed photographs of the South Dakota grasslands decorated the walls.

"Did you take those?" she asked.

A shadow crossed his face. "I did. Once upon a time, I was into photography."

"They're really good. You're talented." She walked over to study one closer. "These are magazine quality."

"Thanks. I don't take pictures anymore."

Though she wanted to ask him why not, something in his closed-off expression told her the question wouldn't be welcome.

"All right then," he said, a bit brusquely. "I'm going

to leave a spare toothbrush on the counter in the bathroom, as well as guest towels and a new bar of soap. I'll leave you my number in case you need anything else."

"I have it. You gave me your card."

Clearly distracted, he nodded. "Perfect. I'll see you later, then."

She followed him down the hall, watching as he let himself out the front door, locking the dead bolt from outside. Goose heaved a sigh and then padded back to the living room. She jumped up on the sofa and gave Layla a look, as if inviting her to join in on the fun.

Actually, it looked pretty darn tempting. Layla went to the refrigerator and grabbed a bottled water. The small kitchen looked clean and lived in, just like the rest of the house. None of her father's high-end designer furnishings, which in her opinion made his house feel staged and uncomfortable.

In the den were several more of the framed photographs. Studying them one at a time, she wondered why anyone this talented would quit. Surely he must have had his reasons, though she couldn't think of any at the moment. Telling herself it was none of her business, she sat on the edge of the couch and kicked off her boots before grabbing the remote and turning on the large TV.

Once she'd gotten settled, Goose moved closer, tucking her long body into Layla's side. Clicking through the on-screen guide, Layla found a movie she'd been wanting to see and settled in with her new companion to watch it. Goose heaved a sigh and began snoring softly, which Layla found adorable and comforting.

She must have fallen asleep. She woke to the sound of the front door opening. Disoriented, she sat up, heart pounding. It took Goose's happy woof to make her realize where she was. Goose jumped down to greet Hunter enthusiastically, while Layla dragged her hand through her hair and wondered how awful she looked.

"You're still up?" Again, that flash of a smile. Then, as he moved closer, he must have noticed her disheveled appearance, because his expression changed.

"I fell asleep." Giving up on trying to smooth out her hair, Layla covered her mouth with her hand as she yawned. "As a matter of fact, I'm going to head off to bed."

She could swear he looked disappointed. Heart pounding for whatever reason, she pushed up from the couch and hurried to the guest room.

As soon as she closed the door, she realized she'd made a mistake. She needed to use the restroom as well as brush her teeth and wash her face.

One deep breath, and then another. Why his late arrival home had suddenly felt unbearably intimate, she couldn't say. Hunter was merely being kind, doing a favor for a woman who'd clearly been panicked and afraid after almost being intentionally run down. Nothing more. He'd given her no reason to read anything else into it. No reason at all.

After giving herself this stern internal talking-to, Layla opened the door and crossed the hall to the small bathroom. Once inside, she felt better. Hopefully as soon as she'd had a good night's rest, everything could return to normal and she'd gain a fresh perspective on all of this.

Instead she found herself standing in front of the mirror crying. Loud, brokenhearted sobs came up out of her chest on their own. She tried to cover her mouth with her hand, but that only made her want to wail louder.

Oh, hell. Hunter might have bitten off a little more trouble than he could chew. He'd certainly not expected to have such a visceral reaction at seeing Layla Colton barely awake on his couch, with her sexy, drowsy eyes and mussed hair. She'd looked, he thought, exactly as if she'd just gotten out of bed after a long night of lovemaking.

And judging from the huge jolt of lust and his body's swift reaction, he needed to get himself under control, pronto. The last thing either of them needed would be that kind of complication.

Secretly relieved when she'd made a beeline for her bedroom, he'd headed for the kitchen to grab a beer and try to unwind after a long day at work. Goose followed right on his heels, of course.

Then he heard it. Gut-wrenching sobs and a low sound of keening. Goose whined before trotting off to the hall bathroom. She sat in front of the closed door, head cocked, before pawing at it.

About to set his beer down, Hunter took a deep drink first. "Layla?" he asked, tapping on the door. "Are you all right?"

"Go away." Her muffled response managed to sound both sad and angry. "I'm sorry I disturbed you."

"You didn't," he replied. "You've had a rough couple of days. I know how it feels. I'll be in the living room if you want some company. No judgment."

With that, he retreated to the sofa and his beer. Goose, however, after giving him what he considered a disparaging look, remained planted in front of the closed door. She'd never been able to turn away from a human in distress. Hunter often thought if she hadn't been such a great police dog, she would have been a wonderful emotional support animal.

"Goose wants to help you," he called out. "She's right outside your door."

"Oh." Making a sound the was part sob, part hiccup, she appeared to be working on getting herself together. "I'll be out in just a moment."

Sipping his beer, he clicked on the TV to give her a bit more cover while she blew her nose or whatever. When she opened the door a few minutes later, he pretended not to notice while Goose did her happy dance.

Clutching a box of tissues, Layla made her way to the couch and sat down at the opposite end. Her red nose and puffy, bloodshot eyes attested to the fact that she'd been crying, but oddly enough, he thought she managed to somehow look cute even then.

"I'm sorry," she began.

"No need to apologize. Like I said, you've had a hell of a time of it lately." He took another drink of his beer and noticed the way her gaze followed the movement. "Do you want one?"

To his surprise, she nodded, so he pushed to his feet to retrieve another can and a glass for her. "Here you go."

"Thanks." She popped the top and tilted the glass slightly as she poured. Fascinated despite himself, he watched as she lifted the glass to her lips and drank deeply. He ached to trace the graceful line of her throat with his mouth.

When she met his gaze, a sheen of tears clouded

her eyes. "I needed that." She sighed. "I don't know what happened to me. I'm so used to being strong—nothing bothers me—but this... In the space of a few days, I've been accused of sexually harassing an employee I can't even stand, learned my own father is the reason our company is failing, realized I agreed to a loveless marriage for false reasons and had someone try to kill me."

"Which would be enough to send someone stronger than you down to their knees," he said.

"Thank you." She took another drink, and he watched her again, wondering how she could make something so common, so simple, into something so sensual.

What the hell was wrong with him? Layla needed comfort, someone to listen and offer support, not some guy who only wanted to jump her bones.

Goose, instinctively understanding this, jumped up to sit next to Layla. Turning in a circle, the dog sighed before settling down with her head on Layla's leg. This coaxed a tiny smile from Layla. "Such a good dog," she crooned, scratching Goose behind her ears. "You're a good girl."

Goose, of course, went into spasms of doggy-heaven pleasure. Tongue lolling, she actually appeared to be grinning.

"Your dog is making me feel better," Layla said, making a half humorous, half pitiful face. "I'm really having to take a close look at my life and my priorities. I've given up so much time—years of my life—to my father's company, and he won't even stand behind me when I'm facing a bogus harassment charge? Though he did hire an attorney to deal with Mark's attorney. So there's that."

"That's good."

"It is. Though I would have hired someone myself if he hadn't. I'm hoping that once the lawyers hash things out, this thing will go away.

"And," she continued, "I find out that Colton Energy would be doing amazing if he hadn't been spending all the profits. And on what? Living the high life. Fast cars, women he refers to as *arm candy*, and jet-setting around the globe."

He nodded, knowing better than to comment. Right now she just needed someone to listen.

"I actually agreed to *marry* Hamlin Harrington so the company could get an infusion of cash. Even though the man sort of makes my skin crawl." The disbelief and disgust in her voice made Hunter want to scoot over next to her and hold her.

Luckily, he had enough sense to know not to do anything as stupid as that. Instead, he gripped his beer can with both hands, almost as if it was a lifeline.

"My priorities are screwed up," she declared. "Maybe it's time to make some changes. Big changes."

He definitely agreed with her on that, though wasn't sure he should say so. He settled on telling her the truth, though not all of it. "You're an intelligent, successful woman. You'd be an asset to any company you choose to work for."

A flash of pleasure lit up her face. "Thank you. Enough about me. What about you? I was always curious why you choose police work over the corporate world. Even though you made it clear how you felt about Colton Energy, you were good at your job and I thought you had a real future."

For a few seconds, he hesitated, and then decided what the hell. Why not. Surely he wouldn't be telling her anything she already didn't know. "It started feeling like selling my soul," he admitted. "I worked closely with your father. There were too many deals that skirted the edge of legality, so many times he asked me to turn a blind eye."

Watching him intently, she nodded. "I get it, I really do. But you could always have said no. I do, all the time. I told him early on that I wouldn't do anything illegal or morally wrong."

"Yet you agreed to marry a virtual stranger for money," he pointed out.

Instead of reacting with anger or a retort, she simply nodded, a thoughtful expression on her face. "You have a point. But tell me, what made you choose police work?"

Again, he had nothing but the truth. "I wanted to help people," he said simply. "My parents were killed in a car crash when I was fifteen. My neighbor, Mae Larson, was kind enough to take me in."

"The Larson twins' grandmother?"

"Yep." He nodded. "She saw a brokenhearted kid in need and stepped up to help. I owe her more than I can say. She helped me work through my grief and never turned her back on me, even when I was a rebellious little snot. She's the reason I always look forward to Thanksgiving. She puts on the most amazing meal. Roasted turkey, corn bread dressing, sweet potato casserole, green beans…just thinking about it make my mouth water."

"What about the Larsons?" She eyed him, her gaze considering. "Are you close to them as well?"

"No. It used to bother me to admit that, but Noel and Evan treated me like garbage. They tried like hell to make my life miserable. I can't tell you how many times Mae Larson got in between us."

"That must be hard, then, with the police trying to build a case against them. I mean, everyone knows they're involved in drugs and stuff, even if no proof has been found."

By *proof*, she meant evidence. RRPD had been trying to catch either of the Larson brothers with drugs. So far, even though numerous witnesses had come forward claiming to have seen one or the other selling or buying, no proof of that had thus far been found. Video cameras conveniently went on the fritz when those two were around. The Larsons' drug dealing might have been common knowledge, but it had begun to take on the status of an urban legend. Not one single shred of evidence had yet to be found.

That didn't mean it wouldn't be. Criminals who used drugs always made a mistake. The Larson brothers would, too, given enough time. When they did, Hunter knew one of his fellow officers would bring them in. Unfortunately, it wouldn't be him.

"That's why I asked to be taken off their case. Sure, the police department is working it, but Goose isn't a drug-detection dog, so I'm not actively involved." He thought about it for another moment, then decided to throw caution to the wind. "Though I—along with every law enforcement officer in the county—am working the Groom Killer case, I've also been assigned to your case, as you know."

He nearly lost the words he'd wanted to say, but didn't. He pushed himself because he figured if he didn't tell her now, he might never.

"And if you'll allow me to, I'd like to help protect you."

Mic drop. She froze, staring at him as if he'd just admitted to being the Groom Killer, or something equally heinous. "Protect me?" she finally managed. "By that, am I to assume you mean you think this will happen again?"

Crud. He hadn't meant to frighten her. But from what he knew of Layla Colton, she definitely appreciated the facts.

"It's possible," he said. "More than that. Highly probable. Someone wants you out of the way. It might be whoever framed you for something you didn't do. If they tried to kill you once and didn't succeed, I think they'll definitely try again."

She swore. Her language made him grin. "Now that's the Layla I know," he said.

Again, the flash of pleasure lit up her face, making him wonder when he'd become so adept at reading her.

It didn't matter, he decided. He could—and would—put this attraction aside and be the police officer she needed him to be.

"Tell me," she asked, leaning forward. "What can I do to help?"

"Just don't take any unnecessary chances. Do you have any vacation days available that you could take?"

For some reason, his question amused her. She laughed, though her eyes shone with the brightness of unshed tears. "Oh, definitely. I haven't taken a vacation in years."

"How many years?" he asked, curious.

"Ever." Grimacing, she shook her head. "While my father's been traveling around the world with his trophy women, I've stayed here to do my job and take care of the company."

He wondered if she recognized the bitterness that came through in her voice. Apparently, she did, because her next comment reflected that.

"In fact, I can't think of a better time than right now to take a break. A few weeks, at least." She grabbed her phone. "I'll leave my father a voice mail right now. He can put that in his pipe and smoke it."

Chapter 6

Layla's bravado lasted about as long as it took her father's voice mail to pick up. She quickly ended the call without leaving a message, her heart pounding. "Anxiety's a pain," she muttered, more to herself than anyone else. She looked up to find Hunter Black watching her, his calm expression somehow reassuring.

He didn't press her or question her. Instead, he got up and left the room, giving her the privacy she needed to do whatever she decided to do.

Palms sweaty, she considered. She needed a break, she deserved some time off and Hunter had hinted that staying away from Colton Energy would help keep her safe. The company would survive without her for a few days—even a few weeks if it came to that.

But what would she do? Sure, she could book a stay at an all-inclusive at a resort somewhere, but doing that sort of thing alone was no fun. Since she'd long ago let any friendships she'd had wither away from lack of attention, the only people she could ask to go with her were family. Patience might do it, but she'd spend the entire trip trying to dissuade Layla from her impending marriage. So, no.

Hanging out in Hunter's house held no appeal, and staying for more than one day would be too intrusive. In all honesty, she felt safer at work than alone in her town house.

Hunter returned, carrying a big bowl of popcorn and two paper plates. Surprised, she smiled. "I didn't smell it popping."

"That's because I didn't pop it. I buy it already made, in big bags." He winked. "It's my secret weakness."

She froze. The effect of that wink hit her low in the belly. If she'd been standing, her knees would have gone weak. As it was, she couldn't catch her breath for a moment.

Instead of the lighthearted, teasing reply that he probably expected, she simply nodded.

"What's yours?" he asked.

You. Of course she didn't allow that response past her lips. "Chocolate," she said instead. "But not just any chocolate. Dark chocolate covered cherries. I'm lucky they only sell them during the holidays. I buy four or five boxes and ration them out, one per day."

Heaven help her, he laughed. Unabashed, masculine laughter, one of the sexiest things she'd ever heard.

Had she lost her mind? What was it about this guy? How had she possibly managed to work with him for a couple of years and never notice how sexy he was?

Goose snorted, almost as if she'd read Layla's thoughts. She nudged Layla's hand with her snout and then rolled over onto her back, presenting her belly, all four legs waving in the air.

This made Layla laugh. "I'm in love with your dog," she said, rubbing Goose's tummy.

His gaze darkened. "That makes two of us." He placed the bowl of popcorn on the coffee table, watching indulgently while Goose got her belly rub.

Finally, Goose flopped back over, apparently satisfied. She got up, shook her entire body, which sent her ears flapping, and then moved to sit next to Hunter.

"I didn't call." She lifted her cell phone again. "I'd like to take some time off, but I'm not sure what I'd do to occupy myself."

"Good point." He grabbed a handful of popcorn and deposited it on his paper plate. "Help yourself."

That was it? Struggling not to show her disappointment, she snagged a small handful of popcorn and sat back. What had she hoped he'd do—offer suggestions to help her decide?

"Do you have a girlfriend?" she asked, wincing slightly.

He tossed a kernel of popcorn at Goose, watching as she caught it neatly, before answering. "Only my dog. Why?"

Heaven help her, but she flushed. "Just wondering."

Then, because she really wanted to know, she let her mouth get ahead of her common sense. "Why not? I mean, you're an attractive man, with a good job, and you own your own home."

He laughed. "If I didn't know better, I'd ask if you were applying for the position."

Though she knew he was only teasing, heat suffused her. Embarrassment mingled with desire and a kind of nervous anticipation that made her go dry in the mouth.

"Maybe I am." She batted her eyelashes at him. Though she'd never been good at flirting, ever, something about this man and the way he teased made her feel comfortable and safe. And wanted.

His gaze zeroed in on her mouth. He scooted closer, dislodging a disgruntled Goose. The basset jumped to the floor and headed off toward the kitchen, probably in search of water.

"You've got a bit of popcorn there," he said, his voice husky. He reached out with one finger to brush it off. Enthralled despite herself, she opened her mouth, her heart hammering in her chest.

"Layla," he groaned. And then he kissed her.

A quick press of the lips at first, but the instant their mouths connected, she felt a flash of fire zinging through her blood. She gasped and then kissed him back with all the glorious, uncertain attraction he made her feel.

His hand tangled in her hair. The kiss—their desire—ran away with them, leveling any chance of rational thought, until only craving remained.

Hot, so hot. His tongue and hers met and mated and explored. Leaving her mouth, his lips blazed a path down her throat to her chest. She arched her back, helpless except for the raw wanting. By silent, mutual agreement, they shed their clothing, quickly and efficiently, until they were skin to skin, still burning.

He covered her with his body, hard and muscular to her soft curves. The force of his hard arousal pressing against her body thrilled her, and she felt herself melting.

"Yes," she managed before he claimed her mouth again. He broke away to retrieve a condom from his wallet, and despite the shaking of her hands, she helped him cover himself with it. Once this was done, he kissed her once more. Deeply, not holding any part of himself back.

Except she needed more. She needed him between her legs and more. As if she'd voiced this thought, between one breath and another he pushed the full, glorious length of himself inside her.

Never in her life had anything felt so wonderful, so good, so damn right. And then he moved and she thought she'd died and gone to heaven.

For once she gave herself over to feeling, without allowing any analyzing or rational thought to intrude. She wanted this, she wanted him, and by all that was right, she deserved it. She'd done nothing but deny herself any kind of pleasure for too damn long.

Starbursts exploded inside her, making her gasp. At first she tried to hold it back, but then she gave over and let herself be swept away.

She cried out, shuddering over and over as her body clenched around the length of him. Tensing, he struggled, clearly trying to maintain control, but a second later he lost the battle. He slammed into her, riding the wave with her, cresting each peak again and again and again until she thought she might die from sheer ecstasy.

He held her while their sweat-slick bodies cooled. Never, ever had she known lovemaking could be like this.

"That was…" he began.

Relieved, she finished for him. "Amazing."

"Yes." He kissed her forehead. "You are one special lady, Layla Colton. But…"

She tensed. She'd suspected there was going to be a *but*. "You're going to say we don't need to do this again."

Chuckling, he shook his head and kissed her again, this time full on the lips and lingering. "Why would I say that? We're both consenting adults. And even though I said earlier this would be a bad idea, I've re-thought that." He cocked his head. "But what about your fiancé?"

"Hamlin? You heard what he said. He doesn't care if I have the hots for another man."

His gaze locked with hers. "Do you?"

"What, care? Or have the hots for another man?"

"Both." One corner of his mouth tugged up in that endearing smile of his.

Her insides cartwheeled. "I don't care, and clearly I want you."

Another kiss, so sultry and sensual she couldn't catch her breath. "That goes for me too, Layla. As long as we're discreet and you're agreeable, that is."

She studied him, fully aware of what he proposed. A no-strings-attached sexual relationship only. There would be no holding hands in public, posting silly pics of them together on Instagram. She was engaged to Hamlin, business deal or not, and many in town knew they were planning to marry once the Groom Killer was caught.

"I'm agreeable," she finally said, feeling bold and daring and as if she'd taken a leap out of a plane with-out a parachute.

"Good. And you should know if at any time, you change your mind and want to end it, all you have to do is say the word."

With that, she felt a bit of herself return. "Sounds perfect," she said, injecting her tone with her usual brusque confidence. She almost didn't recognize the woman she became around him. Pliant and vibrant, giving as much pleasure as she received.

The thought made her grin. "Kiss me again," she demanded.

And he did.

Hunter had never been with a woman like Layla Colton. When he'd worked at Colton Energy, she'd always seemed cool and remote. If she'd had any emotional reactions to anything, she kept them under an ironclad control. Her confidence made her attractive, but those who attempted to get close quickly learned not to. She shut them down, often with a single glance.

If anyone had ever suggested she'd turn out to be this sexy, amazing dynamo in bed, he would have thought they were crazy. Yet she was all of these things and more. He felt so, so glad she wanted to get together again. With a woman like her, once would never be enough.

They cuddled and kissed and talked into the early hours of dawn. Somehow, to his disbelief, passion flared and his body proved ready, willing and able to make love again.

"Are you going in to work today?" he asked her while she drowsily snuggled close to him. Since the clock on his nightstand showed 7:00 a.m., he figured she'd need to get showered and moving if she planned to be at the office on time.

She followed his glance, and her eyes widened. "I can't believe it's this late—or early, depending on your point of view." Closing her eyes, she stretched. "As for work, I don't think I'm going. Though I still haven't decided how much time I want to take off, I don't plan on being there for the next couple of days at least. I'll call and leave my father a voice mail." This time, she covered her mouth to mask a yawn. "What about you? Are you scheduled to work today?"

"No. I'm off. But if I had been, I wouldn't go in until seven tonight."

She nodded. "Do you always work the graveyard shift?"

"Not always. These days, I rarely have to. I've been alternating, sometimes days, sometimes nights, filling in where needed. The chief just switched me permanently to days."

"That's going to be hard to get used to, isn't it?"

"Yep. I'll have to change my entire biological clock. Normally I sleep until noon or so." And damn if he wasn't going to miss that. She yawned again, which made him follow suit. "Layla, if you're not going in, how about we catch some z's?"

Her grin made his heart stutter in his chest. "Sounds good to me."

Of course, he'd barely closed his eyes when his cell rang.

"I know it's early and you probably haven't gotten much sleep," Chief Colton began.

Hunter didn't tell his boss that he hadn't been to sleep at all. "What's up?"

"You might want to get in here," the chief said. "The mayor is here. He's wanting to call a press conference at noon. We're trying to talk him out of it."

"A press conference about what?" Hunter asked, though he suspected he already knew.

"The Groom Killer." Exasperation rang in the chief's voice. "He won't listen. I've told him we don't consider the case locked down yet. Hell, he's wanting to throw Demi Colton to the wolves. She's family, even if Fenwick doesn't like to admit it."

"Damn." Hunter understood the chief's dilemma. "What do you want me to do?"

"Aren't you still working the investigation on Layla? Maybe Fenwick's daughter can talk some sense into him. I'm his family and the K9 chief and can't, so I'm hoping she can. Can you see if she's willing to come in?"

Hunter eyed the woman lying next to him in his bed, wearing nothing but a sheet and a sleepy smile. "I can do that."

"Good. And please, act on it quickly."

Ending the call, Hunter told Layla what was going on.

Her lovely eyes widened. "Of course I'll go talk to him. Wait, maybe I can call him." She grabbed her phone from the nightstand.

A few seconds later, she shook her head. "Voice mail. He never answers his phone. At least, not if he knows it's me calling. I did leave him a message informing him I wouldn't be in the office today."

"Then we need to go to the station." He located his pants and underwear on the floor and pulled them on. "How quickly can you get ready?"

"Give me ten minutes," she responded, surprising him. Keeping the sheet wrapped around that delectable body of hers, he snagged her own clothes off the floor and carried them into the bathroom. "Be right back."

They were in his squad car and on the way to the station in just over ten minutes. Glancing at Layla, he marveled at not only how quickly she'd been able to get ready, but at how put together she looked. One would never guess she'd spent the past several hours making passionate love with him.

They stopped to grab some coffee and a couple of breakfast burritos and pulled up at the police station shortly before eight.

"Isn't it unusual for your father to be out and about this early?" Hunter asked as he parked the car.

She shrugged. "Depends. For all I know, he might have been out all night partying with one of his women."

They got out and headed toward the door. "If he's so busy living large, how does he find time to be mayor?"

This made her smile, though he didn't see any humor in her eyes. "The same way he finds time to run Colton Energy. He delegates."

"I'd wondered if the two of you were close, but didn't want to ask."

"Only when he finds being close beneficial." She grimaced. "That sounds terrible, but it's true. I'm used to it."

By now they'd reached the plate-glass door. Hunter opened it, holding it while Layla went past.

Once inside, he immediately saw the crowd gathered back by the chief's office. Several officers stood on the fringes, while he recognized some of the mayor's office staff in their three-piece suits.

In front of him, Layla sighed. She visibly straightened her spine, squared her shoulders and lifted her chin before sailing forth toward the others.

Two of the mayor's assistants caught sight of her and visibly brightened. She pushed her way past the outer ring of people, Hunter right behind her as she made a beeline for the office where her father and Chief Colton faced off.

As soon as the chief spied Layla and Hunter, he let out a huge sigh of relief.

"Dad?" Layla's sharp voice cut through the crowd like a knife, instantly silencing everyone. "What on earth is going on here?"

Fenwick narrowed his gaze and eyed his daughter. "Layla, why are you here? Don't you have more important things to tend to?"

She shook her head. "Can we talk in private?"

Without waiting for Fenwick's response, Chief Colton shot to his feet. "Clear the room, please. Let's all give these folks some privacy."

Everyone moved away. When Hunter started to leave, Layla shook her head. "You can stay. You too, Chief."

"Who put you in charge?" Fenwick asked, his lip curling in annoyance.

Chief Colton got up and closed the door. Without saying a word, he returned to his desk and took a seat, motioning at Hunter to do the same. Getting the point—staying out of the way—Hunter did exactly that.

Though Layla glanced at Hunter, Fenwick didn't spare him a glance.

"What are you doing?" Layla asked, more quietly this time.

"Doing what our police department won't," Fenwick said. "They know the identity of the Groom Killer. I want to make our citizens aware so their minds can be at ease. Maybe some of them will feel safe enough to resume their wedding plans."

"But they're not safe," the chief interjected. "Even if Demi turns out to be the killer, she's still at large."

"Even if?" Fenwick glared at the other man. "I was informed this was cut-and-dried."

"Informed by whom?"

Though Fenwick's mouth tightened, he didn't respond.

Layla cleared her throat, breaking the tense silence. "You cannot go public with unconfirmed information," she said. "You have a responsibility, not only to the citizens of Red Ridge, but to these hardworking police officers, to keep your silence until they've brought the right person to justice."

The mayor's jaw tightened. "If not Demi, then who?"

"We don't know yet," Chief Colton replied. "It's entirely possible it might be someone else."

Fenwick swore. "This is ridiculous."

"Maybe." Expression implacable, the police chief shrugged. "But don't you agree it's better to arrest the right person? How awful would it be if we arrested someone, say, Demi, and then another groom was murdered?"

"Do your job," Fenwick ordered. "This needs to end before half the hardworking people in our community go bankrupt."

When he turned to leave, he cast a disparaging look at Hunter before focusing on Layla. "Why aren't you at the office?" Making a production of checking his watch, he shook his head. "You're late."

Unsmiling, Layla faced her father. "No, I'm not. Didn't you check your messages? I'm taking today— actually, the rest of the week—off. Maybe more. I'm finally using some of my vacation days."

"Vacation days?" He said the words as if she'd spoken a foreign language.

"Yes. You know, those days away from the office that other people use to do fun things. Well, mine have been piling up, wasted. I decided the time had come to use some of them."

"We'll discuss this later, in private."

"No, we won't." Layla crossed her arms. "This isn't up for debate. I need a break and I'm taking one."

He shrugged. "That won't last long. You'll get bored." Then, without waiting for her to answer, he swept out of the office, back to his entourage.

Chief Colton, Hunter and Layla all watched him go in silence.

"I'm sorry," Layla began.

"Don't apologize for him," the chief ordered. "You're not responsible for what he does. Thank you for agreeing to come and help defuse what could have potentially been an awkward situation."

Hunter cleared his throat. "Chief, we have another problem. Someone attempted to run Layla down last night. I know I should have called it in, but I did make my report." He outlined most of the details, leaving out nothing except how he and Layla had spent the time after he'd gotten home from work.

After listening, Chief Colton nodded. Hunter appreciated that his boss didn't ask if he was certain the attempt had been deliberate rather than an accident. Since Hunter was a trained law enforcement officer, his observations could be taken as fact rather than conjecture.

"Any idea why?" The chief directed his question to Layla.

"To be honest, no." She flushed, looking down at her hands before raising her chin and meeting his gaze. "Just like this thing with Mark Hatton. I have no idea why he'd say such a thing or where he got the photos I supposedly texted him."

"Had you ever seen those photos before? Do you know if someone took them?"

"That's just it. I think they were doctored. Even the video. I never posed for any of them."

Chief Colton nodded. He turned his attention to Hunter next. "What about you? Are you taking steps to make sure Layla stays safe?"

Hunter suspected his boss already knew the answer to that, but he nodded anyway. "Yes, sir."

"Good. And Hunter, about that other lead in the Groom Killer case? I need you to work harder on that, before it's too late. Understood?"

"Understood." Which meant it was time for him and Goose to pay a visit to Devlin Harrington. He just needed to come up with a viable reason.

When they left the police station, Layla seemed preoccupied.

"Where to?" Hunter asked. "I can take you back to my place or we can drive around, or maybe grab another cup of coffee."

"I think you should take me to get my car," she said. "It's still sitting across the street from Pizza Heaven."

He couldn't believe he'd forgotten about her vehicle. "Right. You can park it at my place if you want."

She shot him a considering look. "You know, that might be a great idea. Especially since I'm going to stay there a couple more days."

Her response made him blink, then grin as joy filled him. "That's great," he said, resisting the urge to pull her close for a quick kiss. Not here, in front of the station. No telling who might see.

"That is, if your invitation is still open." She climbed into the passenger side and buckled her seat belt.

"Oh, it most definitely is."

"Great. If I'm going to take a vacation, I might as well have as much fun as I can," she teased.

His body stirred as images of exactly how much fun they'd be having filled his brain. Damn.

On the short drive to Pizza Heaven, he had to fight not to touch her. He couldn't believe how badly he wanted her again, after having spent the previous several hours making love.

"Here we are," he said, his voice a bit raspy as he pulled into the lot across from the restaurant. There were only a couple of cars parked here at this early hour, most likely prep employees, since Pizza Heaven wouldn't be open until eleven for lunch. "Which one's yours?"

Scanning the area, she turned to face him, her expression panicked. "Hunter, I don't see my car. I parked it right here last night. But it's gone."

He searched, too. "What kind of vehicle is it?"

"A white Volvo." Her voice wavered. "Someone must have stolen it."

"Did you have any kind of GPS theft-deterrent device?"

Slowly, she nodded. "I think so."

"Then we can trace it." This was where being a police officer came in handy. "We'll get your car back, don't worry."

Chapter 7

For whatever reason, the theft of her car hit her hard. It felt like the final straw in a gradually increasing pile. Layla usually never cried, at least in public, and this had long been a point of pride with her. But now, after everything that had gone wrong in the last few days, when her eyes welled up and tears started slipping down her face, she just let them fall. Twice in fewer than twenty-four hours meant everything was going very wrong.

"Hey," Hunter sounded concerned. "Please don't cry." A trace of panic edged his voice. "Layla, it's going to be okay."

"Is it?" Sobbing now, she covered her mouth and turned away so he couldn't see. Most of the men she knew reacted to weepy women with varying degrees of horror or disgust. Why should Hunter be any different? She huddled as close to the passenger door as she could, her shoulders shaking, mouth covered as she tried to cry as quietly as possible.

Instead of recoiling, Hunter reached for her. "Come here, sweetheart."

Though she wasn't sure if she should, she half turned, her fist still in her mouth. He pulled her close and then, wonder of wonders, he simply held her and let her cry it out. Inside, she marveled and allowed herself to feel comforted, maybe even loved.

Whoa. Where had that come from? Pushing even the thought away, she sniffed and wiped at her eyes. Like she needed one more thing to worry about. Attraction might sizzle between them, for sure. But attraction and love were two completely different things.

"Here." He handed her a couple of paper napkins he'd gotten from the pocket in his door.

Grateful, she accepted them, blotting her eyes and finally her nose. "I'm sorry," she finally managed, her voice a bit more wavering than she'd have liked. "I'm not really a weepy kind of person. I don't know what came over me."

"Don't worry about it." His easy smile reassured her. You've been dealing with a lot. Having your car stolen…"

"Tops it all off nicely," she finished with a wry smile, still dabbling at her leaky eyes. "To say the least. I really like that car."

"You're going to need to file a police report," he told her. "Luckily, I can take that from you, so you don't have to go back to the station."

"Thanks." She nodded, and then reached for the visor so she could use the mirror to repair the damage.

She hadn't put on very much makeup, so hopefully it wouldn't be too bad.

It was. When she saw herself, she recoiled. "Jeez," she muttered. Bright red nose, swollen red eyes and black mascara streaks, which at least she could wipe off. As for the rest of it... "I don't think that's fixable."

"Don't," Hunter said, his voice warm. "You're beautiful, Layla. Even after you've been crying."

Though she knew he was just trying to be nice and make her feel better, oddly enough, she did. Smiling a still watery smile, she asked for more napkins. Once he'd handed them over, she proceeded to do the best she could to make herself look as normal as possible. When she'd finished, she realized she felt better. Apparently, crying could be cathartic.

"Are you ready for me to make the police report?" he asked. "No biggie if you're not, but I'm thinking we might as well get that done."

"I agree. I'm ready." After she gave him her statement, right there in the squad car in the parking lot, they stopped at her place so she could pick up clothes and toiletries, and then went back to his house to take showers. Separate showers, of course. To her surprise, she toyed with the idea of slipping into the shower with him, imagining the naked fun they could have under the water. But she decided to save that for another day and right now focus on practicality over passion.

Goose greeted her with as much enthusiasm as she did Hunter, which tickled her. She even followed Layla to the guest bathroom, sitting down outside in the hallway when Layla closed the door.

Funny how a nice hot shower made her feel better. She dried her hair and got dressed in a comfy pair of soft leggings and an oversize sweatshirt, electing to go without makeup entirely.

When she emerged, she felt human again. Goose still waited, jumping up and wiggling her entire body when Layla petted her. She saw no sign of Hunter but since his bedroom door remained closed, she knew he hadn't left.

With Goose right on her heels, Layla went to the kitchen and made herself a cup of coffee. She appreciated the choices he had in the variety of coffee pods. She chose a dark roast, added sweetener and a dash of milk, and wandered back out into the living room. She sat down in the overstuffed chair near the window, Goose at her feet.

Looking around the small house, she found herself imagining what it would be like to live here, to raise a family. The holidays, like Thanksgiving, with the countertops groaning with food, small children running around underfoot, friends and family laughing. She knew exactly where the Christmas tree would go, could imagine what kind of decorations would go best with his decor.

All the kinds of things she'd never allowed herself to enjoy. It always seemed a waste to decorate only for one.

Wistful, she shook her head at herself. She'd only seen gatherings like that on television or in movies. Growing up, Thanksgiving meant having a meal catered, eating in the cold formal dining room in uncomfortable silence. Later, her father had decided it would be better to ignore the holiday altogether. Part of her had actually been relieved.

Pushing the foolish thoughts from her mind, she got

up and crossed the room, coffee in hand, and snagged the remote from the coffee table so she could turn on the television. This time, she sat on the couch, tucking her legs up under her, and invited Goose to join her. The happy dog promptly did, curling into her side. Still feeling remarkably at home, Layla watched a program where people searched for the perfect house. For whatever reason, she loved this show. Especially when each spouse wanted opposite things, making her wonder how they'd managed to stay married in the first place.

Hunter's door opened and he emerged, hair still damp and tousled, as if he'd made an attempt to towel it dry. "Hey there," he said, smiling. "Feeling better?"

"I am." She smiled back, her stomach doing a somersault. "I hope you don't mind, but I made some coffee." She loved those crinkle lines around his eyes when he smiled.

"Of course I don't mind. I told you, make yourself at home. Coffee sounds good. Let me grab a cup and I'll join you." His gaze drifted past her to the TV. "I actually like that show."

Surprised, she nodded, dragging her gaze away from him and back to the TV. Goose, who'd raised her head when Hunter had entered the room, settled back down with a contented sigh.

"I think she likes you," Hunter mused, returning to take a spot on the opposite end of the sofa. His amused expression told her he didn't mind. "I always trust my dog's judgment," he continued.

Feeling her face heat—was she actually blushing?— Layla pretended to be engrossed in the drama unfolding between the onscreen couple arguing over which kitchen was better.

Her phone chimed, indicating an incoming call. Her father. She pushed the reject button, sending him straight to voice mail. Grimacing, she shook her head. "I'm thinking the head of Colton Energy isn't too happy that I've taken a day off."

He shrugged. "I'm guessing he'll have to get over it." Expression serious, he eyed the way she kept stroking Goose's fur. "You're good with dogs."

"Am I?"

"At least with Goose, you are. Do you have a dog of your own?"

"No."

"A cat?"

This made her smile. "No. I don't have any pets. I work such long hours, I didn't think it would be fair to them."

He gave her a long look. "You're the boss. Surely you could take a well-behaved dog to work with you."

The thought had never occurred to her. Now that he mentioned it, she probably could. Since her father rarely graced the office with his presence, she doubted he would notice. "Noted for future reference," she said.

"Since you clearly like dogs, have you ever thought about helping out at the K9 training center?"

His offhand question made her heart skip a beat. "I'd love to do that, but I wasn't aware they'd let anyone volunteer."

"You're not exactly anyone, are you?" His grin took any sting off the words. "I mean, your mother's trust got the training center up and running. At least that's what I've heard."

She nodded. "This past year I've been involved in the funding since the trusts ran out. Colton Energy donated quite a bit of money, and I solicited more from some of the other companies we did business with." Thinking for a second, she took a deep breath. "I'd love to help out there while I'm off work. I could ask my half sister Patience, but as the veterinarian for the training center, I doubt she's too involved with the volunteers. Do you know who I'd need to contact to see if such a thing might actually be possible? Sarah Danvers?"

"She'd be a great place to start," he replied. "I'm sure there's got to be something she needs help with."

Suddenly, the prospect of a week or two away from Colton Energy felt energizing, full of promise. "I'll call her after I speak with my insurance company," she told him. "Would you mind taking me to get a rental car? I'm going to need something to drive until mine is found."

If it was found. She could only hope for the best.

Once all the calls had been made, Layla's mood greatly improved. Though the insurance company said she'd need to wait until twenty-four hours after the car had gone missing to file a claim, her agent had told her she carried rental reimbursement, which would pay her back for a rental car. She'd reserved a small, four-door sedan, which would be much different than her Volvo SUV. And best of all, Sarah Danvers had sounded overjoyed at the prospect of Layla volunteering. She'd asked Layla if she could start in the morning. Layla enthusiastically agreed, even though she had no idea what tasks she'd actually be performing.

"Wow," she told Hunter after ending the call. "Thanks for the suggestion. I start tomorrow. It feels really good to take a leap of faith." And to be doing something for her own satisfaction, rather than her father's, though she kept that to herself.

After dropping Layla off at the car rental agency, Hunter and Goose headed into the police station. Hunter filed Layla's stolen car report and thought about what the chief had said about finding the actual Groom Killer. Hunter decided to go ahead and make some sort of move.

Pretending to be acting as a private citizen rather than a police officer, he called Devlin Harrington's office and made an appointment to meet with him. Though at first Hunter's request was met with frosty disapproval by Devlin's secretary, once Hunter had given the reason for his call, she immediately booked him a slot that very afternoon.

Hunter had done a little bit of digging and learned the youngest Harrington was an avid collector of rare sports memorabilia. In one of the K9 unit's recent drug busts, they'd confiscated a good-size collection of old baseball cards. Hunter went into impound and slipped a couple in their protective sleeves into a hard, plastic sheath which he placed in his coat pocket, signing them out to be safe, even though he had every intention of returning them later. For now, he'd pretend to be selling them to the highest bidder. Not only would that gain him entrance into Devlin Harrington's office, but it would give him an idea of what made the other man tick.

Whistling for Goose, who'd gone roaming the office, greeting her legion of fans, Hunter smiled when she came running full speed down the hallway, long ears flying. She skidded to a stop right in front of him, gazing up expectantly.

"Want to go to work, girl?" he asked, bending down to scratch behind her ears. Instantly, she perked up, since he'd used a familiar word, if not the actual phrase. He snapped her leash on and together they headed for his car.

He'd made his appointment with Devlin at two and he hadn't mentioned that he planned to bring his dog. Goose had her breed and her looks to her advantage. No one ever suspected her of being a police dog, despite her being one of four dogs in the country trained to detect SD cards and thumb drives. She had longer legs and few skin folds.

To Hunter, Goose was the most beautiful dog who'd ever existed. He didn't really care if the rest of the word thought she looked goofy. He slipped a voice-activated recorder into his pocket and he was ready to go.

The receptionist at Harrington Inc. blinked when he entered with Goose on leash. Hunter leaned on the counter to talk to her, turning up the charm full strength, and she eventually forgot about chiding him over the dog.

She called upstairs, reaching Devlin's secretary, who told her to send Hunter right up. "Top floor," she said, and then handed him a yellow sticky note with her name and phone number scrawled on it.

He stuck it in his pocket and headed toward the elevator. As soon as they were inside, he crouched down near Goose. "Ready for work?" he asked. The phrase was one of the cues he used to let her know what she had to do. "Time to go to work."

Immediately, Goose began checking out the elevator. He chuckled. "At ease. Not yet, girl. Not yet."

Devlin Harrington's secretary looked up when he entered the room and frowned. She wore her steel-gray hair in an austere bun, which matched her prim, no-nonsense dress. "I'm sorry, no pets are allowed in here."

Since Hunter noticed Devlin himself watching from inside his corner office, Hunter shrugged. "Maybe you should ask your boss. You know that the two of us have something important to discuss. Since I don't go anywhere without my dog, I'll have to leave. I really don't think he'd like that."

Pursing her lips in a tight line, she glared at him. "One moment, please." Spine stiff, she marched into Devlin's office. A moment later, she returned. "You may go on in. Along with your...animal."

Grinning, Hunter decided why the hell not, and winked at her on his way past. Her face turned a dull red, but one corner of her thin lips twitched in the beginnings of a smile.

Finally. Hunter had schemed for weeks for a way to gain entrance to this office. He greeted the younger Harrington with a courteous hello.

As Hunter entered his office and approached the desk, the younger man jumped to his feet and pumped Hunter's hand a bit too enthusiastically. His gaze dropped to Goose and he frowned.

"What's with the mutt?" Devlin asked, sniffing the air as if he smelled something foul.

"She's not a mutt, she's a purebred basset," Hunter replied, keeping his tone mild. "Insult my dog, insult me. She quite enjoys going to *work* with me. Right, Goose? Work?"

The golden combination words of *Goose* and *work* had Goose's nose working overtime. With her on lead, Hunter took a stroll around the large office. "You got some nice pieces," Hunter commented, studying the collection of autographed baseballs, footballs, jersey and photographs, many of which Devlin kept under glass.

Goose pawed at one display case, her signal to Hunter that she'd detected the unique scent of some kind of data-storage device. He made a mental note and moved on.

As eager to show off as most collectors, Devlin sat back and watched, beaming with pride while Hunter took in the scope of his collection. Which, even though he knew next to nothing about sports memorabilia, Hunter had to admit seemed quite extensive.

One more wall to inspect. Goose signaled once more, tilting her head and looking up at him as she waited for her reward. He dug in his pocket, retrieved one of her favorite liver treats and gave it to her. He knew he'd want to check out those places in the near future. He just had to come up with a legal way, otherwise whatever he found wouldn't be admissible in court.

When he returned to where Devlin still sat, Hunter took a seat in one of the plush chairs across from the desk. Goose stuck close and sat, too, her side touching Hunter's leg. Alert, ears slightly back, she didn't wag her tail as she watched the other man. She was telling him, in her wordless, canine way, to be wary around Devlin.

Good to know. As if he wasn't already.

"You have something to show me?" Devlin asked, rubbing his hands together in anticipation.

Hunter nodded. Reaching into the inside pocket of his coat, he removed the baseball cards. He placed those on the desk and slid them over to Devlin. "I'm taking bids," he said. "I've got several people who are interested. The highest bidder takes all."

Picking up the first one, Devlin's eyes widened. "This is a 1955 Topps Roberto Clemente. The last one known sold for over four hundred grand."

"I know," Hunter replied. He'd done his research. Lucky for him, that particular drug dealer had expensive taste in baseball cards. Next up was a 1954 Topps Ted Williams. While that particular card was worth about fifty thousand dollars, it was about the same value the rest of the rare and coveted cards in the collection.

"A 1967 Topps Rod Carew," Devlin breathed. He looked through the others slowly, trying to maintain a stoic expression, though he failed. Perspiration beaded his forehead, and he kept licking his lips.

When he finished studying the cards, Devlin set the stack down on his desk. "This is over a million dollars' worth of cards," he said, his tone suddenly flat. "Mind telling me how you, a police officer, came by them?"

"I took them from our evidence locker," Hunter replied easily. He'd learned long ago that the truth always worked best. "We got them when we took down a large drug operation a few months ago. One of the top guys was a collector. There are a lot of them, so these won't be missed."

Devlin considered his words. "That means you can get more, right?"

Hunter hadn't expected this response. But when he considered what he knew of Devlin Harrington, a flagrant disregard for the law fit right in. "Maybe," Hunter allowed. "I have to be careful. I don't want to get caught."

"True, true." Devlin picked up the cards again, slowly leafing through them. "I'm prepared to make a cash offer, right now."

Goose suddenly stood, her entire posture alert. She moved forward, sniffing the front of the heavy oak desk. When she lifted her paw, almost like a pointer, Hunter dug out another liver treat and gave it to her.

When Hunter looked up again, Devlin continued to watch him intently, oblivious to the dog. "Go ahead and make your offer and I'll take it under consideration," Hunter said easily, reaching across the desk and retrieving the cards. "Like I said, I'm dealing with numerous interested parties."

"I'll beat any other offer." A thread of desperation ran though the other man's voice. "Promise me you'll at least give me the opportunity to do that."

"Sounds good." Hunter pushed to his feet, careful to promise nothing. He scooped the cards up, dropping them carefully into the card sleeves he'd transported them in. After placing them inside his coat pocket, he stepped back. "You've got my email. Shoot your best offer over to me that way. I'll be back in touch."

Goose by his side, Hunter strode out of the office, slightly worried that Devlin would attempt to stop him and take the cards by force.

But once he and his dog rode the elevator down, his

heartbeat steadied. "Three places, eh, girl?" he said. Goose looked up and wagged her tail. While he had to be careful, as an illegal search would completely undermine any case, at least he knew Devlin Harrington was hiding some sort of electronic data storage. For now, that would have to be enough.

Back at the office, he checked in with his crew. Nothing new in the search for Demi Colton, which surprised no one. Demi had once been a very successful bounty hunter. If anyone knew the best places to lie low, she did. Hunter didn't expect her to be found anytime soon.

"Fenwick Colton has gone on a rampage," one of the guys told him. "Seems his daughter Layla has disappeared. He's wanting to file a missing-persons report and have us find her."

"What?" Hunter couldn't contain his shock. "I just took a stolen vehicle report from her, not more than a couple hours ago. She's not missing."

"The mayor says she won't return his calls and she's not home." The other detective shrugged.

"Sounds like more of a domestic dispute than anything else," someone else chimed in. "But you know Fenwick. Always trying to pull strings."

"Since you're the last one to see Layla," Chief Colton said, walking into the squad room and pointing at Hunter, "I'd like you to call him and calm him down."

Hunter winced. Ouch. "Will do," he replied, picking up his phone. He had to be careful what he said, as he didn't want to betray Layla's confidence. He also couldn't lie to the mayor.

The call went about as he expected. A lot of yelling

on Fenwick Colton's end, pretend hysteria about his daughter's safety along with a clear disbelief that Layla appeared to be avoiding him. "She won't even take my calls," Fenwick complained at least five times, injured pride making his voice more irritating than usual.

"I'm sorry, sir," Hunter said, though he wasn't. "But I spoke with her earlier today and she was just fine." He also didn't want to tell the other man that Layla's car had been stolen.

Finally, Hunter appeared to get the mayor to understand that the police department couldn't help him mend his rift with his daughter. Layla was an adult, so at this point there wasn't much Fenwick could do.

Since he wasn't officially on a scheduled shift, Hunter left shortly after dark. He stopped at the Chinese place and got some fried rice and sweet and sour chicken—enough for two, just in case Layla hadn't eaten.

Funny, but he found himself eager to get home and tell Layla about his day. Though he had no idea if she would even still be there, he truly hoped she'd stay at least one more night. Preferably more.

When he turned down his street and saw a little rental car parked in his driveway, a rush of happiness filled him. As he parked, he took a moment to consider how he felt. While he didn't know for sure where this thing with Layla might be going, or even if it was going anywhere at all, he understood he had a choice. He could obsess over nothing or take it one day at a time and see what happened.

When Mae Larson had taken him in after his parents' deaths, she'd seen right away how worried about his future the teenaged boy had been. He'd wailed about his grief and his pain, not sure how he'd get through the rest of the school year.

One day at a time, she'd told him. *Put one foot in front of the other and keep going. That's the only choice you have.*

She'd been right. He'd be forever grateful to her for that. He'd had a clear choice: to follow one path or to take another. He'd studied hard and graduated near the top of his class. His SAT scores were high enough to get him a partial scholarship to college, and Mae had helped him apply for several others. She'd made up the difference herself. When he'd graduated with a business degree from South Dakota State, she'd been there, as proud as if he really was her kin. He'd pretended not to mind that the rest of her family claimed to have forgotten about his graduation.

He'd stayed in Sioux Falls for several years after college, working in accounting for a large legal firm. To his young and idealistic astonishment, the executives and attorneys he'd worked with were consumed with jostling for power. He'd witnessed firsthand so much backstabbing and outright corruption, he'd known he had to get out.

When the position at Colton Energy had opened up, he'd applied, thinking it would be good to move back to the place where he'd grown up.

Unfortunately, working there had been more of the same, just on a much smaller scale.

He'd told Layla the truth when she'd asked why he'd chosen to go into law enforcement. He truly felt as if his job made a difference in other people's lives. Sure, he might see a lot of bad actors and criminals, but at least as a police officer he could bring them to justice.

Getting out of his car, he glanced at his house. The yellow light shining from his windows filled him with warmth. For the first time since he'd moved away from Red Ridge, someone waited for him at home.

He'd need to be careful not to get too used to that.

Chapter 8

Trying to relax on Hunter's couch, Layla found herself missing both Hunter and his dog, though not necessarily in that order. Or so she told herself.

It surprised her how comfortable she felt in someone else's home. Safe, even as she had to wonder if someone had truly been trying to run her down. They could have been after Hunter, for all she knew. After all, he'd probably made more than a few enemies while arresting criminals.

Still, every sound made her start, which was why she wished she had Goose there with her. The dog's ever-vigilant hearing would alert her should any trouble arise.

Not, she reminded herself, that she expected any. In fact, to be perfectly honest, her jumpiness might just have to do with a certain tall, reddish-brown-haired man with bright blue eyes. Her attraction to him was off the charts. Amazing and wonderful, true. But also, frankly terrifying.

When headlights swept the front window and his car pulled into the driveway, her heart rate sped up. Now what? Hurrying to smooth down her hair, she glanced around frantically. She didn't want to appear as if she'd been waiting up for him, even if she had, so she grabbed the book about dog training she'd been reading earlier that she'd originally picked up from his coffee table.

He came through the door—broad shouldered, narrow hipped—and every cell in her body buzzed alive. Mouth dry, she watched him walk across the room, holding a large bag from which wafted delectable smells. Chinese? She'd opened her mouth to ask, but then Goose spotted her on the couch and gave an excited bark. The dog launched herself at Layla, tail wagging furiously, seemingly overjoyed to see her.

Layla laughed, gathering the wiggling bundle of canine joy close. "Well, hello there to you, too," she crooned. "Were you a good dog today?"

The deep, rich sound of Hunter's masculine laughter sent a tingling warmth through her. She looked up from his dog and let her eyes drink her fill of him.

"She was a very good dog," he said fondly, gazing at his K9 partner. "Come on, Goose, let's get you your dinner."

Apparently understanding every word, Goose abandoned Layla and trotted into the kitchen, tail wagging, head up, in search of food. Hunter poured some kibble into a bowl and put it down. "Here you go, girl."

Not sure if she should stay put or join the man and

the dog, Layla got up. Since she despised indecision in others, she refused to allow herself to vacillate. What to do, how to act? While she wasn't sure what it was about Hunter Black that got to her, she definitely didn't plan on letting her attraction to him interfere with her essential nature or personality.

But damn, he was easy on the eyes. She especially liked the way he moved, full of confidence. She found that sexy as all get-out.

"Productive day at work?" she asked, leaning her shoulder against the door frame. Though her entire body hummed with the need to touch him, she tried like hell to seem casual.

She thought her attempt at casual worked well, until their gazes locked and bam—she forgot how to breathe. All rational thought fled at the heat blazing from his bright blue gaze. He felt it, too, she knew he did. If she just took a few steps toward him, she knew she'd end up in his arms.

Tempting. So tempting, she swayed.

This could easily become a habit. She wasn't quite sure if that was a good thing or bad.

"Come here," he said, his voice rough as he opened his arms.

No indecision at all—she did exactly that. His big, muscular body felt amazing, making her conscious of her own petite size and softness. He merely held her close, safe and warm in his strong embrace, nothing more. Somehow, that was enough. More than enough. Her eyes stung and her throat ached as she realized how much she'd missed simple human contact.

Except with Hunter, it was so much more than that.

Heart hammering in her ears, she raised her head,

intending to initiate a kiss. Instead, to her surprise, he released her and stepped away. "I'm starving," he said without a hint of apology. "I picked up some Chinese. Would you like some? There's enough for both of us."

"No, thanks." Taking a seat at the table, she watched while he opened the various cartons. It smelled delicious and she felt the tiniest bit of regret for not asking for some herself.

Instead, she rested her chin in her hand and watched him eat.

In between bites, he told her about his visit to Devlin Harrington.

"But why?" she asked once he'd finished. "What crime do you think he could possibly have committed? I don't know Devlin all that well, but from what I can tell, both he and his father take visible pride in their reputations being above reproach."

Hunter didn't respond at first, clearly considering his words. "Sometimes, what people show the outside world isn't exactly the truth about who they really are."

She nodded. "True." She thought about Devlin, with his pompous attitude and vain certainty that he was the best-looking and smartest man in town. He hadn't handled it well when he'd learned of her engagement to his father. He'd hit the roof, ranting about how she planned to try to usurp him in his father's company.

Swallowing hard, she passed that on to Hunter.

"Not too surprising," he allowed, flashing a grin that caught her low in her stomach.

"Do you really think Devlin did something illegal?"

"I don't have any proof," Hunter finally allowed, "and there's not a judge in the county that will allow a search warrant based on gut instincts. But in here—"

he touched his chest "—I know. I just need him to give me a valid excuse for a search warrant. Goose has already alerted me that he's hiding something. But I can't do an actual search without a warrant."

"That makes sense." She took a deep breath. "Could Devlin be behind Mark Hatton's accusations against me?"

"Possibly." He grimaced. "Right now I'm one of the only cops in Red Ridge who thinks there's a strong possibility Devlin might be the Groom Killer."

Stunned, Layla couldn't find anything to say to that.

Clearly spotting her skepticism, Hunter changed the subject. They chatted about inconsequential things, but Layla kept going back to what Hunter had said about Devlin.

Finally, she couldn't stand it any longer. "Devlin doesn't want me to marry his father."

Hunter nodded. "So you said. Something about him fearing you wanted to take over their company."

"Yes. But there's more. Devlin had the nerve to come on to me right before he started dating my sister—half sister—Gemma, and I said no. With his huge ego, my rejection was hard enough for him to handle. But then when his father rubbed his nose in it by bragging to the public that he and I were engaged... Well, Devlin lost it."

Gaze sharpening, Hunter leaned closer. "When you say he lost it, what exactly do you mean?"

"He confronted me." She'd told no one about this, not her father, especially not Hamlin. "Showed up on my doorstep one night. He'd been drinking, and at first, I couldn't decide if he was hurt or if his pride was injured. Stupidly, I let him in."

"If he laid a hand on you..."

The icy menace in Hunter's voice felt oddly reassuring. "He didn't," she replied, not saying that it hadn't been for lack of trying. "He ranted and raved, slurring his words."

Still Hunter watched her, his expression inscrutable. "Did you feel threatened?"

Reluctantly, she answered. "A little. Okay, a lot. He pinned me up against the wall and demanded to know why I didn't want him. He rambled about his dad being old and told me the company would pass to him eventually. His insinuation was that I was marrying his father to gain control of Harrington Inc. I tried to brush him off, especially since it was the opposite, but he pinned me and tried to force his tongue down my throat."

Saying the words made her shudder.

Judging from Hunter's furious expression, Devlin ought to be glad he wasn't in the room.

"And then?" Hunter prodded. "What happened?"

"And then I brought my knee up and got him right in between the legs." She shook her head. "I've never heard a grown man make a sound like that. He doubled over in pain and I ushered him right out the door. I told him I'd call the police if he didn't leave, ditto if he ever came back. And that was the end of that."

Silence. And then Hunter laughed, the kind of deep, masculine laughter that made her feel warm all over. "Good for you," he managed in between laughs.

"And when Devlin started dating Gemma, I tried to get her to listen to reason, but of course she refused to hear a word I said. Thank God she got rid of that toad and found her prince in Dante Mancuso." Dante was also a K9 officer.

Though she smiled, she had to point out the obvious. "Apparently, I made Devlin my enemy. I can see how he'd set up something like the Mark Hatton thing in order to get even."

Now Hunter's smile vanished. "Yet when I asked you earlier if you had any enemies, you failed to mention this entire incident."

"I told you I considered Devlin one of them. Sort of."

"You only said you'd overheard him talking to Hamlin and that he was against you two marrying. Not any of this. Christ, this is motive."

"Judging from the accusation in your tone, you think I withheld vital information on purpose."

"Did you?" he shot back, frowning.

"No, not at all. He came by the office and begged me not to tell anyone. I agreed. And I haven't. No one else knows about this, except you."

His frown deepened. "Layla, that doesn't sound like you." He flushed, but set his jaw and continued. "I mean, what I know of you. Why would you keep something like that quiet? What if he did that to someone else?"

Instead of answering, she waited, knowing he'd make the connection. When he did, she knew instantly.

"Because you didn't want to do or say anything that might affect your marriage agreement with his father." The flatness in his voice told her what he thought of that.

Refusing to be ashamed, she lifted her chin. "I did what I thought I had to. My family's company was— is—in trouble. I agreed to marry Hamlin to save it. That was before I knew my father's out-of-control spending was the reason."

"And now that you know? Does that change anything?"

"I'm not sure." She realized she wanted it to, for reasons she didn't want to examine too closely yet. "Colton Energy still needs an infusion of cash. The charges against me aren't helping our public image, either, though we've managed to keep most of it out of the press. It's between the attorneys now."

"I see." Pushing up from the table, he carried his plate to the sink. His rigid spine and stiff movements told her what he thought of her answer.

She opened her mouth to speak and then thought better of it.

"I'm going to go out for a while," he said, excruciatingly polite. "Goose will be here to keep you company."

He left without a backward glance. Layla got up and went to the window, watching him drive away. That was when she understood the bubble of her fantasy had just burst. She couldn't continue staying at Hunter's house. Time to go back home and deal with her life the way she always tended to.

Head-on and facing reality. Luckily, the media frenzy appeared to have died down and no one would be staking out her house.

Hunter couldn't believe how badly he'd allowed himself to be taken in by Layla's pretty face. To be fair, she'd been nothing but honest with him, but still… to think she was still actually considering going ahead with that sham of a marriage, even now that she was aware of what her father had done.

He wanted to punch something. And, though he

wasn't really dressed for it, he knew just the place. The gym. Luckily, he kept a gym bag in the trunk.

An hour later, drenched in sweat, he felt immensely better. Clearheaded, able to think beyond the constant press of his desire for Layla. Yet her refusal to see reality drove him crazy.

It shouldn't matter to him at all what she did. Her life choices were hers alone. He hadn't been involved with her long enough to have a say. However, he couldn't seem to make himself not care. Marriage was permanent, or should be, for Pete's sake. One should marry for love, not money, or in hope of pleasing a parent who clearly had long withheld affection.

Getting in his car, he took a deep breath. While truth be told, he wanted to go home, pull Layla up against him and kiss her senseless, he knew he couldn't. Not with something like her engagement between them. He'd never been the type of guy who poached on another man's woman, nor would he start now. He'd only kissed her at all because he'd honestly believed once she felt the strength of the chemistry between them, she'd end her sham of an engagement. That hadn't happened. No matter what the reason for it, Layla had agreed to marry Hamlin Harrington. If she still planned to go through with it, she would be off-limits, as far as Hunter was concerned.

Now he just needed to convince his body of that.

When he pulled up to his house, the first thing he noticed was the absence of her rental car. Slightly concerned, he parked and headed up to the back door, which was locked.

After he unlocked the door and stepped inside, Goose greeted him with her usual enthusiasm. He flipped on the lights, let his dog out in the backyard for a potty break and picked up the note Layla had left on the kitchen table.

"I thought it best if I went back home," it said. "Thank you so much for your kindness and hospitality. Give Goose a hug for me. Layla."

Of course. As usual, her actions made perfect sense. Why had he expected she'd stay longer?

After letting Goose in, he sat down in the living room but didn't turn on the TV. Instead, he pulled out his cell phone, toying with the idea of calling her. Only the lateness of the hour dissuaded him.

When his phone rang, his heart stuttered. But caller ID showed it was one of his buddies at the police department. Hunter almost didn't answer, but he knew Tim Lakely wouldn't call if it wasn't important.

"Hey, I know you just got added to the Layla Colton case," Tim said. "A neighbor just called in a break-in at her home. Apparently, Layla surprised an intruder midburglary."

Damn. Jaw clenched, he struggled to respond. "Was she hurt?"

"No, at least nothing life-threatening. I'm on the scene now and she's pretty shook up. She's asking for you."

"I'll be there in a few." Hanging up, Colton snagged his car key and told Goose he'd be back. As he hurried to his squad car, he wondered why Layla hadn't called him herself. He guessed he was about to find out.

When he arrived at her town house, he noted two marked squad cars parked outside. After pulling up alongside them, he hopped out and headed up the sidewalk.

The front window had been broken from the inside

out. Glass crunched underfoot. A uniformed police officer stood in the open doorway. Tim. When he spotted Hunter, he motioned him inside.

"She's in the other room talking to the Greg," Tim said, keeping his voice pitched low. "He's taking her report. She's pretty upset."

"Thanks for calling me," Hunter said. He headed toward the kitchen, where his colleague Greg stood, making notes on his pad. When Layla saw Hunter, she jumped to her feet and took a step toward him before apparently rethinking that. "Hunter," she said, relief in her expression and tone. "I'm so glad you came. I would have called you, but my phone got broken in all the craziness."

He pretended not to notice the way her voice wobbled at the end of her sentence. "Is anything missing?"

"No. And that's the weird part. This guy was going through my stuff, but he didn't take anything. It was almost like he was searching for something specific."

"Like jewelry, maybe?" Greg put in helpfully.

"Maybe." But she sounded doubtful.

"Do you have anything else you want me to add to my report?" Greg asked.

Slowly, Layla shook her head. "I think I've told you everything."

"Well, if you remember anything else, here's my card." Greg handed it to her. "You can give me a call, or just tell Hunter, okay?"

"Thank you." Layla didn't move. She and Hunter watched in silence as the other two policemen left.

Once they were gone, she sighed. "I've already called a glass repair company, but they can't get out here for a couple of days."

He matched his tone to hers. Friendly, a bit impersonal. "I don't suppose you have any plywood?"

"No."

"I'll go get some. It won't take long to nail it up to cover that window." He turned to go.

"Wait." She grabbed his arm. "I'd like to go with you."

Staring down at her long fingers clutching the sleeve of his jacket, he reminded himself of his earlier resolve. "No need. You stay here and clean up. I won't be gone that long."

"Please, wait." Instead of letting go, she moved closer. "To be honest, I'm afraid to stay here by myself. I'm not sure why I'm being targeted, but first someone tries to run me down, my car is stolen, and then my home is broken into? That doesn't sound like a coincidence to me."

It didn't to him, either. "Did the intruder try to hurt you?"

"Not really," she admitted. "I think somehow, whoever was behind it knew that I wasn't staying at home. The guy seemed surprised. Since I was between him and the door, he shoved me hard. Into the window." She swallowed. "I broke it." Releasing him, she held up her hands, revealing a series of bloody cuts. "The EMTs wanted me to go to the hospital. But they cleaned out all the glass and none of these cuts are very deep, so I refused."

A horrified shudder ripped through him at the thought of what might have happened to her. "You need to go get checked out, just in case. I'll drive you."

"No." Her smile didn't touch the fear in her gaze.

"I'm fine. Let's go get that plywood so we can fix my window."

Again, he wanted to pull her close and hold her, reassuring himself that she truly would be all right. Exerting every ounce of his willpower, he managed to keep his hands to himself, even though they were clenched in fists at his sides.

"Fine, let's go." He eyed his squad car, and then her rental. "I don't suppose you know anyone with a pickup truck?"

Her eyes widened as she realized what he meant. "We have no way to get the plywood here."

He nodded. "Let me make a call." He got a hold of another of his coworkers, quickly outlined what he needed and secured Jesse's promise to meet them. After passing that information along to Layla, they got in his car.

As they drove to the home improvement store in silence, he ran a thousand different scenarios through his mind. She could stay with her father, except she couldn't. She'd already told him that she had no close friends. That left him, and his place, with all the temptations having her there would bring. But in the end, it all came down to one thing: keeping Layla safe.

"You're staying with me," he told her, his tone leaving no room for argument. "Until we either apprehend whoever is after you or figure out what exactly is going on."

"Thank you." The relief in her soft voice nearly undid him. He had no idea what it was about this woman, but she got to him in ways no other ever had.

At the home improvement store, he purchased a large sheet of plywood and wheeled it out front, where

Jesse waited as promised with his pickup truck. Jesse followed them back to Layla's town house and dropped it off, cheerfully refusing any offer of payment.

With Layla's help, it didn't take long for Hunter to have the window covered. Luckily, she kept a fully stocked toolbox, including a hammer and nails.

"Go ahead and gather your things," he said. "Goose will be happy to have you back."

She nodded and hurried off. He supposed he should be glad she hadn't asked him how he felt. Because despite giving himself a stern talking-to, he couldn't help but feel glad to have her back, too.

Once they arrived at his place, he helped her carry her bags inside. This time, she'd brought considerably more with her. Goose, of course, greeted Layla as if she'd been gone for weeks rather than hours.

Once they'd stowed her bags in the guest bedroom, Layla trailed after him toward the kitchen, Goose hot on her heels.

"I'm sorry to be such an imposition," Layla said. "I can pay you rent, if you'd like. You name the amount, but make sure it's enough to repay you for me putting you out."

"Don't insult me," he replied, his mild tone revealing none of his tangled emotions. "You're no bother. Truth be told, I actually enjoy your company."

He turned in time to catch the look of surprise on her face. "Why does that shock you?" he asked, genuinely curious.

"I don't know." Clearly flustered, she looked away. "I guess I just assumed things between us were more physical than anything else."

He touched her shoulder, a quick squeeze, not trusting himself to let his hand linger. "I'm not going to lie, Layla. I want you. But I also like you. A lot."

Her gaze darkened, and she parted her lips. He held up his hand, forestalling her before she could speak.

"And while I mean every word of that, I have to insist on one thing. The attraction between us is pretty damn powerful, but it's completely off-limits as long as you're still engaged to Hamlin Harrington."

Not immediately responding, she appeared to consider his words. "Like friends?" she asked, her voice flat.

"Exactly." And though the next words he spoke might be a lie, they had to be said. "I think we can be great friends, if we put our mind to it." As long as he could somehow make himself stop wanting her. Which wasn't going to be easy. Every time he looked at her, his entire body caught fire.

"You know what?" Tilting her head, she nodded. "Challenge accepted. Friends it is."

She spun on her heel and left the kitchen without waiting for a response. A moment later, he heard her door close. Hard. Not exactly a slam, but pretty close.

Looking down at Goose, who appeared startled, he grinned. Layla's reaction made him feel a bit better. At least it appeared he wouldn't be the only one suffering.

Chapter 9

Once she got to the sanctuary of her temporary room, Layla sat on the edge of the bed and took several deep breaths. She didn't know why she felt so upset. What Hunter had said made absolute sense. Despite the incredible sex they'd had, she could understand and even respect the way he felt. In fact, she would have had the same sentiments if the situation had been reversed. People who were engaged shouldn't even want to do what she and Hunter had done. She actually should have had to wonder why she did.

Except she knew. So did Hunter. She didn't love her fiancé. And Hamlin didn't love her, either. Not for the first time, she pondered what else her father had offered the older man in order for him to want to marry her. Not once had Hamlin looked at her with affection, only desire. Any conversations they'd shared had been cursory and banal, like two strangers in line at the grocery store chatting about the weather.

They'd never held hands, never mind kissed. To be honest, when her father had come to her in desperation, begging for her help to save the company, she'd agreed without really considering what that might mean.

She might have gone into this with zero illusions, well aware Hamlin considered her a prize, a trophy— or so he'd told her many times. But while Layla knew she was pretty, she certainly wasn't on the same level as the vapid models her father liked to sport on his arm. If Hamlin wanted a trophy wife, he'd do better with one of them. There certainly didn't appear to be any shortage of gorgeous young things throwing themselves at her father.

So what then? He planned to infuse Colton Energy with a huge amount of cash. A shrewd businessman, Hamlin would have asked for partial ownership, which would be fair.

Then why the marriage? Simply because the older man wanted her? The thought made her shudder. As did the idea of actually having to sleep with Hamlin once they were married, which he'd surely expect.

Or would he? Judging from his lack of enthusiasm for anything physical, at least with her, she'd wondered if theirs would be a sexless marriage.

Once, she'd told herself she might have been able to live with that. Now, after the explosion of passion between her and Hunter, such a life seemed unimaginably bleak.

Hunter had asked her if she still planned to go through with the wedding. She truly didn't know. Based on what she'd learned of how her father's actions had nearly bankrupted the company, she felt much less inclined to offer herself up as a sacrificial lamb.

With the Groom Killer still at large and all weddings put on hold, she had plenty of time to decide. That was, if she could survive being around Hunter so much and not being able to touch him.

A few minutes later, slightly embarrassed by her reaction to Hunter's declaration of the rules, she forced herself to emerge from her room. She marched on down the hallway to the living room, where Hunter sat on the recliner with Goose curled in his lap. He appeared engrossed in a late-night crime drama, though he looked up when she entered.

"Hey," he said. "Everything okay?"

Noting that he appeared wary, as if he feared she might insist on rediscussing their talk, she grimaced. "Yes. How about you?"

"Fine." He returned his attention to his show.

And there, she thought as she took a seat on the couch, was a perfect example of how to maintain one's distance. Aching, she wondered how long she'd be able to take it. At least she had her new volunteer job to occupy her time while she was on vacation from her real job.

Her real job. Her real life. Both suddenly seemed as false as the sham of her engagement.

Dangerous to even think like that. As soon as seemed reasonable, she got up and told Hunter good night.

Barely looking at her, he responded in kind. Her heart sank, even more than she would have believed possible, but she kept her chin up as she turned to go.

"Layla?"

Slowly she turned. He flashed that smile, the one that turned her insides to mush and had her entire body buzzing. "Yes?" she managed.

"It's going to be all right. Everything will work out in the end, I promise."

"I'm sure it will," she responded, even though she wasn't. "Right now, I've got to get to sleep so I can get up early for my volunteer shift at the K9 training center tomorrow."

And she took herself off to her room, hoping sleep would come quickly.

The next morning, Layla woke before the alarm, surprised to find that she'd slept uninterrupted by doubts or worries. Jumping up out of bed, even her normal early-morning energy seemed multiplied, as if she'd already drunk several strong cups of coffee. This was a good thing. She hurried through her shower and got dressed in jeans, a T-shirt and a long-sleeved flannel shirt, plus her scuffed boots. Putting her long hair into a neat braid, she grinned at herself in the mirror, scarcely able to contain her eagerness.

In a few hours, she'd start her unpaid job at the K9 center, which felt like a dream come true. Surprisingly so. The last time she'd felt like this, she'd been a newly minted college graduate, eager to start work in her father's business.

Even the fact that she'd slept alone in the guest bed, waking to be momentarily super-conscious of the gorgeous man still asleep in the other bedroom, did little to dim her anticipation.

Sauntering into the kitchen, she stopped short at the sight of Hunter sitting at the kitchen table with a cup of coffee, working a crossword puzzle. Not asleep, then. Her mouth went dry.

He wore a tight white T-shirt that fit his muscular chest like a glove.

"Morning." Glancing up at her, he smiled, clearly oblivious as to his effect on her.

"Good morning," she chirped, wincing at her overly bright tone. She busied herself making a cup of coffee, and while it brewed, she wondered what—if anything—she should eat for breakfast. No matter how many times he told her to make herself at home, she still didn't feel entirely comfortable raiding Hunter's refrigerator in front of him. And something smelled wonderful, though she wasn't sure what, exactly.

Goose immediately came over and leaned against her leg. She bent down and spent a moment making a fuss over the dog. "There's the beautiful girl," she crooned. "How's sweet Goose today?"

When she finally looked up, she caught Hunter watching her with a strange look on his face.

"She's a good dog," she said, straightening and trying not to feel self-conscious.

"Yes, she is." He dragged a hand through his hair. If anything, the ruffled look made him even sexier. "Are you hungry?" he asked. "I went out earlier and picked up some kolaches and sausage rolls." He gestured at a white box sitting on the counter.

Grateful, she smiled. "That's what I was smelling. And yes, I'd love some, thanks. I'm a little nervous and a whole lot excited."

He studied her while she grabbed a plate, a couple of the sausage rolls and one fruit-filled pastry.

"You're a natural," he told her, gesturing at Goose, whose attention had shifted from Layla to the food.

Warmth filled her at his kind words. For the first time since he'd declared himself off-limits, hope filled her. Maybe they could do this friend thing. Once she trained herself to stop wanting him, that is.

"Glad you're enjoying those," he commented, helping himself to a sausage roll.

"Oh, I am. If I keep eating like this, I won't be able to fit into my clothes," she said after finishing her entire plate. "As it is, I need to squeeze in a couple of workouts."

"Not hardly." Again, the warmth in his gaze made her body respond in kind. "A few extra pounds would hardly hurt you."

Not sure if he was teasing, especially since her father continually harped on how much weight she needed to lose, she simply shrugged and took a sip of coffee. "Ahh." She gave a satisfied hum. "The first taste of coffee in the morning is always the best." Next, unable to help herself, she went for seconds, taking another sausage roll and one more kolache. "These are amazing," she told him, refusing to apologize as she bit into her treats. Again, she made a sound of pleasure, eating it slowly and savoring every bite before starting on the pastry.

It wasn't until she'd devoured everything, washing it down with coffee, that she looked up to realize Hunter still watched her, the expression on his face intense.

"Do you realize," he rasped, "how sexy you are when you eat?"

Again, a blast of heat filled her. Desire, longing and

a sense of being too close to losing control. *Trouble*, she told herself. Best to cut it off immediately.

"Funny," she responded, managing to laugh off his words. "Especially since you said sexy was off the table." She pushed to her feet, finishing off her coffee. "Anyway, thanks for breakfast. I've got to get running. I don't want to be late the first day."

As she sailed off to her room to retrieve her purse and the rental car keys, she wondered if staying with Hunter was even going to work. Maybe she'd need to consider an alternative, like a hotel. But she knew she wouldn't be safe. Even if she were, she wouldn't *feel* safe without him.

So there was that. She'd much prefer to stay here for as long as he'd have her.

They were both adults. Surely they could figure out a way to coexist. Right?

Arriving at the K9 training center, she parked. Telling herself to calm down, she exited the car and went inside.

The first thing she noticed was the noise. Dogs barking, people talking and the whirr of some kind of machine that might have been a vacuum.

"Can I help you?" an older woman asked, her tone pleasant.

"I'm looking for Sarah Danvers," Layla replied.

"That would be me. And you must be Layla Colton." Smiling, Sarah studied her. "I'm very happy to meet you. Some of the other trainers have told me you were instrumental in keeping funding going for this place."

Relaxing slightly, Layla nodded. "The K9 training center has always been important to me. I'm glad to see it's doing so well."

Sarah led the way to a small office. "Yes. We train police and TSA dogs for all over the county. Some of them send pups here to be trained, others simply purchase one of our dogs."

"I'm eager to help out." Now inside the office, Layla waited while Sarah closed the door.

"Take a seat," Sarah invited, going around to the back side of a messy desk. She shoved a few stacks of paper over so she could steeple her hands in front of her. "Now tell me about your experience working with dogs."

"I have none."

Sarah's brows rose. "Interesting. I guess I just assumed..."

"But I love dogs and I'm a fast learner," Layla interjected. "I work hard, no matter what the task."

"Even if it's cleaning out dog runs?" Sarah laughed, though her steady gaze seemed serious.

"Even so. Whatever you need, I'm game."

"All right then. We appreciate that." Standing, Sarah started for the door, but she turned before reaching it. "Just a few things. Since you have no experience working with dogs, please don't make any sudden moves, especially around their faces. If a trainer asks you to do something, do it immediately, no questions asked. I don't want you or one of our dogs getting hurt. Understand?"

"Understood." Layla rose and followed the other woman out the door. They left the small reception/office area for a large, covered ring that reminded Layla of an indoor riding arena. Several dogs and handlers worked here, all in separate areas.

Sarah stopped walking, letting Layla take it all in

before touching her arm. "I'm going to put you with Clarice Kutchison. She's not a K9 trainer—she helps with our dogs' care, the grooming, feeding, exercising and such. I think that would be an excellent place for you to start."

Smiling, Layla nodded. "I can't wait."

Working the night shift, Hunter's usual days off had been Monday and Tuesday. Now that he'd be transitioning to a day shift, he still had his Monday off but would report to work on Tuesday. His other day off would probably be Sunday, though specifics still hadn't been discussed.

Either way would be fine. Living alone, Hunter hadn't really cared. In fact, on more than one occasion he'd gone up to the station when he hadn't been scheduled to work.

Not this Monday. Today he planned to work around the house and yard while Layla was at the K9 center. And then he planned to make big pot of spaghetti and Italian sausage, which was one of his specialties, for them to eat once she got home.

Home. While his house had long been his place of refuge, he wondered at how easily Layla seemed to slide into his life, as though she were the puzzle piece he'd long been missing.

This sort of thinking could get a man in trouble. He snorted at himself, and then got busy cleaning the kitchen while washing a load of laundry.

His cell phone rang just as he was about to tackle the bathrooms. Caller ID showed city hall. Which could only mean the mayor was calling him.

Resigned, Hunter answered.

"Where is my daughter?" Fenwick Colton demanded, skipping any pretense at pleasantries and cutting straight to the chase. Hunter swore he could detect a hint of panic underneath the bluster in the older man's voice.

"She's not here at the moment," Hunter answered, keeping his tone civil. "I'd be happy to take a message. Or you could simply call her yourself."

"She hasn't been answering her phone. I've left several messages." Now the older man didn't even attempt to hide his desperation. "Is she staying with you?"

"Yes, for her own safety."

"You are aware that she's engaged?"

"I am," Hunter replied. "And you should know that she's staying in my guest bedroom, alone. In light of the attempt on her life and the break-in at her town house, this seemed the safest bet."

"Why you?" Fenwick sounded bewildered. "She certainly is welcome to come home. She knows that."

No way was Hunter going there. Family dynamics needed to stay exactly that—between the family.

"Again, sir, I don't know what to tell you. I suggest you take it up with Layla."

Once he'd ended the call, Hunter had to wonder who'd given the mayor his private cell number. If someone from the police department had done such a thing, Hunter would need to address the serious breach in confidentiality. He didn't care who was asking, be it the mayor or even the governor—personal information should never be revealed without his permission.

Shrugging off his annoyance, he continued to catch up with his household chores, intent on making the most of his day off. Since he started his new day shift tomorrow, he'd forced himself to get up earlier than normal, hopefully to help his system become adjusted to a completely different schedule.

His phone rang again, making him groan out loud. This time caller ID showed Harrington Inc. A bit wary, he answered anyway, hoping it would be Devlin rather than Hamlin.

"I'm prepared to make my offer," Devlin said, keeping his voice low. "I'm interested in purchasing the entire lot of cards. I can give you—"

"Not over the phone," Hunter cut in smoothly. "In writing, like I told you."

"Okay." The other man barely missed a beat. "What's your email address? I can't find it."

Since Devlin couldn't see, Hunter rolled his eyes and rattled it off. "Make sure and be specific."

"Oh. All right." Though annoyance colored Devlin's tone, he kept it civil. No sense in ticking off the guy who had what you wanted. "Will you let me know where I stand once all your offers are in? I might be able to raise my bid."

Hunter let several seconds go by before he answered. "That's not usually how an auction works. The highest bidder wins."

"I see. However, I really want those cards. It's a win-win for you, too, since I guarantee I'll top any higher bids, as long as you can prove they're real."

Again, Hunter shook his head at the other man's naïveté. For all Devlin knew, Hunter could write up his own bids, each of them higher than Devlin's, and use them to get more money. Which, if Hunter truly was the type to steal valuable evidence from the evidence locker and sell it at a personal profit, he'd probably do.

"I'll consider your request," Hunter finally said.

Since he wouldn't actually be selling the baseball cards, there was no way he could let Devlin win them, no matter how high the bid. He also still needed to fill the chief in on what he'd done.

He ended the call and glared at his phone. He didn't plan on answering it again unless Layla called. Glancing at his watch, he figured it would be time to start cooking soon. She'd probably be back shortly after five.

The knowledge that he'd see her soon energized him. It shouldn't, he knew. Better to keep his distance until she figured out what she wanted to do with her life. Until he knew for certain that she wanted him in it, he knew he shouldn't get too used to her presence.

Nevertheless, picturing her reaction to a home-cooked meal made him grin. He'd never cooked for a woman before, but Layla wasn't just any woman. She was his houseguest. And as long as he could keep her in that category, he'd be just fine. No danger of losing his heart that way.

Spending an entire day working with dogs had been pretty damn perfect. At the end of her shift, which had flown by in a completely different way than her days at Colton Energy, Layla felt a pleasant sort of exhaustion.

The dogs had been amazing. Their handlers, too. Her job had been comprised of menial tasks such as feeding and exercising and, to her surprise, playing with them. Apparently, canines also needed to blow off steam. She'd enjoyed that part the most.

Many times during the day, Layla had found herself filled with joy and grinning from ear to ear. That *never* happened at Colton Energy. And while she knew if a paying position came up here it wouldn't offer anything close to the salary she currently earned, she'd managed to amass an amazing investment portfolio, as well as significant savings. Having no life outside her job had that particular benefit, at least. The only things she spent money on were necessities like her mortgage and utilities, food and clothing.

Humming under her breath as she exited the building, she practically skipped to her car. She couldn't wait to tell Hunter about her day. Since he was a dog person, she knew he'd understand.

"Layla."

Key fob in hand, she froze, cursing herself for not noticing the shiny black Mercedes parked two vehicles down from her. Just like that, her ebullient mood deflated. "Dad. What are you doing here?"

"Chasing you down." Wearing an expensive, custom-made suit and long overcoat, Fenwick looked as if he'd just finished a photo shoot for a magazine. "Luckily, your sister mentioned she'd seen you up here, so I didn't have to look too long."

Her half sister Patience was the K9 training center veterinarian. If her sister hadn't stopped by to say hi, she must have been very busy with patients. Patience didn't miss an opportunity to try to talk Layla out of marrying Hamlin.

"Why are you looking for me?" she asked her father. "I told you, I'm on vacation."

Instead of acknowledging her words, he gestured toward his car. "Do we have to have this conversation in the parking lot? That wind has a bite. Let's sit inside my car instead."

Instead of moving, she eyed him. "What conversation? I don't think there's anything to discuss. I'm off for this entire week. I just spent the day doing volunteer work here at the training center. I'm exhausted and I'd really like to get home and shower."

"Home? By that I take it you mean your boyfriend's house? What are you trying to do, scare Hamlin Harrington off for good? First this thing with Mark Hatton, and now you're shacking up with a police officer? I raised you better than that."

Great. It figured her father would manage to completely ruin her day. For once, she wasn't going to let him demean her or take away her burgeoning self-confidence.

Anger flared, warring with tiredness. "You know what?" she replied, lifting her chin and locking gazes with him. "Maybe we do need to have a talk, after all. But I think it can be right here, in this parking lot, because I don't think it's going to take very long."

Clearly believing he had the upper hand, Fenwick crossed his arms and waited, his arrogant, smug expression begging to be taken down a peg.

"Well?" he demanded when she didn't immediately speak. "What do you have to say for yourself?"

"I know what you've done with Colton Energy's profits." She kept her tone crisp and professional, careful to keep any emotion out of it. "I finally went up to accounting and took a look at the books. You're the reason the company is in trouble. How dare you ask me to marry someone I don't love to save the company when you're the one who created the mess to begin with?"

"I'm the owner. I can do whatever I want with the profits *my* company generates." His tone indicated he found his response perfectly logical. "You work for me. What I do is none of your concern."

"It is when you ask me to marry someone to help out our company and don't reveal the reasons behind the financial difficulties we're having."

"The reasons?" He sneered. "Do they really matter?"

Throat tight, she managed to nod. What had she expected, her egotistical father to break down and admit what he'd done, begging for forgiveness? Maybe not, but at the very least, he owed her an explanation. She said as much to him.

"You want an explanation? Fine. The cash flow is messed up. That's all. Anyway, I'm doing you a favor. Clearly, you're unable to find a man willing to marry you on your own. This way, we all benefit. You get a wealthy spouse and a second company where you can dabble. And Colton Energy gets a much-needed influx of cash."

"*Dabble?*" She could barely get the word out. "Is that what you think I do?"

He flashed an indulgent smile. "Layla, I created your position especially for you. I assure you, Colton Energy has always run just fine without you."

A furious sort of triumph had her smiling a cold smile. "I see. Then surely you won't mind if I take a second week off from my unessential position. I might even take a third—maybe even an entire month. I certainly have more than enough unused vacation days built up."

He knew she had him then. He opened and closed his mouth. Then, narrowing his eyes, he shook his head. "I'm so disappointed in you. Don't bother to come for Thanksgiving."

"Thanksgiving?" She'd had more than enough. "Since when have you ever hosted a get-together at any holiday? Last year you were in Grand Cayman. The year before, Punta Cana."

He shrugged. "You never know. Maybe I decided to stay home this year."

"Right. Have you? Decided to stay home and serve turkey, I mean."

At least he had the grace to look ashamed. "No. I'm going to be staying with a few friends at an all-inclusive in Montego Bay."

"Have a nice week," she told him, for once not over-analyzing her feelings as she turned to go. Hands shaking, she got into her rental car, pressed the start button and shifted into Reverse.

She drove away without a backward glance.

At least the drive to Hunter's house gave her time to cool down. One thing was for sure, she'd definitely undergone a significant change in her own attitude. Usually all her father had to do was express disapproval and she'd fall all over herself to try to please him. Not today. She'd finally become aware enough, just now, this very moment, to realize she likely never would.

Sobering. And liberating, too. For the first time she understood she needed to take a hard look at her life and consider making some changes.

Chapter 10

Filled with the mouthwatering aromas of spaghetti sauce and Italian sausage, the entire house smelled amazing. To Hunter, it was the aroma of home. Certain scents—bread baking, chicken roasting, spaghetti simmering on the stove—brought back many of his childhood memories, both before and after his parents' deaths. Mae Larson, the kind woman who'd taken in fifteen-year-old Hunter, had loved to cook. Since her own grandchildren hadn't expressed any interest in learning, she'd taught Hunter. He'd found not only did he enjoy assembling the ingredients and experimenting with seasonings and flavors, but the entire process relaxed him.

He couldn't help but hope a simple, home-cooked meal might also assist in making Layla feel more at ease.

Pouring each of them a glass of red wine, Hunter

kept one eye on the front window so he'd see Layla pull up. Not only had he managed to finish all his usual day-off chores, but he'd made a quick run to the store for a bottle of Chianti and a loaf of crusty French bread. He'd made a huge bowl of salad, which now chilled in his fridge.

His stomach growled, reminding him that he'd skipped lunch. No worries, as he planned to eat his weight in pasta tonight.

The instant he spotted her rental car heading down the street, his heart kicked into overdrive. He took another sip of wine, stirred the sauce and popped the bread into the oven to warm.

Layla came bursting through the door, her hair flying behind her. A few steps in, the aroma apparently hit her, because she slowed, lifted her chin and sniffed the air. "Wow," she said, sauntering into the kitchen. "A man of many talents."

"Thanks." Grinning, he handed her a glass of wine. "I've been craving pasta all day, so I made it, plus salad and bread. I figured it'll be the perfect kind of meal for a chilly night like tonight."

The warmth of her smile made his entire body heat. "It really is. And a nice way to end a good day. Plus, I'm starving. I can't wait to tell you about my day."

Like friends. Or partners.

He smiled back. "I can't wait to hear about it."

"Let me go clean up and change," she said, taking another sip of her wine. "I'll be right back."

Watching her walk away, a giddy sort of possibly dangerous happiness filled him. Whatever, it felt good. He'd been right. Sometimes all it took was a simple thing to get people to move past the awkwardness.

She reappeared just as he finished tossing the salad and getting the bread out of the oven. "What can I do to help?" she asked. She'd put on black leggings and a long, faded blue sweatshirt, as well as a pair of fluffy, furry slipper-boots. Eyeing her, he lost all appetite for food. He craved her. Only her.

"Hunter? Is there anything you'd like me to do?"

Blinking, he swallowed back what he really wanted to say and shook his head. "Nothing," he told her, gesturing at the table. "Sit, relax a minute and then we'll eat."

Following his instructions, she sipped her wine and watched while he got out the salad and some dressing, removed the bread from the oven and sliced it, and then drained the pasta, mixed it with the sauce and cut up sausage into a huge bowl. To top everything off, he'd shredded some mozzarella cheese.

"Amazing," she commented, her blue eyes wide. Goose, always hopeful for handouts, assumed her position in between their two chairs. This made Layla laugh again, the brightness of the sound bringing another smile to Hunter's face.

"I must have really needed time off," she said. "I haven't felt this happy in a long, long time."

His chest constricted at her words. Part of him wanted to tell her he thought her sense of well-being was more than simply taking time off from a high-pressure job. The possibility existed that she'd finally had a chance to do the kind of work she was meant to do. He well knew how incredibly fulfilling that could be.

But he kept his mouth shut. It wasn't his place to make judgments on her life. Layla was a smart, educated woman. No doubt she'd reach the same conclusion without his help.

"Dig in," he said, nudging the salad toward her.

"I believe I will." Her cheeks were flushed. "I'm incredibly grateful. This is the first time anyone other than one of my father's cooks has ever cooked a meal for me."

"What about your mom?"

"I barely knew her. Once her marriage to Fenwick ended, she wanted nothing to do with me. I haven't seen her since I was four." Then, because she wanted to keep things light, she picked up her fork. "That looks amazing."

"Taste it first," he teased. "You might just change your mind." Even though he'd made this exact dinner numerous times and knew it would be delicious.

With another laugh, she dug in.

While he'd prepared dinners for other women, none of them had ever felt like this. Before, he'd used them as a prelude to seduction—candlelight, slow music playing softly on the stereo, rushing through the meal to get to what would hopefully happen after. He'd never met a woman he craved as much as Layla Colton. He wanted to get to know every inch of her, not just her admittedly delectable body but her mind, too.

Oblivious to his tumultuous thoughts, she ate with the same sensual appreciation she always did. Mouth dry, he pretended not to watch her while he tried to eat.

In between bites of food, she told him all about helping out with the dogs, excited when he also knew several of the canines by name. He listened and watched her while she talked, wondering if she realized how she glowed with enthusiasm.

"Sounds like you really liked it," he commented, the vibrant beauty of her spirit making him ache to touch her. But he didn't want things to get off track, so he kept his hands busy with slicing more bread, refilling their wineglasses and offering more pasta.

"I'm stuffed." She tilted her head, a mischievous glint in her bright blue eyes. "Please tell me you made tiramisu for desert."

He pretended to smack himself in the forehead. "I knew I was forgetting something. I should have picked one up at the bakery or something. Here's the sad truth. I can cook, but I can't bake. At all. And believe me, I've tried."

"I'm sorry." Expression serious now, she leaned across the table and touched his arm. "I was joking. I'm so full after all this, there's no way I could eat anything else. Thank you for making this wonderful meal for me. It was delicious and the perfect end to my day."

"Sounds like you had a good one." Again, the ache to touch her. Or better, to pull her into his arms and kiss her. Instead, he pushed to his feet and began clearing the table.

Immediately, she jumped up to help him.

"No need," he said firmly. "Get some more wine and go relax. I've got this."

Again, her warm smile slayed him. "I will, then. And thank you."

Instead of going into the living room, she sat back down at the table. Sipping her wine, she watched him, her expression pensive. He tore his gaze away and focused on the task at hand.

Glad he could stay busy, he rinsed their dishes off

and placed them in the dishwasher. He covered up the leftover spaghetti and carried it to the fridge.

"That'll be even better tomorrow," she commented, surprising him.

"Yes, it will." He chanced a quick look at her and instantly regretted it. The wine had given her porcelain skin a soft flush. As he watched, she took another sip. Her lips parted as she exhaled, and all he could think about was how badly he wanted to taste that wine off her lips.

Instead, he covered the leftover salad, carried it to the fridge and then poured himself another glass of wine. Now he'd run out of busywork, so he'd have to figure out another way to keep his hands to himself. It really shouldn't be this difficult, especially since he wanted to get to know her better. And of course, there was her engagement to Hamlin Harrington in the way as well.

"Did you happen to run into Patience at the center? You haven't mentioned her. You two aren't close?"

Her smile faded, making him regret asking. "Patience has made her feelings clear about my engagement, so I guess we've both been avoiding each other. But she apparently saw me at some point, since she told my father I was there. He was waiting for me in the parking lot when I left to come home."

Ouch. He grimaced, imagining how that must have gone. Then he realized she'd used the word "home." A bit of tentative joy flooded him, though he kept his expression neutral. "Is everything all right?"

She considered, and then shrugged. "You know what? I think so. He was irate and out of control, but I dealt with him. My father's been bullying me for a really long time. He told me today he was doing me a favor by arranging my marriage to Hamlin Harrington, insinuating that I'd never find another man who would want me otherwise."

Shocked, he took a step closer to her. "You know he's wrong, right?" The compulsion to touch her had grown even stronger. If he hadn't wanted so badly for them to get to know each other apart from just physically, plus prove his point with her fake engagement, he wouldn't have been able to resist proving to her just how misinformed her father was.

When she didn't answer, he forced himself to move away, pretending an urgent need to wipe down the kitchen counters. He knew he could tell her how badly he wanted her, but at this point, that went without saying. He knew she wanted him, too. Just not enough. Yet.

"I know he's wrong," she finally said, which allowed him to exhale in relief. "It bothers me, though. Seriously, what kind of man says something like that to his own daughter?"

"The kind who's trying to manipulate her." Since there was no more busywork to occupy him, he refilled both of their glasses. Luckily, he didn't have to go anywhere and neither did she. A quick glance at the indoor/outdoor thermometer revealed the temperature was steadily dropping. November in South Dakota could often be like that—unpredictable. "How about I build a fire and we sit out there and talk?"

To his relief, she nodded. "Sounds perfect. And cozy. My life's been short on that lately."

Cozy. At least she hadn't said "romantic." It took

every ounce of his self-control to keep amorous feelings buried. Layla made it so damn difficult.

Puttering around with the fireplace, he retrieved several pieces of wood from the pile outside. While he kept busy getting the fire going, he gave himself a stern talking-to. He could do this. Until she broke things off with Hamlin Harrington, he *would* do this. And it shouldn't be this difficult. Despite his overwhelming attraction to Layla, she was definitely a woman worth getting to know more than physically.

Intimately. Another dangerous word. He gave himself a mental dressing-down. He need to chill out, relax and stop letting his libido govern his interactions with Layla.

With a fire roaring in the fireplace, Hunter took a seat in his chair, opposite where she sat on the couch. Though Goose normally joined him, the little traitor chose to snuggle with Layla instead. Judging from Layla's contented expression, this suited her just fine. She stroked his dog's fur, putting Goose in a catatonic sort of doggy bliss.

Hunter couldn't help but think about how good it would feel to have her slender hands stroke him.

And there he went again. "Tell me more about your day," he prompted, genuinely interested. He dealt with the K9 training center every day, so it would be interesting to hear the fresh view of someone not as familiar with it.

Brightening, she launched into more stories about some of the dogs and handlers she'd worked with. It helped that he knew exactly which dogs were which. He was able to explain some of the training methods when Layla asked. To his astonishment, the more they talked, the more he relaxed. Though desire simmered in the background, he found he wasn't constantly battling himself.

This could work. Whether short term or long term, he could truly enjoy having Layla stay in his house. As yet, he didn't allow himself to actually think of them as having any future. They couldn't, not while she remained engaged to another man.

Layla swirled her wine in her glass and smiled at Hunter, who appeared unaware that he'd been glowering at her. She wasn't sure exactly why, though she suspected it might have something to do with his declaration that anything physical between them would be off-limits as long as she was promised to another man.

Right now, with her entire body pulsing with longing for Hunter, she knew she'd need to be careful. As badly as she ached for him, she could promise just about anything if he'd touch her the way he had earlier.

Whoa. She took a tiny sip of wine, aware she'd need to switch to water after this glass. She could tell from the rosy glow and the way her thought process seemed a bit fuzzy that she'd had enough.

"What a wonderful night," she mused out loud. "I can't thank you enough for everything you've done for me."

His gaze darkened, sending a shiver of need up her spine. And then, because she knew she had to do something to stop this runaway train before it completely jumped the track, she took a deep breath. "It's really awesome having a friend like you."

A stiffening of his jaw was his only reaction. Pretending not to notice, she continued. "Right now, friends are one thing I'm short on. I confess, it's my fault. I let my blind loyalty to my job, my obsession with the company, take up every ounce of time in my life, leaving none for anything or anyone else. That's going to change, starting now."

After a moment, he nodded. "That sounds like the same kind of epiphany I had when I left Colton Energy to go to the police academy."

Stunned, she realized he was right. Once again, she owed part of her realization to him. And while she knew he was right about her marrying Hamlin Harrington to save Colton Energy, she wasn't ready to let go of her stupid hope just yet. While intellectually she understood she'd never be able to somehow earn her father's love and respect, she didn't know how to make herself stop trying. Or caring. On the outside, she might be a whip-smart, capable career woman, but on the inside lurked that little girl wanting her father to love her. She didn't know how to make that little girl go away.

Pushing away her maudlin thoughts, she placed her wineglass on the table.

"What are you doing for Thanksgiving?" he asked, his voice casual. "It's in three days, in case you didn't realize."

"I don't know." She shrugged. "Thanksgiving isn't a big deal to my father, and my siblings are all leaving town for the holiday. I'm not close to the other branches of the family." In other words, no one had extended an invitation to her to eat with them. Most likely they had no idea that her father always abandoned her.

"Still, you're doing something, right?"

"I am. Maybe I'll go see a movie or something. As long as the theater isn't anywhere near a shopping

"FAST FIVE" READER SURVEY

Your participation entitles you to:
* 4 Thank-You Gifts Worth Over $20!

Complete the survey in minutes.

Get 2 FREE Books

Your Thank-You Gifts include **2 FREE BOOKS** and **2 MYSTERY GIFTS**. There's no obligation to purchase anything!

See inside for details.

Dear Reader,

Since you are a lover of our books, your opinions are important to us... and so is your time.

That's why we made sure your **"FAST FIVE" READER SURVEY** can be completed in just a few minutes. Your answers to the five questions will help us remain at the forefront of women's fiction.

And, as a thank-you for participating, we'd like to send you **4 FREE THANK-YOU GIFTS!**

Enjoy your gifts with our appreciation,

Pam Powers

To get your
4 FREE THANK-YOU GIFTS:

✷ Quickly complete the "Fast Five" Reader Survey
and return the insert.

"FAST FIVE" READER SURVEY

1	Do you sometimes read a book a second or third time?	○ Yes	○ No
2	Do you often choose reading over other forms of entertainment such as television?	○ Yes	○ No
3	When you were a child, did someone regularly read aloud to you?	○ Yes	○ No
4	Do you sometimes take a book with you when you travel outside the home?	○ Yes	○ No
5	In addition to books, do you regularly read newspapers and magazines?	○ Yes	○ No

YES! I have completed the above Reader Survey. Please send me my 4 FREE GIFTS (gifts worth over $20 retail). I understand that I am under no obligation to buy anything, as explained on the back of this card.

240/340 HDL GM37

FIRST NAME

LAST NAME

ADDRESS

APT.#

CITY

STATE/PROV.

ZIP/POSTAL CODE

READER SERVICE—Here's how it works:

center. I like to stay away from those crazy Black Friday crowds."

He stared at her like he thought she'd lost her mind. "Aren't you and your *fiancé* doing something—even for show?"

The slight emphasis he put on the word "fiancé" clearly reflected his distaste, which made her smile. "Hamlin and I don't spend much time together," she replied, aware of how awful that probably sounded. "Neither of us is pretending this engagement is something more than what it is. A business arrangement." Odd, but actually saying the truth out loud made her want to cry. Instead, she swallowed hard and forged on. "What about you? What are your plans for the holiday?"

"Usually I eat over at the Larsons'," he replied, frowning slightly as if still puzzling over her response. "Though if the twins are home, I'm not always welcome. Mae still invites me, of course. But it's usually pretty uncomfortable if Noel and Evan are there."

He gazed at the fire. "They don't always go to Mae's for the holidays, but when they do, they make it clear that I'm the interloper."

She didn't know why this shocked her, but it did. Learning other people also had dysfunctional families always surprised her. "Seriously? I mean, you lived with them, right?"

"Yeah, but they didn't appreciate their grandmother taking me in. We were all teenagers, and I didn't run with the same crowd." He grimaced. "No matter what I did, they never warmed up to me. Eventually I stopped trying. Now we all just endure each other when we have to—especially since I'm a cop and they have reason to be wary of me. I try to make sure we don't have to deal with one another often. The only exceptions I make are the holidays. I try to help Mae as much as I can. She's getting older and can't do as much as she used to."

"I get that. Are you going this year?"

"I was thinking about inviting her over here and cooking the meal myself. That is, only if the twins weren't planning on going to Mae's. I won't have them in my house." He cocked his head, eyeing her. "I usually have to work part of the day anyway. But if I do have Thanksgiving dinner here, I'd love for you to join us."

Touched, she had to swallow to get past the ache in her throat. "I'd like that," she allowed. "But when will you know? It's awful short notice, isn't it? Three days?" Privately, she thought if Mae Larson hadn't invited Hunter by now, she'd made other plans that didn't include him.

"I know. I've been procrastinating, though I have already bought a turkey. It's thawing in the fridge. The only problem is Goose. Mae claims to be allergic to dogs."

Since he'd used the word *claims*, she figured that meant he didn't believe her. "So put Goose in the bedroom while Mae's here. That should take care of that, right?"

"It depends. She's said she can't even be around dog dander. No matter how much I clean, I doubt I can eliminate that 100 percent."

"Probably not. What kind of allergic reaction does she have?"

"I don't know." Hunter shook his head. "She's never

been around Goose—or any other dog—that I know of. I've never seen her have any sort of reaction."

She understood his skepticism. "If she truly was allergic to dog dander, wouldn't it be on you and your clothes? She'd get some on her when she hugs you."

"Exactly. As unimaginable as it might sound, I'm thinking maybe she just doesn't like dogs. The twins managed to steal two dogs from the training center and had them for months before your sister Patience stole them right back. Noel and Evan must have had dander on them, too, but I saw the three of them together before that and Mae wasn't sneezing up a storm. Yeah, I think she just doesn't like dogs."

The mournful tone in his voice, along with the sparkle in his blue eyes, made her smile. "That's a shame."

"Especially since Goose is part of the family." He eyed his dog, currently curled into Layla's hip. "I always just leave her at home when I go over there. But if I invite Mae over here, I'm not sure she'll come."

"I'd think since she's older, she'd really appreciate someone else offering to cook the meal," Layla commented.

Hunter laughed. "Oh, not Mae. She likes to be in control at all times. I'd have to insist she stay out of the kitchen entirely. Otherwise, she'd simply push me out of the way and take over."

"Then why even try? Why not just do it the way you've always done and simply go to Thanksgiving dinner at her house? Even if she hasn't mentioned it, maybe she's just assuming you'll go."

He met and held her gaze, his intense. "Because I want to spend Thanksgiving with you. No one should be alone on a day that's supposed to be all about family."

Touched, she slowly shook her head. "There's no need for you to worry about me. I'm used to spending holidays alone. It's not that big a deal to me."

Even she knew how pathetic that sounded. Except she'd never really minded, or so she'd always told herself. Until now. The prospect of spending Thanksgiving with Hunter made her feel dizzy with longing.

To hide this, she turned her attention to Goose, who'd fallen asleep. "She's such a good dog."

"Come with me," Hunter said, surprising her. "Whether I cook a turkey here or go eat at Mae's, join me. Please." Stunned, she slowly raised her head to find him watching her with the same intense expression. "I mean it, Layla. I enjoy your company. Having you share the day with me would make it that much more special."

Her mouth went dry. Not sure what to think—was this pity, or did he really mean it?—she searched for a response and came up short. "I don't know what to say."

"Say yes," he urged.

She wanted to—oh, how badly she wanted to. But this seemed like the sort of thing people who were in a relationship did. "You confuse me," she admitted. "You drew a line in the sand. As long as I'm engaged, we can't—"

"We can't be friends?" he interrupted. "Is that what you were going to say?"

Friends. It hadn't been, and she suspected he knew that. Did he really think they could merely be friends, with the crazy attraction simmering between them? The more time they spent together, the better they got to know one another, the greater the chance that they would eventually end up in each other's arms again. In fact, if she hung out at his place too long, she figured lovemaking would be inevitable.

Evidently, he didn't see things the same way.

Friends. Though her chest felt tight, she straightened her shoulders. If he could do it, so could she. "I could really use a friend right now," she admitted. "And I'll think about your offer for Thanksgiving. Let me know once you've firmed up your plans."

"Okay." Still, he watched her, as if trying to get inside her head. "I'll decide by tomorrow and let you know. Either way, I promise you I'll tell Mae up front that you're only a friend. That way, she won't jump to any conclusions and start discussing weddings or babies with you."

Just the thought of weddings or babies made her breath catch. She'd always put the notion of having a child into the same category as having a puppy—no time. Which wasn't quite the same thing as no desire.

Hamlin had made it clear up front that he didn't want any more children. He had a grown son, and that was all he needed. Since the idea of procreating with him made her skin crawl, she'd actually been relieved.

But somewhere deep inside herself, she'd always secretly longed to have children of her own one day. She wouldn't go so far as to say she'd longed for the tired old white picket fence, husband and two kids, but pretty darn close. Except when she did think about it—which she hadn't for a long, long time—she had dreamed of a partner with whom she shared equal responsibilities and dreams.

Somehow, without her realizing or even caring, her job had become her substitute for a rich, full life. She'd let everything else go—her friends, a social life and a chance at finding love—all in the name of Colton Energy.

And for what? A CEO who cared so little about the family business that he brought it to the brink of ruin with his spending? A father who cared so little about his own daughter that he was willing to broker her to a much-older man for money, just like he was selling a prize cow?

Hurt flooded her, along with embarrassment and shame. She'd been blind. Hunter had seen, Hunter had known. He'd been right all along. Her eyes stung with tears and her throat closed. What a fool she'd been.

Refocusing her attention on Goose, who opened one eye sleepily when Layla began petting her, she struggled to get her emotions back under control.

She'd never been one to spend a lot of time worrying about the future. One day at a time, with the exception of work, since she had to always plan ahead for marketing campaigns. At thirty-one years old, she'd figured she was still young enough to have lots of time to make major decisions. When her father had made his case for her to marry Hamlin Harrington, she'd been so eager to finally please him that she'd agreed without considering the ramifications for her entire future.

Now she understood she wasn't willing to settle for a loveless marriage or a future with a man to whom she'd only be another possession he'd managed to acquire. She wanted more.

What this eye-opening realization might mean, she wasn't sure. The one thing she knew for certain was if she chose to make a change, her life would be altered drastically.

As would her relationship—whether they were friends or otherwise—with Hunter.

Chapter 11

One of the hardest things Hunter had ever done was keep his hands and words to himself as he watched Layla struggle with some inner revelation. Her breath caught in an audible gasp, and before she looked down, he saw the bright sheen of tears in her beautiful eyes.

More than anything, he ached to comfort her, to wrap his arms around her and offer her his shoulder to cry on if she needed it, but knew he didn't have the right. This thing between them—whatever it might turn out to be—was still too new, too uncertain.

After all, Layla still intended to go through with marrying another man.

Her fiancé should be the one to comfort her. She deserved that, as well as a man who would love her more than anything else, who would hold her close on wintry nights and celebrate her victories, large and small.

All of which, Hunter realized, he himself longed to do.

This should have stunned him, but it didn't. He'd known since the first time he touched her that Layla Colton was special. She just didn't realize it yet.

Hopefully, he'd be around when she did.

Pushing up out of his chair, he went into the kitchen, eyeing the almost empty wine bottle and deciding to pass it up in favor of water. "Do you want the rest of the wine?" he called out. "There's probably enough left for one more glass."

"No, thanks," she said, her voice a bit wobbly. "But I'd love a glass of water if you don't mind. For some reason, wine makes me dehydrated."

He poured two tall glasses of ice water and carried them back into the living room. "Here you go," he said cheerfully, handing one to her. She raised her head and thanked him. At least she didn't appear to have been crying.

"Everything's all going to work out, you know," he told her, even though he had no idea of the nature of her inner struggle. "It always does."

"True." Sipping her water, she considered him. "You know what? Once I get back home, I'm thinking it's time to get a dog of my own."

She couldn't have surprised him more if she'd tried. "Really? You'd have to cut way back on your work hours or hire someone to come let him or her out."

"I know." Her serene smile told him she'd clearly reached some kind of inner resolution. "I've actually realized that the time has come to make a lot of changes to my life."

He waited for her to elaborate, but instead she

started talking about how eager she was to get back to work at the K9 center tomorrow. Since he knew better than to push her, he didn't. She'd tell him whenever she felt ready to.

Because they both had to be up early the next morning, they watched the evening news and said their good-nights. As he walked to his room, Hunter marveled how easily they clicked together, even when it wasn't about sex.

He could get used to this.

Since that kind of thinking felt way too dangerous, he pushed the thought from his mind and went to bed.

The next morning, Hunter staggered into the kitchen with the intention of grabbing a cup of coffee. Caffeine first, then a hot shower. Hopefully, those two things combined would help wake him up. Even when he'd been younger, he'd never been much of a morning person, and switching from working graveyard to the day shift would take a bit of an adjustment. To put things mildly. It didn't help that he and Layla had sat up late just talking.

He enjoyed her company. Even putting aside the constant attraction simmering between them, he admired her intelligent wit, her sense of humor and the passion with which she discussed things that mattered to her.

Since he could hear the sound of her shower running, he knew he'd have the kitchen to himself, which was exactly what he wanted. He made his coffee and escaped to his own room.

After his coffee and his shower, he felt a lot more human. Dressed in his uniform and ready to go, he made his way back to the kitchen to grab a second cup of coffee and something to eat.

Layla looked up and smiled when he entered. "I hope you don't mind, I made a pot of oatmeal," she said. "There's more on the stove if you want some."

Grateful, he nodded. "Thanks. That sounds a lot better than the bowl of cold cereal I was planning on having."

Outside, the sun had not yet risen. The wind howled around the edges of the house, making the window screens rattle. He shuddered. "Sounds cold."

"It is. I checked the weather on my phone," Layla told him. "A cold front came in earlier. It's snowing. They're predicting three inches." Since snow in South Dakota wasn't unusual this time of year, no one was surprised.

"At least it's just a dusting." However, since this would be only the second snowfall of the season for Red Ridge, he envisioned numerous accidents. People appeared to completely forget how to drive on snow over the course of a summer.

Because of that, he went back to his room and replaced his shoes with snow boots. When he returned to the kitchen, Layla had just donned her down parka. A soft violet color, it looked both warm and expensive.

"Nice coat," he told her.

"Thanks." Pulling a pair of gloves from her pocket, she slipped them over her hands. "Stay warm today."

"You too." He didn't tell her he'd probably be working some accident scenes, depending on how the chief wrote the assignments. Since it had been a good while, Hunter figured he was due to take a turn.

Once he stepped outside into the howling wind and

near whiteout conditions, Hunter realized the weather forecast had been wrong. No way was a snowstorm this intense only bringing three inches. Hell, from what he could tell, four inches had already fallen, and the snow continued to come down in a steady curtain of flakes.

Despite the as-yet unplowed roads, Hunter arrived for work early, which was good, since he wanted to have a word with the chief. The night shift—his former coworkers—were just getting off, and they greeted him with waves and a few teasing comments about how soft he'd be now that he worked days. He teased them back and then asked how the last couple hours had been for traffic incidents.

"Most people are still home" was the reply. "Everything will start rocking and rolling for rush hour."

Just what he'd been afraid of. Hopefully, people would wake up with the common sense they'd been born with and it wouldn't be too bad.

Since Chief Colton always showed up early to have a few words with the graveyard shift before starting his day, he already was in his office, drinking black coffee out of an oversize mug and skimming through the newspaper. The board on the wall still held last night's assignments, so Hunter didn't know if he'd work traffic patrol or not yet.

In the meantime, he wanted to talk to the chief about Devlin Harrington.

Hunter poked his head in the doorway. "You got a minute?"

"Of course." Putting down the paper, the chief waved him to a chair. "What's up?"

Hoping he wouldn't get in too much trouble for playing fast and loose with valuable evidence, Hunter filled his boss in on what he'd done with the baseball cards and Devlin Harrington. When he finished, Chief Colton pinched the bridge of his nose and considered.

"But what exactly are you hoping to accomplish?" he asked.

A reasonable question. "Goose alerted me three times when I visited Devlin's office. He's got some computer storage devices stashed there. We just need a valid reason to ask for a search warrant. If we could set up a sting operation, with me selling him the valuable baseball cards and then having me get busted, we could search there, since he knowingly bought stolen inventory. I brought a small recorder and I have it all on tape."

To Hunter's relief, the chief didn't immediately discount his plan.

"It might work," the older man finally allowed. "We'd have to bring a few of the others in on it. Let me ask you this. What exactly are you hoping to find on these storage devices?"

"Evidence that will incriminate Devlin for the Groom murders."

Chief Colton whistled. "That's a tall order."

"True," Hunter admitted. "But my gut instincts are rarely wrong."

"You know, you might have something there. Yesterday when you were off, we received an anonymous tip. One of the murder weapons is supposedly buried on some land Devlin Harrington owns. A team is going out there with their dogs to search this morning."

Hunter wanted to go, but that kind of search wasn't Goose's specialty, so he'd only get in the way. Despite the rush of triumph that flooded through him at the news, he kept this to himself. "Please let me know if they find anything," he said instead.

"Will do." The chief glanced at him. "Any news on the two incidents with Layla?"

"No. I'm frustrated. Whoever is behind them is too good. We don't have any prints or witnesses. Nothing."

"I hope something turns up." Returning his attention to his computer, Chief Colton dismissed him.

Back at his own desk, Hunter sifted through the case files he'd brought with him from nights. He had a possible embezzling case to bring Goose to, which she'd love. The company had requested help locating evidence that could prove what they already suspected.

And the Mark Hatton/Layla Colton case. That would move slowly, and most of the interaction would be between the individuals' attorneys. Of course, Hunter still had hope he could find real evidence to disprove Hatton's claims.

When assignments went up, Hunter saw he wasn't on traffic. Both relieved and surprised, he figured the work he'd been doing on Devlin Harrington had to be the reason.

At noon, after a morning spent pushing paper, Hunter stretched and headed out to grab something to eat. He'd take it home with him, just as he'd done on the graveyard shift, so he could spend time with Goose and let her out. She loved snow.

Outside, the snowfall had tapered off to flurries. It looked like the streets had been plowed, too, and traffic appeared steady. As he trudged through snow to his vehicle, he glanced over at the K9 training center and wondered how Layla was doing. Briefly, he considered stopping in and saying hello to her, but he knew that would likely cause speculation and gossip.

Instead, he drove slowly down Main Street. The sky continued to sporadically spit out snow. He picked up a burger and fries and headed home. As usual, Goose greeted him with enthusiasm, but since she was used to sleeping during the day, she appeared a bit confused. He let her out, standing by the back door since he knew she would stay outside too long if he didn't call her in due to her love of the white wet stuff.

As he'd expected, she romped and burrowed, making tunnels in the snow. But when he called her, she returned to the door in record time, shaking the white flakes off her coat. Once inside, she shot him a mournful look before circling around to lie in her bed near the fireplace. Even though there wasn't a fire, this was her favorite spot. She'd been known to drag her bed back there when he moved it elsewhere.

After he finished his lunch, he ruffled his dozing dog's fur, which earned him another look, and headed back to work. On the way there, he passed a fender bender. Two of his coworkers worked it, both appearing miserable in the cold wind. He waved and one of them raised his gloved hand and flipped Hunter the bird, making him laugh.

As soon as he walked through the door to the squad room, he knew something was up. The entire department buzzed, and the energy level felt high. He'd barely made it to his desk when Detective Carson Gage bustled over. "Did you hear? We found the Groom Killer's murder weapon."

"Wow. Good work." Hunter stared. "Where?"

"Some vacant land owned by Devlin Harrington."

Carson grimaced. "A couple of the guys went to talk with him. He claims he has no idea how it got there."

"Of course he doesn't." Hunter didn't bother to hide the sarcasm. "Are we going for a warrant to search his home and office?"

The detective glanced toward the chief's office. "Chief is working on it with the DA's office, but apparently the DA wants more evidence."

With difficulty, Hunter suppressed a groan. Then they'd have to go with his plan involving the baseball cards. He'd honestly been hoping there'd be an easier way.

Ten minutes later Chief Colton summoned Hunter to his office. "Close the door," the chief ordered. Judging from the steely glint in his blue eyes, he was furious. "I just got off the phone with Judge Kugen. He declined to grant us the warrant. So we're going with your idea. Pick two guys who you'd like on your team and we'll get them in here and fill them in. I want to get the ball rolling on this."

"Yes, sir." Hunter headed back to his desk to mull over which two officers he wanted to work with. Though he hadn't been on day shift long enough to know them well, he'd dealt with several of them over time. He should be able to make a smart choice and get this operation up and running.

Layla's second day at the K9 training center went by just as quickly as the first. While she knew most people would find it odd to spend one's vacation doing volunteer work, she could honestly say she enjoyed it more than a week lounging on the beach at one of her father's luxurious beach resorts.

Not only did she love being around all the dogs, but it felt fulfilling to be a part of something that contributed to the greater good. These canines would go on to become police and bomb-sniffing dogs. Watching the handlers train the animals put an itch inside her to learn what they knew so she could do it herself.

Which would be a total career change. And she had no clue what such a job might pay.

Still, as the day went on, she couldn't shake the idea. She asked a lot of questions, earned some approving and curious looks, and paid attention. As possibilities went, she realized the logistics seemed staggering. At thirty-one, she'd not only have to attend the police academy and pass, since all trainers were also police officers, but she'd have to attend classes on dog training. And even once she'd done all that, she had no guarantee that they'd even hire her.

Yet she hadn't gotten this far in her life by being a quitter. Despite her father owning Colton Energy, Layla had worked damn hard to get where she was today. And she'd continued to work hard to stay there. Long hours combined with a dedicated work ethic kept her at the top. And now that she'd gotten where she'd always wanted to be, was she really willing to chuck it all for something completely different?

An early midlife crisis, perhaps? She grinned at the thought. Was such a thing even possible at thirty-one? More likely, she'd finally opened her eyes and realized all she had to show for her hard work was an empty life. No pets, no friends, no special someone. Spinning like a hamster on a wheel trying to please a narcissistic father. Oh, and she'd also allowed herself to get engaged to a man she barely knew, someone she could not imagine spending the rest of her life with.

In short, she was a mess.

Today, everyone at the training center was talking about Thanksgiving. Sharing recipes, bragging about the size of their turkey or how many people were coming over. To her surprise, they included her in their discussions, even though she had little to contribute. She knew better than to volunteer how she usually spent her holidays and didn't feel comfortable mentioning that Hunter had invited her to spend Thanksgiving with him, so she simply listened and nodded a lot.

She even asked for a recipe when one of the trainers described a particularly mouthwatering apple-caramel cheesecake she made. Though Layla wasn't much of a cook, since Hunter didn't bake, maybe she could take care of dessert. The thought of making something for him filled her with a warm, fuzzy feeling.

When she asked who trained the dogs like Goose, who were able to detect hidden computer storage devices, the group's reactions surprised her. Apparently, there were only a few dogs like Goose in the entire United States, and that type of specialized training only took place in a facility on the East Coast.

Hunter had gone there and learned the technique. Then he'd applied that technique and trained his dog himself.

"Does that mean he hasn't trained any others?" Layla asked, looking around at the group. One by one, they all shook their heads.

"When he started with the Red Ridge PD, he wasn't part of the K9 unit," one of the men explained. "He bought that odd little basset from a breeder and trained

her himself. With a dog like that, he could have gone
to work anywhere. The FBI, the DEA and a half dozen
police departments from around the country all wanted
him. Yet he choose to stay here once he was offered a
spot as a K9 officer."

"Wow." As she looked from one admiring face to
another, Layla realized Hunter had done something
difficult and made it look easy. "I take it Goose must
be good at what she does?"

Several people laughed. "Let's just say that little
dog's talents are in high demand. Hunter is constantly
fielding requests to assist in various investigations,
usually FBI."

Impressed, Layla changed the subject before someone asked her why she seemed so interested in Hunter.

Walking outside into the fenced enclosure with one
of the dogs, she saw the snow wasn't falling as heavily,
though when she looked past the chain link, all the cars
in the parking lot were covered in white. The roads
looked good, though, which meant they'd been recently
plowed. South Dakota residents were used to winter
weather. Most natives even relished it, at least at first.
By March, almost everyone had cabin fever and wanted
the snow gone.

Hunter Black fascinated her. Where another man
might have bragged about his own accomplishments,
he'd only lauded his dog. From what she'd seen, the dog
trainers were all a highly supportive—though slightly
competitive—bunch, and even they hadn't failed to
give credit where credit was due. They'd spoken of
Hunter with such affectionate reverence, indicating he
was not only well liked, but well respected.

She'd never met a man like him. She doubted there

were many. Physical lure aside, his strength of character and dedication to his dog and his job doubled his attraction to her.

Tired of so much deep thinking, she took a deep breath, enjoying the bite of the frigid air. Exhaling, she decided to try to simply live in the moment. At least for the rest of the day.

Right before it was time to leave, Clarice Kutchison called her into her office. "How are you liking things so far?" she asked, motioning at Layla to take a seat.

Feeling comfortable, Layla smiled at the other woman. "I'm enjoying myself," she said. "So much so, I'm wondering what kind of training I'd need to make this a full-time occupation."

Clarice's eyes widened. "You do seem to have a natural affinity for dogs," she mused. "Of course, you'd have to attend a training academy with a specialty in dogs. There are two nearby. Not everyone makes it through the rigorous K9 part, but if you pass, perhaps Danica, our lead trainer, would hire you part-time until something full-time comes up."

"Part-time?" Layla swallowed. "Do you have any idea for how long?"

"That depends on the need and how well you do. As a rookie trainer, you'd be assigned to shadow various trainers here and study their techniques. Of course, we only use positive reinforcement, as well as NILF."

"NILF?"

"Nothing in life is free. It's a method of teaching dogs that they have to work for everything. We've had great success with it, especially with some of the behavior issues we see in animals coming here from a shelter."

"Clearly, I need to do some reading up," Layla said, smiling.

"And think very long and hard how serious you are about this," Clarice continued. "This is the opposite of corporate management, the type of work you do now. You'll never get rich working with dogs."

"Getting rich has never been a dream of mine." Aware her honest answer could still be misconstrued, Layla elaborated. "My family has money, and as far as I can tell, it's never brought any of them happiness."

Clarice laughed. "Said by someone who has no idea what it's like to be truly poor. I've been there and never want to live like that again." She shuddered. "Not knowing where your next meal is coming from, how you'll manage to keep the electricity on…"

"I'm sorry," Layla said. "I didn't know."

"Hey, it's all in the past. No worries." Reaching across the desk, she touched the back of Layla's hand. "But it's something to keep in mind, too. I mean no offense, but you're a Colton. I know your sister, and she's good people. She's dedicated to what she does here."

"It runs in the family." Layla smiled. "I can assure you I'd be equally dedicated."

"I'm sure you would. But you work for your dad. Carrying on the family business and all that. On top of that, your father is the mayor." She took a deep breath. "He could make things pretty awful for us if he didn't approve of you making a career change."

Stunned, Layla could only stare. "My father doesn't control my life. Anymore, anyway."

Clarice's arched eyebrow spoke volumes. Layla's stomach churned.

Clarice opened her mouth to reply, but Layla held up

a hand before she could speak. "He doesn't seem to understand that I'm a grown woman and capable of making my own decisions." With a massive effort, Layla managed to keep her voice steady. "I can assure you," she continued, "while my father might sign my current paycheck, he doesn't have the right to say what career choices I make or what I do with my life." Taking a deep breath, she briefly debated whether to continue, but she hadn't gotten to be a top-notch executive, regardless of what her father thought, by avoiding tackling difficult things. "I have to say, I'm disappointed. I find it appalling that you would let my father dictate who you could or could not employ."

Instead of reacting defensively or with anger, Clarice laughed. "I'm glad to hear that." Clarice flashed a brilliant smile. "To be honest, what Fenwick Colton does or doesn't want has never been a factor in any of our hiring considerations. But I've heard you were a daddy's girl and would do whatever he ordered. I'm glad to know I heard wrong."

Though Layla could well imagine where the other woman had gotten such information, since all of her siblings had always been critical of her relationship with their father, she didn't take offense. How could she? Because up until recently, even the prospect of her father's disapproval would have had her scurrying to find a way to please him.

No longer. It felt weird to actually understand what her brother and sister had been telling her all along—that no child should have to earn a parent's love.

Clarice stood. "It's been great talking with you," she said, her expression earnest. "You're doing great and I've heard good things about you. You're welcome to volunteer as long as you'd like. And if you decide you truly want to pursue a career training police dogs, you have my stamp of approval to work here once you've made it through the police academy."

Pushing to her feet, Layla smiled at the other woman. She felt like she'd just aced a job interview. "Thank you so much. I really appreciate all your help and your insight."

This made Clarice laugh. "Someone had to tell you, just in case you didn't already know. It's never good to have a super-controlling parent running around behind your back trying to undermine you."

"True." Layla stuck out her hand.

After they shook, Clarice walked with her to the door. "Remember, we're closed Thursday and Friday for the holiday. You're welcome to come in on the weekend, but it will be a skeleton staff until Monday."

"Do I need to let you know?"

"No. I'll expect you on Monday, but if you do decide to show up this weekend, just ask around and see how you can help."

Layla thanked her and left. As she made her way back to the training arena, she reflected on what Clarice had said. *A super-controlling parent running around behind your back trying to undermine you.*

Exactly. Fenwick Colton had damn well better back off, or she might just decide to take an indefinite leave of absence. Right now, even the thought of returning to her once beloved job at Colton Energy made her feel queasy.

Chapter 12

After reviewing his choices, Hunter picked two other officers to join him on his operation. Tim Lakely, because he knew the other man well, and Brittney Tower. Brit had a reputation for being adaptable and level-headed, which were always good qualities to have on any operation.

He asked them both to join him in one of the interrogation rooms, which they did, no questions asked. Taking seats, they listened intently as he explained everything.

"I like it," Tim enthused. "Though I have to say, until the murder weapon was found on his property, I never once considered Devlin Harrington a suspect."

"Seriously?" Brit eyed him. "Please don't tell me you jumped on the Demi Colton bandwagon. That woman had nothing to do with any of this."

She'd voiced the exact argument currently raging in their squad room. Men and women who worked side by side as partners had taken sides over this. Finding the Groom Killer had become more than catching a murderer and saving their town. Finding the Groom Killer would also restore unity to the Red Ridge Police Department.

However, right now, Hunter damn sure didn't want to hear that same old argument again.

"Whether she did or she didn't," Hunter interjected, "we need to take a look at Devlin. Judge Kugen didn't feel we have enough evidence for a warrant, so we've got to go at this another way."

"Great thinking," Brit said, clapping him on the back. "I still can't believe anyone would pay that much money for a baseball card."

"I admit to being shocked myself." He grinned. The more he interacted with her, the more certain Hunter became that Brit had been a good choice for the team. And she and Tim had a chemistry that he hadn't picked up on before now. This could be good or bad, depending. As long as no one let their attention get diverted from the task at hand.

"Now here's what we're going to do," he continued. And then he outlined his plan to arrest Devlin. The other two suggested changes, they discussed every aspect and finally he felt ready to go.

With Tim and Brit listening in, Hunter called Devlin. "I have great news. It looks like you won the auction," he said.

"Fantastic." The confidence in Devlin's voice spoke to his absolute certainty that he'd win.

Hunter took a deep breath and continued. "I'll need

the payment in cash. How long do you need to raise the money?"

"Raise the money?" Devlin chuckled. "I've had it sitting here in a briefcase ever since you showed me those cards."

The thought of leaving that kind of cash lying around boggled the mind. But Hunter kept his mouth shut. Instead he asked the other man where he'd like to meet.

"You can come here," Devlin replied. "I mean, you're positive no one knows you stole the cards, right?"

"Right." Inwardly, Hunter winced. Since the entire conversation was being recorded, Devlin's admission that he knew full well he'd be purchasing stolen property would be damning. Even if they couldn't use the recording in court, they could present it as evidence to a judge in order to obtain a search warrant. Which was the entire point.

"When can you bring the cards by?" The eagerness in Devlin's voice made him sound like a kid about to open Christmas presents.

"This afternoon." Hunter wanted to swing by and pick up Goose. He needed her expert nose to make sure Devlin hadn't moved his stash of data, even though he couldn't yet legally extricate it. One thing was for sure, whatever data the other man was hiding, had to be big. Hunter had a feeling it would be Devlin's downfall. In fact, he was betting this entire investigation on exactly that.

Call concluded, Tim and Brit high-fived. "Success," Brit crowed.

"Yeah." Hunter cleared his throat. "Let's go over everything one more time. We can't afford any mistakes."

After reviewing the instructions with his new team and standing still while he was outfitted with a wire, Hunter left to get Goose. As soon as he asked her if she was ready to work, she immediately got even more excited. He took her out back, giving her a minute or two to calm down. Goose worked best cold, without a lot of prior preparation, so he didn't mention working again. Not yet. He'd save that for when they arrived at Harrington Inc.

Once they exited his house, he led Goose to his personal SUV. Though he'd taken the squad car the last time he visited Devlin's office, he wanted to make it look more like personal business this time. Out in the street, Tim and Brittney sat in an unmarked van. They'd follow him, listening in on the conversation and recording everything.

When he arrived, the receptionist clearly had been instructed to watch for him. She rose gracefully and greeted him with a welcoming smile, a far cry from his last visit, and told him to go right on up. She said Mr. Harrington was expecting him.

Like before, Hunter carried the baseball cards in his inside coat pocket. When he stepped off the elevator, Devlin waited for him, practically bouncing on the balls of his feet. He'd slicked his dark hair back, and the custom suit he wore probably cost several months of Hunter's salary.

"Not the dog again," Devlin complained, wrinkling his aristocratic nose in distance.

"I told you, my dog goes everywhere with me," Hunter replied. "Even to *work*. Right, Goose?"

Though she wagged her tail, Goose looked up at Hunter as if to ask him if this guy was for real.

"And you talk to your dog."

"Of course I do." Hunter let a trace of annoyance show. "If you don't like me bringing Goose, the two of us can always leave."

"Not until we've finished our business." Tone placating, Devlin gestured toward his plush office. "And your dog is always welcome. She can even sit on the chair. The cloth one," he elaborated. "Not the Italian leather."

Which made Hunter want to ask Goose to hop up on the forbidden chair.

Though the thought made him want to laugh, he wouldn't. Instead, he maintained his poker face and followed the other man to his office. His feet sank into the thick carpet.

Once inside, while Devlin closed the door, Goose glanced at Hunter, clearly waiting for him to give her the silent hand signal or the verbal cue. He'd already said the word *work*, which had alerted her.

This time, he used his hand as he let go of her leash. Roaming around, sniffing, Goose sat with her nose out toward Devlin's desk, adopting the posture meant to alert Hunter to the presence of some sort of data storage device.

He felt a little thrill of pride. His dog had never been wrong, not once since completing her training.

"Good girl." Hunter signaled her off. Immediately, she returned to his side, though with her head up and her nose twitching, she clearly wasn't finished working. Nor did he want her to be. But he couldn't send her to do a full office search. Not yet, since they couldn't do anything legally without the search warrant, which hopefully would be obtained soon.

"Well? Do you have them?" Devlin asked, all but rubbing his hands together with glee. His cuff links flashed in the light. Were those actual diamonds?

Hunter squelched his instinctive dislike for the other man and nodded. "I do. What about the money?"

Reaching under his desk, Devlin retrieved a battered leather briefcase and placed it in front of him on the desk. He clicked the metal fastenings and opened it, revealing neat stacks of hundred-dollar bills. "It's all right here. The exact amount. Would you like to count it?"

"That won't be necessary," Hunter began, which was the cue to send his teammates rushing in to make the arrest.

Both men turned toward the door at the sound of a commotion out in the hallway.

"Sir, ma'am, you can't go in there," Devlin's secretary shouted, just as the door to his office crashed open. Talk about a dramatic entrance. Hunter had to look down to hide his grin.

Exactly as planned, Tim and Brit rushed through, their service weapons drawn. "Nobody move," Brit ordered.

"What's going on?" Devlin asked, even as he tried to nudge the briefcase to the side. "I don't understand—"

"We've got you on tape." Brit's cold stare had been known to fell hardened criminals.

Devlin merely frowned. "On tape for what?"

"You're under arrest," Hunter elaborated. "For purchasing stolen goods. Officer Lakely is going to read you your rights."

"Oh, yeah?" Devlin's eyes narrowed. "What about you? You're the one who stole them and then tried to sell them to me. You might be a cop, but you're also a thief. If anyone's going down, it's going to be you."

Hunter shook his head. "Not this time, Harrington. This was part of a sting operation. The cards will be returned to evidence immediately." He indicated the briefcase. "The cash is in there."

"Entrapment," Devlin shouted. "I won't stand for this. It's nearly Thanksgiving, for Pete's sake. I have plans! I demand I be allowed to call my attorney."

"You will be, in good time." Brittney snatched up the briefcase, despite Devlin's efforts to keep hold of it.

"Come on," Tim ordered, going up behind Devlin and cuffing him. "You have the right to remain silent..."

Hunter took the opportunity to take another stroll around the office with Goose after quietly giving her the hand signal to work.

Again, the little dog alerted Hunter to several locations, which made him itch to get his hands on that search warrant. Since everything would soon be shutting down for the holiday, he knew they'd have to move fast. Hopefully, they could get in the request this afternoon and have the warrant by morning.

While that was in the works, he had to firm up Thanksgiving plans. No doubt since he hadn't heard from her, Mae simply assumed he'd come to dinner there, like he always did. Which would be fine. He'd simply sound her out on the possibility of him bringing a guest.

On the drive back to the office, he called her. Mae

answered on the second ring with that usual combination of annoyance and affection in her gravelly voice.

"There you are," she said. "I kept wondering when I was going to hear from you. I thought maybe you'd gone out of town for Thanksgiving."

He laughed. "Nope, I'm still here and still working. I've been trying to adjust to working days."

"They switched you off graveyard shift?"

"Yep." After exchanging a few small pleasantries, Hunter finally got around to the point of his call. "How would you feel about having Thanksgiving at my place? Kind of give you a break this year."

"Are you kidding me? I've already started cooking. You can't wait until the last moment and then expect me to switch plans. Do you have any idea how much work goes into this meal?"

And then she started her familiar litany of complaints. Since griping was a habit of hers and everyone who knew her well was familiar with this particular character flaw, Hunter paid her little mind. He simply listened and waited for her to wind down.

Once she finally paused for breath, he asked her what she wanted him to bring. After that, he figured he'd mentioned that he'd like to have Layla accompany him.

"I'm sorry," Mae finally said, after a brief—and thoroughly unlike her—silence. "The twins are bringing their new girlfriends and they specifically asked me to tell you not to come."

"What?" Stunned, Hunter pushed back the shock and hurt. "Are you kidding me?"

"That's why I didn't call you," she admitted. "I kept

hoping they'd change their minds. I hope it's not too late for you to make other plans."

Part of him wanted to tell her it was and demand he be allowed to show up for the holiday meal, just like always. The other part of him, what little remained of the vulnerable boy who'd lost his entire family, refused to beg for something that should have been his right.

"As it turns out, I did make other plans," he said, forcing a cheerful nonchalance into his voice. "That's why I invited you over. I have a lady friend coming to eat, plus a few other people that I invited." Or would invite. He knew there were several at the station who spent the holiday alone. Occasionally, they got together and had dinner out and saw a movie. It might be late notice, but he figured they might want to have a home-cooked meal at his place. If not, he'd cook for just himself and Layla.

"Good." Of course Mae sounded relieved. This would be the first time since Hunter had gone to live with her as a teenager that he wouldn't be welcome at Thanksgiving. No doubt Christmas would be the same. The message was clear: time to move on with his life.

"I'll let you go," he said, clearing his throat, again pushing away the hurt and anger.

"Okay." She sighed. "Please do stop by and visit soon. Maybe Friday, when the twins aren't here."

"We'll see." He waited for more, for her to apologize for letting her rotten grandsons rule her life, but she only murmured goodbye and ended the call.

He sat for a moment, holding his phone, trying to process what had just happened. Dumped by the people he thought of as family, while admittedly dysfunctional, right before his favorite holiday of the year.

Immediately he thought of Layla. This sort of thing, being alone on Thanksgiving, had long been her norm. Not this year. It might be short notice, he thought with a bit of grim determination, but he could think of a few other people at work and around town who might welcome coming over for a home-cooked meal on Thursday. If he got busy, he figured he could turn this into a Thanksgiving Layla would never forget.

It took two tries, but Layla finally managed to make that caramel-apple cheesecake. She threw away her first attempt, which she'd managed to overcook so badly it had cracked down the middle, and started over.

She had to admit, she felt pretty darn proud when she removed it from Hunter's oven.

"Smells great," he said, finally entering the kitchen. She suspected he'd deliberately stayed away to give her space while she baked. "And looks even better. Well done."

His praise made her beam with pride. "Thank you. Now tell me, what can I do to help you?"

"You might be sorry you asked." He rubbed his hands together. "But let's get started."

For the next several hours, following Hunter's instructions, she chopped and sautéed, mixed and blended. He made a homemade dressing, a sweet potato casserole and green beans with almonds. He also showed her how to make the cranberry relish and mix up the turkey brine so he could soak the bird overnight. Goose watched all of this from her place on the rug near the back door, clearly hoping they'd relent and toss a scrap of something her way.

"Not today, girl," Hunter said, smiling at his dog. "But tomorrow you'll get a nice slice of turkey."

Goose chuffed happily, as if she understood his every word. This made Layla laugh, earning a grin from Hunter before he went back to cutting cheese for a cheese platter.

Thanksgiving meal was going to be a feast, she thought, exactly like the ones she'd read about or seen on TV. Hunter appeared determined to go all out. The only thing he wasn't making from scratch, as far as she could tell, were rolls. Two bottles of a nice riesling were chilling in the fridge.

While he put the finishing touches to some sort of pea salad, she set the table. Four others—one from the K9 training center and three from the police department—had RSVP'd that they were coming. Including Hunter and Layla, that made six total.

Hunter hadn't elaborated as to the reason for the change in plans. When she'd asked about Mae Larson, he'd only said that she'd made other arrangements. She'd noticed his carefully controlled tone and wondered but figured he'd tell her what happened when and if he was ready.

"This is going to be epic," he said when they finally finished. He grabbed them both a beer, twisting off the tops before handing a bottle to her. Accepting it, she followed him into the living room and dropped onto the sofa with a sigh. Goose followed and jumped up next to her, turning a couple of circles before settling in place.

"Wow," she mused. "That was intense."

"But getting to eat it tomorrow will make it all worth

it." The twinkle in his blue eyes started a slow warmth low in her body.

"True, I guess."

"You guess?" He took a long drink of his beer before grinning at her. "There's a reason Thanksgiving is my favorite holiday. All that delicious food." He kicked his feet up on the ottoman. "Makes all the work worthwhile, I promise."

Again that sizzle of attraction buzzed through her veins. Never would she have believed a man who could cook would be so damn sexy. But more than that, she really liked him the more she got to know him. She found herself wishing they were sitting next to each other with his arm around her. She thought how good it would feel to rest her head on his shoulder, to curve herself into his body.

"What's your fiancé doing tomorrow?" Hunter asked.

And just like that, reality came crashing back in. "I'm not sure," she said, realizing she hadn't heard from Hamlin at all. "I haven't talked to him in a while." Nor had she even spared him a thought.

"Then you aren't aware that his son was arrested?"

"Devlin?" Shocked, she tried to imagine how that had gone. "What for? I can't stand the man, but I don't think he's a criminal."

"Oh, he is." The certainty in Hunter's voice made her take a second look at him. "He tried to purchase stolen property, for starters."

"Maybe he wasn't aware it was stolen."

"He knew." Narrowing his eyes, Hunter studied her. "Are you defending him? Maybe because he's going to become part of your family?"

She'd already started shaking her head before he'd even finished talking. "Not at all. But I can imagine his father must be upset, what with Devlin in jail over Thanksgiving."

"He's not in jail. He bonded out already. The rules rarely apply to people with that kind of money."

The bitterness in his voice concerned her. Mainly because people usually lumped her into that same group. "Oh," she replied rather than questioning. "Then Hamlin is probably relieved."

"Don't the two of you talk at all?" Hunter asked, his expression watchful.

Her situation with Hamlin was the last thing she wanted to discuss the night before her first real Thanksgiving. Yet something about the hunger in Hunter's gaze urged her to tell him the truth. "I'm thinking that entire thing might not work out."

He tilted his head and took another drink. "Pretty vague statement, don't you think? Want to elaborate?"

Instead, she jumped to her feet and took the chicken's way out. "Not tonight. I'm pretty tired. Since it's after ten, I think I'll head to bed." And beer in hand, she fled to the relative quiet of her room.

The moment she closed the door, she missed Hunter. She knew what he wanted to hear, which was the same thing she wanted to do, but she didn't want to do it because of him. If she broke things off with Hamlin, it would have to be on her own terms, in her own timing. Her father would be furious and her decision would definitely impact Colton Energy.

As for Hamlin himself, she sensed he wouldn't really be affected, at least not emotionally. Aside from his wanting her sexually, the rest was all a business decision to him, not personal. Once she'd rejected him, she doubted he even cared if he ever saw her again. He could always find another trophy wife.

The next morning, she woke up at six, jumped in the shower and then hurried to get ready. She knew Hunter had planned to put the turkey in early since they were eating at one, but she wasn't sure when.

Hair dried, makeup done, she dressed comfortably in worn jeans and a long-sleeved T-shirt before hurrying to the kitchen. Goose greeted her with a soft woof and a tail wag. Hunter sat at the kitchen table with a cup of coffee and a muffin.

"There's more muffins over there," he said, pointing. "I confess I used a mix to make them, but they're still good." As if using a mix was a sin.

Her stomach growled, right on cue, loud enough to make him smile. "Sounds like you could definitely use a couple," he teased. "Help yourself."

The rest of the morning passed in a blur. Working side by side like an old married couple, he directed and she followed his directions. They cooked or heated everything they'd made the day before, and by the time the doorbell chimed to announce the first guest, the entire house smelled fantastic. For the first time, Layla truly understood Hunter's obsession with the holiday. Her mouth watered and she could hardly wait to taste everything.

Soon everyone had arrived. Layla recognized the only other woman from the K9 center, where she was a trainer. The rest of the group were other police officers, two younger, single guys with families far away, and one older man who said he was a widower.

Hunter set up everything on the kitchen counter, buffet style. Once he'd carved the perfectly browned turkey, he invited everyone to help themselves. Which they did.

Laughing, talking, sharing stories, passing the rolls around the table and eating, of course. Eating and more eating. No one appeared reluctant to have seconds. And when Hunter brought out the cheesecake Layla had made, everyone groaned good-naturedly and dug in.

It was the best Thanksgiving Layla had ever had.

Sitting back, her stomach and her heart full, she took it all in and wondered how she could have lived thirty-one years without every experiencing a day like today.

The one subject they'd all agreed not to discuss was work. On this day of celebration and hope, Hunter said, no darkness should be allowed to tarnish the meal.

Though they weren't related by blood and Layla barely knew them, by the end of the meal, they felt like family. Mort with his shiny bald head, telling wistful stories about his wife and her many botched holiday meals. She'd been gone five years, he'd said, and he still missed her every day.

The younger guys, Shannon and Gray, tried to one-up each other with who could eat the most, jostling each other with boasts about the one time they'd…fill in the blank. Cara the dog trainer spent a lot of time interacting with Goose, who'd parked herself under the table in case anyone dropped food.

As host, Hunter interacted with them all. There were lots of laughs, and the sense of camaraderie actually made Layla's throat close up more than once. She hadn't realized how much she'd missed. She hadn't realized how lonely she'd been. When Shannon voiced the hope that this would become an annual tradition, every single one of them agreed without hesitation.

After her cheesecake had been devoured, the guys decamped to the living room to watch football. Still marveling over her happiness, Layla began clearing the table, intending to do the dishes. Cara shook her head, muttered something about gender profiling and went to watch the game with the men. Grinning, Layla waved her away. Truly, she didn't mind. She relished the chance to be alone with her thoughts. Though to some of the others, today might have seemed ordinary, to her the meal had been a revelation. She needed some quiet time to process her thoughts and emotions. Continuing to gather up plates and silverware, she stacked them next to the sink.

Seeing this, Hunter returned. He went right past Layla and began rinsing off plates before stacking them in the dishwasher.

Layla couldn't help but stare. Neither her father nor any of his friends could be bothered to help clean up anything. "What are you doing?" she asked, even though it seemed obvious.

He barely even turned. "Rinsing the plates. What are you doing?"

"Touché." She couldn't help but laugh. "Go watch the game," she ordered. "You did most of the cooking. I can handle this."

He glanced at her over his shoulder, expression intense. "I'd rather be with you," he said.

Chapter 13

The instant the words left his mouth, Hunter regretted saying them. Truthful, for certain. He meant them with all of his heart. But they'd been dancing around their mutual attraction ever since he'd drawn the line in the metaphorical sand. As long as she remained engaged to another man, Hunter would consider her off-limits. No matter how difficult that might be.

Once the dishes were all in the dishwasher, he helped Layla put up the leftovers and then they joined the others watching the game.

For such a smart woman, he wondered how she could be so blind to the truth. She didn't belong with Hamlin Harrington.

She belonged with him.

The next morning, Hunter and Layla drank coffee and munched on a delicious coffee cake one of their Thanksgiving guests had brought.

Though Hunter still felt relaxed and at peace, Layla seemed restless. She gulped her coffee and paced, only stopping long enough to devour a slice of cake. Finally, she announced that she wanted to stop in at the K9 training center and see if there was anything she could do to help the skeleton crew charged with taking care of the dogs who were still in residence. He didn't question her, simply nodded and told her to have a good time. He suspected yesterday might have been as life changing for her as it had been for him, and if so, she had her own way of dealing with the realization.

As for him, he figured he'd go with the flow. Relax and enjoy the day off.

He'd just stepped out into the backyard with Goose when his cell rang. Mae Larson. Figuring she most likely had suffered a bit of guilt over the way she'd treated him, he really thought she should stew in it.

But since her rejection had turned out to be a blessing in disguise, he went ahead and took the call.

"Happy belated Thanksgiving," he said instead of hello.

"Oh. Right. Happy belated Thanksgiving to you, too." Mae sounded both frazzled and exhausted, even more so than normal. He guessed having extra guests at her table had proved more work than she'd expected.

"Are you all right?" he asked.

"Sure. I'm right as rain." The hard edge to her voice told him she wasn't. "They finally went home. The twins drank yesterday and their girlfriends were fighting. The second they pulled out, I escaped to the backyard with a brand-new bottle of Jack. I haven't opened it yet, but I'm seriously considering it."

And thus the reason for the call. Mae had been sober

for sixteen years, ever since the day she'd taken him in. She relied on Hunter occasionally to pull her back from the abyss.

"You know you don't want to drink that," he said. The old familiar line. And as usual, she responded the same way she always did.

"You know what? I really do."

"It's not worth it. You've done so well all this time. I know you can get past this. It's just a small bump in the road."

The analogy made her laugh, a gravelly sound that testified to her two-pack-a-day cigarette habit. "I missed you yesterday," she said, surprising him. "Did you have a good meal somewhere?"

"I did. Turned out I had a houseful of people. It was a nice day. Very relaxing."

"Oh." For once, she appeared to be at a loss for words. But she recovered soon enough. "I'm glad. I just wanted to check in. Maybe you could stop by later if you get a chance. I have lots of leftovers and you can have lunch."

He made a noncommittal sound, not bothering to tell her he had plenty of his own leftovers. Her rejection still stung, even though because of it he'd had one of the best Thanksgiving meals ever. Not being allowed to spend the holiday at the Larson house had actually shown him that the time had come to branch out on his own, to start making his own memories. For that, he would always be grateful.

Once the call had ended, he looked down to see Goose sitting directly in front of him, her head tilted as she listened to his side of the conversation.

"Sorry, girl." He bent down and ruffled her fur. "Let's get back inside where it's warm."

He resolved to put Mae and the Larson clan out of his mind for the rest of the day.

When he went back inside, Layla was already dressed, clearly intending to head out.

"Are you going to the training center?" he asked, pouring himself a cup of coffee.

"I'm not sure." She shrugged. "I'm thinking I might poke my head in there. I enjoy helping with all the dogs, and I definitely need to work off some of the calories I consumed yesterday."

That made him laugh. "Have fun."

"What about you?" She eyed him curiously. "What are your plans?"

He swallowed and made a quick decision. "Though I know I should probably give Mae more distance for a longer period of time, I'm not the type to hold grudges," he said, shrugging. "So today, the day after Thanksgiving, when most of the town will be out searching for bargains on Black Friday, I'm going to visit her."

"Good for you." Her warm smile made him feel better about his decision.

After breakfast, he drove over to Mae's house. But not alone. This time, despite Mae's so-called allergies, he brought Goose.

Pulling up in front of the small cape in the run-down section of town, he parked. Mae like to tell everyone how she'd lived in that house for forty years with her dear husband. She'd stubbornly refused to allow either Hunter or her grandsons to make any changes or improvements to the place, claiming she liked to see it stay the way it had looked the day she'd moved there after getting married.

Ever since then, Hunter had made only necessary repairs for her. Her grandsons, the Larson twins, refused to touch anything, claiming they were honoring her wishes. Privately, Hunter knew they were lazy, but of course Mae usually couldn't see anything bad about them ever. Except when they started drinking. Then she got annoyed.

Snapping on Goose's lead, he got out and then helped Goose. Digging his phone from his pocket, he dialed Mae's number, intending to let her know he was there along with his dog. He wanted to finally show Mae how sweet Goose was and that she'd like the basset if she gave Goose a chance.

No answer.

As he walked up the driveway, he froze. Despite the chilly breeze, the side door swung back and forth, clearly open.

"Come on, girl." Hunter broke into a run, Goose easily keeping pace.

Pushing through the door, he caught sight of Mae, lying on the kitchen floor, unconscious.

His training kicked in. No blood, which meant she hadn't hit her head or been shot. Next, he checked for a pulse. Once he'd located that, he dialed 911 and asked for an ambulance. After he hung up, he noticed Goose nosing around the basement door, which was usually locked but now sat ajar.

As soon as his dog realized he was paying attention to her, Goose spun in two quick circles. She stopped, then pawed at the door, opening it a bit wider. Her signal, though not for electronics. He'd also trained her to detect weapons and drugs.

Weird. Why would Goose do that here? While everyone in law enforcement knew the Larson twins were involved in illegal activities, he doubted they'd be stupid enough to stash anything here in their grandmother's house. Even if they were, no way would Mae allow it.

But then why did she always keep the door locked? Sorely tempted to peek, he checked on Mae again, then listened for the ambulance siren. They weren't close yet. No surprise, since they'd be coming from the other side of town. An officer from Red Ridge PD would also likely back them up.

Now or never. He'd always wondered what secrets Mae kept in her basement, which had been off-limits to everyone as long as he could remember. She'd once told Hunter it was where she kept her late son and daughter-in-law's old furniture and possessions, items she couldn't bear to part with and that the twins might want someday. Noel and Evan's parents had died in a car accident when they were young, but being orphaned hadn't brought them any closer to Hunter.

Since Goose had alerted at the basement door, Hunter decided to check it out. Mae would never know. One fast look and he'd lock it back up with no one the wiser.

Whistling for Goose, he opened the door and flipped on the light before heading down the stairs, his dog hot on his heels.

At the bottom he stopped and stared, feeling sick. Goose went crazy, signaling over and over until he called her to his side. To his left, cases of automatic weapons, one open. Stockpiles of drugs. Cash—duffel bags full.

He staggered backward, unable to believe his eyes. The Larson twins had kept their stash here all this time?

Did Mae know? Logic told him she had to.

Hands shaking, heart racing, he trudged back up the stairs. Now he could hear the siren, whether from ambulance or police car, he wasn't sure.

Either way, this discovery was big. Huge. He had no choice but to call it in. Quickly, he called Dispatch and requested additional backup.

Mae began to stir a bit by the time Hunter opened the back door to let the EMTs in. They knelt beside her, checking her vitals and asking her questions. When she asked for a glass of orange juice and some nuts, one of them complied. She gulped down the juice and ate the nuts quickly. Right about then, two patrol cars pulled up, followed by another. It wasn't every day that the RRPD made a bust of this size.

"I'm fine, I'm fine," Mae protested, attempting to brush off the paramedics. She caught sight of Hunter and started to smile, but then her gaze slid past him to the open basement door. "Hunter?" she croaked. "Tell me you didn't go down there."

Just then, the uniformed officers rushed inside. Hunter pointed, stepping aside to allow them past him.

Two stayed with Mae. After questioning the paramedics, who still wanted Mae to go with them to the hospital for further checks, they informed her that she was under arrest and read her rights to her.

Meanwhile, she continued to glare at Hunter. "After all I did for you," she said, her voice both brittle and cutting. "This is how you repay me? By turning us in?" Spots of color bloomed high in her cheeks when she caught sight of Goose, sitting obediently by Hunter's side. "Why is that *animal* inside my house? Get. It. Out. Now."

Hunter ignored her.

More police cars arrived. Someone said they'd notified the DEA, who were on their way.

Again, the EMTs asked Mae if she'd go to the hospital. "No," she snarled. "I forgot to eat and my blood sugar must have gotten low. After the orange juice and nuts, I feel better. Leave me the hell alone."

The two EMTs exchanged glances and then wordlessly began packing up their equipment. When they'd finished, the taller man shook his head at the police officer. "We'll leave her to you, then," he said.

Chief Colton arrived. "Good job," he said, clapping Hunter on the shoulder. "We've sent men to pick up the Larson twins. It's about time we're finally able to make some charges stick."

Hearing that, Mae's entire complexion went red. "I demand to speak with my lawyer."

"All in good time," the police chief replied.

Jaw clenched, she swung around to face Hunter. "You know they'll kill you for this," she told him. "You're a dead man walking."

Hunter opened his mouth and closed it. Throat tight, he still struggled to reconcile the Mae he knew with all of this. Clearly, not only had she known what her grandsons were up to, but she'd aided and abetted them in their criminal enterprises.

"Threatening an officer of the law is also a crime,"

Chief Colton scolded her. "Cuff her and take her to the station, boys. I'll be there shortly."

Hunter watched as they led Mae away, his chest aching. Right now, he recognized several of the emotions swirling around inside him—shock mingled with anger and disbelief.

"Come on, Officer Black. Show me what you found." The chief gestured toward the basement stairs. "I know this had to be rough on you, but good job."

Though the praise didn't make him feel any better, Hunter nodded. "Thanks." Bending down to scratch Goose's neck, he gave her the hand signal to go to work. She rushed past him, down the stairs. "Who knows what else she might find," Hunter told his boss. "There's a lot down there, right in open view. But there might be more hidden. Let's go and see."

Aware she couldn't avoid her emotions forever, Layla threw herself into exercising the dogs she was assigned. These canines hadn't yet completed training and either weren't matched with a handler or were due to be shipped back to their various police departments once they were ready.

It didn't help that her father hadn't even bothered to call and wish her a happy Thanksgiving. In the past, at least he'd done that. Pitiful as it might be, she usually looked forward to his call, considering it proof that their tenuous family tie still mattered to him.

Instead, she'd heard from all four of her half siblings. They'd all been pleased she'd finally made plans to do something with people for the holiday, since she'd always declined their occasional invitations to join them and their significant others. Though she'd tried to be careful not to mention Hunter's name, Patience worked closely with the RRPD as the training center vet, and since he'd extended an open invitation to the officers and training center staff, she'd connected the dots. Her sister had been full of questions about whether this meant she was going to marry Hamlin, but Layla had said no comment, much to her sister's annoyance.

To Layla's surprise, no one mentioned the elephant in the room—their father. While they were all used to his disappearing on holidays, everyone had to know she'd taken some time off from the family business. Even Gemma, who liked to poke her nose in everyone's business, didn't mention it. Which was actually fine with Layla. She wanted to avoid making an actual decision just a little bit longer.

Right now, she found it easier to take things one day at a time. Her nature had always been super-analytical—her own father had often told her she was a born accountant. But she knew if she sat down and analyzed all the changes she'd been thinking about making, she'd panic. This wasn't just a simple tweak to her lifestyle. She'd be turning her entire life upside down.

Again, she pushed the thought away, focusing on the regal German shepherd she needed to walk. Elsie had just turned one year old and begun her training recently. Due to her youth, she needed frequent walks. Layla had gotten permission to take her out of the training center yard, down Main Street and onto one of the trails that led up into the woods. Since these trails were used frequently, by both joggers and walkers alike, Layla felt this would be help socializing the young dog.

She stuck her phone in her back pocket, clipped her little canister of citronella spray to her belt, double-checked the dog's harness and set off. Since Elsie had recently completed basic obedience, she heeled like a dream, walking alertly in perfect position at Layla's left side. Layla had been instructed to bring the citronella spray as a precaution, as it could safely break up a dogfight.

Despite the brisk air, with the sun shining and only a few clouds dotting the blue sky, it was a perfect day. Most of the snow had melted. Surprised at the relative emptiness of the trails, Layla guessed most people had chosen shopping or hanging out with family rather than enjoying the outdoors. Still, she supposed there'd be enough foot traffic to suit her purpose, which was to see how Elsie reacted.

The first jogger they encountered didn't have a dog. Elsie watched him go past, alert with her ears forward. She didn't growl or bark or otherwise react, so Layla praised her effusively.

The trail wound through a heavily forested area and along the edge of a stream. Layla loved coming here in every season, spring, summer or fall, but often the trail was inaccessible in winter due to deep snow.

Elsie growled, drawing Layla's attention. As far as she could see, no one was ahead of them or behind them. The dog growled again, louder this time. Slightly alarmed, Layla checked out the underbrush on both sides of the trail. Hopefully, whatever threat Elsie felt would turn out to be wildlife of the not harmful kind.

Just in case, Layla unclipped the citronella spray from her belt and kept it in her hand.

As they rounded a curve in the trail, Elsie came to

a sudden stop, which made Layla stumble. To her left, she saw a flash of movement. She'd barely started to pivot when someone jumped her, slamming her into the ground and knocking the wind from her.

A man. Black hoodie, ski mask over his face. He covered her mouth with his gloved hand, making it hard for her to breathe or scream. Though dazed, she struggled.

And then the dog took hold of him, all eighty pounds of her focused on defending Layla.

The assailant screamed as the shepherd sank her teeth into his leg. This gave Layla enough space to scramble out from under him. She used her citronella spray on the thug and, heart pounding, attempted to call Elsie off. She prayed the dog had learned enough to listen.

Luckily for them all, Elsie had. She released the now blubbering and bleeding man, though she stood guard over him with her teeth bared.

Layla dialed 911. Giving her location as succinctly as possible in her shaking voice, she left the line open, as the dispatcher instructed, while waiting for the police and EMTs to arrive. Someone must have notified the K9 training center as well, because two of the male trainers on duty came sprinting down the trail. They arrived before the police did and gave Elsie the command to leave it. She obeyed, albeit reluctantly, trotting to their side and sitting for a treat.

The rest happened in a blur. EMTs tended to the man's leg wound, the police took Layla's statement, the trainers checked Elsie over for wounds. Then her assailant was taken away, whether to go to the hospital or to the police station to be booked, Layla had no idea.

She wanted Hunter. Hands still shaking, she called him, but it went straight to voice mail. Instead of leaving a message, she hung up, intending to try again later. Maybe by then she would've regained her composure.

One of the officers asked her if she was all right. Layla nodded, then ruined it by crying. She turned away, hoping the other woman wouldn't see.

"Come on, honey. Let's get you someplace warm." The female officer slipped her arm around Layla's shoulders, gently steering her back toward Main Street.

Instinctively, Layla looked for Elsie, since the dog was in her charge, after all. But one of the trainers now held the leash, and when he saw Layla eyeing him, he gave her a small nod and told her to go. "We've got this," he said.

As Layla walked back toward the training center with a uniformed police officer at her side, she once again longed for Hunter. These attacks—three now— were getting far too numerous. How had that man known she'd be out on the trail walking? Or had him jumping her just been random? Like a weird twist of fate. Nope, way too coincidental for her liking.

Once they reached the training center, the officer left her with several of the trainers. It wasn't until she was gone that Layla realized she hadn't even gotten the other woman's name.

Shakily, she explained what had happened. Just as she finished, the others arrived back with Elsie. Of course everyone rushed to examine the dog, which gave Layla the opportunity to leave unnoticed.

But once in her car, she sat frozen with indecision. The trembling had returned and she could barely get the key in the ignition. She needed to leave, but where should she go? Hunter clearly was out somewhere, so his place would be empty. Not home, as her town house no longer felt safe. Not to her father's, since she knew he was still vacationing in the tropics. The last thing she wanted right now was to be alone. Then she thought of Goose and understood if she went to Hunter's, even with him gone, she wouldn't be alone. Goose's happy acceptance would be exactly what she needed to feel better. Even if what she really wanted was for Hunter to wrap her in his strong arms, hold her close, and tell her it was going to be all right.

She'd just pulled into Hunter's driveway when her cell rang. Her heart squeezed as she checked caller ID, hoping it would be Hunter.

Instead, the display showed Hamlin Harrington's aristocratic photo. Wondering what on earth he could possibly want, she answered.

"I heard you were mugged," he said, his cultured tone sounding concerned.

Surprised, she took a deep breath before answering. "More like jumped. The assailant didn't appear to be after any of my belongings."

"Then what possible reason could he have for attacking you?"

She held her silence for a moment, hoping he'd think about his question and maybe the answer would magically sink in.

Instead, he seemed to take her lack of response for something else entirely. "Are you ashamed?" he asked. "Is that why you didn't immediately call me?"

"Ashamed?" She practically spit out the word. "What on earth would I possibly have to be ashamed about? That makes absolutely no sense whatsoever."

"I'm your fiancé." His stern tone admonished her. "I know you've got a lot going on, fending off those sexual harassment allegations. Do you really need to add soliciting sex from strangers to the list?"

This statement so boggled the mind that she wanted to call him a few choice curse words before ending the call. Instead, she took another deep breath. "Hamlin, this isn't going to work out."

To her disbelief, he chuckled. "You're telling me. I can get everything cleaned up for you, but after you become my wife, I'm going to require a bit more discretion."

"That's not what I meant. *We* aren't going to work out. You and I. Being engaged. We need to end it now. I'm not going to marry you."

"Of course you're not. Not yet, at least. But I promise you, once that Groom Killer sicko is caught, I'll let you have the most lavish wedding you ever dreamed of. I know you're a bit shaken up, but I don't want to hear any more foolish talk."

Surely he wasn't that stupid. Which meant he was being deliberately obtuse. "It's over, Hamlin. I'm not going to marry you. Not now, not when the Groom Killer is caught, not ever."

Silence, which meant her words had finally sunk in.

"Does your father know?" he asked, anger threading his voice. "I'm guessing not. How about I call him? I guarantee he'll be on your doorstep ten minutes after I give him the bad news."

There were so many ways she could answer that statement. Instead of giving in to temptation, she simply told Hamlin to have a nice day and ended the call.

Surprisingly, she felt as if a huge weight had been

lifted from her shoulders. And since Hamlin had never gotten around to giving her an engagement ring, she didn't have to deal with returning that.

Once she let herself into Hunter's house, Goose came bounding over with her usual effusive greeting. After letting the dog out back, she gave Goose a treat and changed into a pair of comfortable leggings and her favorite flannel shirt.

Then she and Goose cuddled on the couch while she watched a home improvement show. Finally, Layla felt safe and warm and…at home. Stiff and sore, she told herself things were looking up now. The only other thing that could make the day better would be Hunter coming home. Hopefully, he would soon. She had a lot to discuss with him.

Chapter 14

When Hunter stepped into the squad room, the entire place erupted in cheers. By now, everyone had heard about his bust. They'd been after the Larsons for a long time, after all. His discovery was what they'd been searching for—the evidence to get an unbreakable conviction.

"We finally got them!" more than one officer exclaimed. Fist bumps and high fives made Hunter smile. Despite his lingering pain that Mae had clearly never been the person he'd believed her to be, shutting down those awful grandsons of hers had long been a dream. Now that dream had finally come true. Assuming they'd been rounded up. He wouldn't put it past the sneaky bastards to have fled to Canada, letting their grandmother take all the heat for their actions.

"Are the Larson twins in custody yet?" he asked,

crossing his fingers. When informed they were already being processed down at the jail, he grinned and gave the thumbs-up sign. He continued to smile until he remembered Mae would be there with them. While the thought of the older woman being locked up among hardened criminals disturbed him, he knew she had to make restitution for what she'd done. Of course, the entire family would probably bond out before they went to trial. The twins kept on retainer several expensive attorneys who were no doubt working hard behind the scenes to make sure they weren't held too long. He hoped they weren't immediately successful. He wouldn't put it past the twins to simply disappear.

Once all the celebratory comments had died down, Hunter turned to make his way to his own desk and begin the arduous paperwork such a bust required. When he was halfway there, the chief stuck his head out and called Hunter to his office.

"Take a seat."

A cold chill settled over him. He made no move to sit. "Don't tell me something went wrong with the Larson bust," he began.

"It's not that." Chief Colton gave him a long, considering look. "There's been another attempt on Layla Colton," he said.

Hunter froze. "What? When? I just saw her this morning." Heart pounding, he gripped the edge of the door frame so hard his knuckles turned white. "Is she—"

Chief Colton held up his hand, interrupting. "Sit down. She's fine."

Legs weak, Hunter dropped into a chair. "What happened?"

"She was walking one of the police dog trainees. Some idiot tried to jump her from behind a tree. The dog took care of him." He shook his head. "What kind of idiot tries to attack a woman when she's accompanied by an eighty-plus-pound German shepherd?"

He had a point.

"Even stranger, it's the same guy who claimed he witnessed Demi killing Xavier Wesley."

"Paulie Gaines?" Stunned, Hunter leaned forward. The small-time drug dealer with a long rap sheet had been considered a barely credible witness at best. "This could be huge. Do we have him in custody? If so, I'd like first crack at him."

The chief tilted his head and studied him. "I don't think that's wise. This is personal for you. I'll have someone else question him."

About to protest, Hunter realized the other man was right. Any attempt on Layla Colton was personal as hell. "Of course, I don't want to jeopardize the investigation in any way. But I'd like to at least sit in and observe."

"Behind the glass. Lucas Gage is in charge of this one." Judging from the set of Chief Colton's jaw and his no-nonsense, take-it-or-leave-it tone, that was as good as it was going to get. Lucas was a deputized bounty hunter for the RRPD and had gone after Paulie Gaines in the past, so they had something of a connection.

"I'll take it," Hunter responded. "Behind the glass."

"Then you'd better head down to interrogation room three. He's in there now, and Lucas is about to start questioning him."

"Thanks." Hunter took off. He arrived just as Gage took a seat across from the suspect. Paulie looked about the same as he had the last time Hunter had seen him. Permanently red eyes, with his face riddled by bloody marks where he'd picked at it, marking him as a tweaker—in other words, a meth addict. He wore a green sweatshirt with the hood pulled up.

Following standard procedure, Lucas asked Paulie to state his name, age and address. Instead, Paulie jumped to his feet. "Let me out of here," he demanded. "You got nothin' on me."

Lucas motioned him back to the chair. "Sit. Because you're wrong. Not only is the woman you attacked able to identify you, but a trained police dog took a chunk out of your leg. Let me tell you, our dogs don't do something like that unless they have good reason. Do you follow?"

Slowly, Paulie nodded. At any moment, Hunter expected him to demand an attorney. But Paulie was either too cocky or too stupid, because he smirked at Lucas and then sat back down.

"I wanna make a deal."

Even Lucas blinked at that. "What kind of a deal?" he asked.

"I know stuff," Paulie boasted. "I can give you information in exchange for you dropping all my charges."

"That's now how this works," Lucas replied. "First, how do I even know your information is accurate, never mind useful? And second, we can maybe discuss reducing the charges, not dropping them."

Silence while Paulie digested this unwanted information. "Oh, yeah? Well, how about this? People have paid me to say and do things." And then he sat back and crossed his arms, clearly pleased with himself.

As ambiguous as that statement might be, Hunter hoped Lucas realized the potential and pursued further.

"Paid you to do things?" Lucas frowned. "You mean like work? At a job?"

"No, man. Other things."

Now Lucas pushed to his feet. Hands flat on the table, he leaned over the smaller man. "Back in January you claimed you saw Demi Colton shoot Bo Gage dead. Then you claimed you saw her shoot Xavier Wesley. Are those among the things?"

With a defiant smile, Paulie shrugged. "Could be. But you'll have to make it worth my while if you want me to say anything else."

"Oh, yeah?" Lucas snarled. "Bo Gage was family. So help me, if you lied about what you saw and who you say you saw kill him, you'd better speak up right now. Or things are going to get a hell of a lot worse for you."

Judging from the way Paulie appeared to shrink back into his hoodie, he believed every word. Hunter had to hand it to Lucas. That was the mark of a good interrogator.

"Well?" Lucas demanded when Paulie didn't speak. "Did you really see Demi Colton shoot Bo?"

Slowly, Paulie shook his head. "No."

Damn. Hunter had to give Lucas credit. There went the basis of the hunt for Demi. Yet Lucas remained professional, his stone face giving nothing away.

"Then why'd you say you did?"

"Money, dude. I got paid five large to say that." Paulie's dreamy smile told them exactly what he'd done with his payment.

"By who?"

"Dunno."

Hunter could imagine how Lucas must be grinding his teeth. The frustration was mutual.

"What do you mean, you don't know? How were you paid?" Lucas asked.

"Cash. A bag full of it. I talked to the guy on the phone—no idea how he got my number. Once I'd done what he wanted, he sent a bag full of money by some courier service. It was cool. I signed for it and everything."

Hunter could see Lucas making notes. Another lead—a damn good one, in fact. It could be entirely possible that the actual Groom Killer had hired Paulie to frame Demi. Meanwhile, Paulie appeared to have no idea of the impact of what he'd done.

On top of that, Lucas still hadn't gotten to Paulie's attack on Layla.

"You're in a lot of trouble, you know," Lucas informed the younger man. "Lying about a shooting is bad enough, and I can promise you we'll come back to that. But I also want to know why you attacked Layla Colton."

Paulie made a face. "Isn't it obvious? Duh. More money. Even though she had that stupid dog with her, it's worth it for another five grand."

At this, Lucas sat up straighter. "The same person who asked you to lie about witnessing a murder wanted you to jump Layla?"

Another half-hearted shrug. "I guess. Yeah, I mean it was the same deal. I got a phone call, told what I needed to do and promised payment. Only I ain't gotten my money yet, on account of being arrested." He glared at Lucas, as if to say he felt it was the other man's fault.

Unable to contain himself any longer, Hunter rapped three times on the window, one of the signals RRPD used to let an interrogator know someone wanted to share information.

Lucas glanced at the mirrored glass and nodded. After ordering Paulie to sit tight, he popped around the corner into the viewing room.

"Hunter." Lucas shook his head. "Did you hear that? Sorry about Layla. I know you and she are—"

"Friends," Hunter interjected. "And thanks. She's actually been attacked several times, so I'd be interested to know if Paulie was behind all of them."

"I can sure ask."

"Thank you." Hunter exhaled. "But that's actually not all of what I wanted to talk to you about. Paulie claims he only knows this guy by his voice. Would you mind playing a recording for him and seeing if it's the same guy?"

"Sure." Lucas appeared intrigued. "Who do you have in mind?"

"Devlin Harrington," Hunter replied. "And since we just arrested him on something else and are waiting for the warrant to go through so we can search his office, I just happen to have a recording of him on the phone. Let me go get it from my desk."

Lucas nodded. Hunter wondered briefly why the other officer didn't appear surprised, but figured maybe he hadn't been the only one who'd thought something was off with Devlin.

After jogging to his desk and back, he found Lucas still waiting. "It's good to let the little bastard cool his heels." He jerked his head toward Paulie. "You know, I really wondered why someone was trying to harm

Layla. She isn't a threat to anyone. But when you throw Devlin Harrington into the mix, it all starts to make sense."

Hunter nodded. "Right? Clearly, Devlin doesn't want her marrying his father."

"But what about the rest of it? Why would Devlin want to frame Demi Colton as the Groom Killer?"

Handing Lucas the thumb drive for him to insert into a small audio player, Hunter grimaced. "Guess we'd better not get ahead of ourselves. First, we've got to make sure it actually *was* Devlin calling Paulie and giving him orders. Once we know that for sure, then we can speculate as to motive."

Lucas nodded and carried the audio player back into the interrogation room. The rest of Hunter's thoughts went unsaid. There could only be one reason, and both men knew it. If Devlin Harrington wanted everyone to think the Groom Killer was Demi, it would be because he wanted to hide the true murderer from the authorities. Which meant Hunter's suspicions had been right all along.

Turning to watch, Hunter listened as Lucas asked Paulie to listen and tell him if the voice on the recording was the same as the one who'd hired him.

When Paulie said yes without hesitation, Hunter silently fist-bumped the air. Finally. Now if they could get Paulie to admit to breaking into Layla's house and also stealing her car, they were golden.

Trusting that Lucas would make sure Paulie was questioned and charged for all crimes, as well as making sure they got his sworn statement, Hunter rushed off to see if it was too late to amend the search warrant request from the judge. If the original request citing purchasing stolen goods hadn't been enough, Paulie's statement was sure to be.

The sound of the garage door opening made Layla sit up. She must have fallen asleep, despite her phone's constant vibrating. Anticipating her father's reaction when he learned about Hamlin, she'd put the ringer on Silent.

As if on cue, it vibrated again. She shook her head. No way was she dealing with her father right now.

Goose jumped down and ran to the kitchen so she could greet Hunter the instant he came inside.

Swinging her legs over the side of the couch, Layla stretched. She felt stiff and sore and figured she probably would have a few bruises. But she considered herself lucky it hadn't been worse. She didn't know how she'd cope with broken bones or something like that right now.

The instant the door opened, Goose began wiggling, simultaneously spinning in circles. Hunter crooned a greeting to his dog, bending down to fuss over her. When his eyes found Layla, her entire body tightened.

"Are you okay?" Hunter asked.

She wanted to shout out her news that she'd broken the engagement to Hamlin, but she didn't. They needed to deal with one thing at a time.

"Yes," she answered softly. "I'm really thankful for Elsie. She's the dog I was walking. She took the guy down."

"Yeah." His voice sounded rough. "We have your attacker in custody. I watched his interrogation."

"Did he say why he wanted to hurt me? I have no clue why I keep getting attacked."

Hunter nodded, crossing the room to sit beside her on the couch. "Devlin Harrington is behind all of this. Apparently he really doesn't want you marrying Hamlin."

Though shocked, she wasn't surprised. Her phone buzzed again. When she made no move to pick it up, Hunter eyed her. "Are you going to get that?"

"No." She shook her head. "It's only my father, freaking out. As a matter of fact, now might be the perfect time to tell you my news. I broke off the engagement. I'm not going to marry that man after all."

He didn't move. "Because of Devlin?"

"Not at all." She let herself smile, hoping he could see the hope in her gaze. "Because I don't love him. I'm done trying to live my life for my father."

He gazed at her, searching her face. "Are you sure?"

"One hundred percent." Taking a deep breath, she decided to tell him the rest. "There's one more reason I broke off the engagement. I can't marry Hamlin because of you. You've made me realize that I want—"

Reaching for her, he didn't even let her finish. Covering her mouth with his, he showed her how he felt with a deep, sensual kiss that rocked her to the core.

When they finally broke apart, both were breathing hard. Hope bloomed inside her, along with a desire so tender the depth of it brought tears to her eyes.

"I want you," he told her. "And now that you're free, you get to choose."

"That's easy. I choose you." She ran her hands up his strong biceps, leaning in just enough to lay her hand tenderly alongside his cheek. Though she didn't say the rest out loud, she knew that from this day forward, she would always choose him. Someday, maybe she could tell him that.

Hunter didn't move, though a muscle worked in his jaw. His gaze had darkened. She couldn't tell if her words or actions had moved him or not. Either way, her entire body ached for him.

Trembling, she touched her mouth to the hollow just below his throat, where she could see his pulse beating strong and steady. "I want you, Hunter Black. Right here, right now."

"Damn," he groaned. Fascinated, she watched as he relaxed his apparently ironclad self-control. "You have no idea what you do to me, Layla." And he proceeded to use his hands and his mouth to show her exactly what he meant.

Later, still wrapped in each other's arms, Hunter simply held her. With her head on his chest, Layla thought if there really was a heaven, this had to be it. Goose, who'd fallen asleep on the armchair, woke and jumped down, whining softly, nudging Hunter's bare foot as she demanded her dinner.

With a husky laugh, he grabbed his boxer shorts and stepped into them. Tucking the throw blanket around Layla, he headed into the kitchen to take care of feeding his dog. Sated, warm and comfortable, Layla snuggled under the blanket and let herself doze.

A sharp rapping on the front door startled her, making her jump. Whoever it was continued to pound the door, not letting up. Goose ran in, growling and barking, turning circles in front of the door.

Hunter rushed into the room, frowning. "What the…" He looked out the peephole and recoiled. "It's your father."

"No way. He's out of town." Fenwick Colton didn't take no for an answer. Since she hadn't been taking his calls, had he decided to simply fly back home show up and try to force her to see reason?

"Don't answer it," she started to tell him, but then changed her mind. "Wait. Just a second." More pounding, as if he beat on the door long enough he thought it would magically open.

She snatched up her bra and panties and put them on. Hunter grabbed his jeans and shirt and did the same. Once she'd shimmied into her leggings and buttoned her flannel shirt, she took a deep breath and nodded. "Okay. Go ahead and let him in."

The second Hunter unlocked the door, Fenwick burst through. His mottled complexion and furious gaze attested to his mood. "I knew I'd find you here," he shouted.

Hunter cleared his throat. "I suggest you lower you voice."

Ignoring him, Fenwick advanced on his daughter. "What the *hell* where you thinking?" he yelled.

Hunter grabbed the older man's arm and spun him around. "I said lower. Your. Damn. Voice. My house, my rules."

Clearly not sure how to respond, Fenwick blinked. "All right," he said, his tone normal. "Now, if you don't mind, I'd like to talk to my daughter. Alone."

"He stays," Layla interjected. "Hunter can hear whatever you have to say."

Fenwick swallowed, clearly biting back a retort. "This is family business, Layla. And this man, whatever he may be to you, is not family."

"He stays or you go." Layla gave a shrug, hoping

her father couldn't tell how fast her heart was pounding. To go from making love with Hunter to having to defend her life choices to an infuriated parent—talk about ruining what had been an amazing day.

"Fine." Fenwick glared at Hunter before returning his furious gaze to his daughter. "I got a call from Hamlin Harrington. He says you broke off the engagement."

"That's right," Layla replied, amazed at how calm she sounded. "What are you doing here, anyway? I thought you were in Jamaica for the holiday weekend."

"I was." He grimaced and gave a dramatic sigh. "But I had to cut my trip short after you told Hamlin you weren't going to marry him. You know how badly Colton Energy needs that money."

"I guess you'll have to figure out another way to get it. You can't just auction me off like a prizewinning heifer."

Recoiling, Fenwick actually appeared hurt. "I would never do that."

"Yet you did." Amazingly, her confidence returned. Not in tiny bits, either, but in a huge rush. Due, no doubt, to actually knowing she was in the right. What kind of parent would ask such a thing of their daughter?

Her father opened and then closed his mouth. Scratching the back of his neck, he glanced at Hunter. "What about you?" he asked. "Do you have something to say? Otherwise, why don't you give us a little privacy?"

Shaking his head, Hunter looked past him. When his gaze found Layla's, she smiled. "It's okay," she said. "I'll be fine. This shouldn't take long."

Hunter nodded. He located his boots and socks and

sat down in the chair to pull them on. Then he whistled to Goose. "Let's go outside," he told his dog. Goose chuffed happily.

The instant the back door closed behind them, her father dropped all pretense of civility. "Layla, I've been trying to be supportive. I granted you unplanned vacation days, didn't say anything when you shacked up with the cop. But I cannot let you throw away your future with Hamlin Harrington. Do you not understand how rich and powerful you will be?"

"That's not the point," she explained with exaggerated patience. "He doesn't love me and I don't love him. If there actually is a better reason not to marry, then I sure as heck don't know it."

"Love?" Fenwick repeated, his eyes bulging. "You're ruining everything over love? I know you're young, but true love doesn't really exist."

"Yes, it does." Thinking of Hunter and how he made her feel, she smiled. "I'm sad that you've apparently never experienced it."

"That is not the point." He stamped one foot, a childish display of frustration. "We have an agreement, Hamlin and I. I can't go back on my word."

She eyed him in disbelief. "Dad, this isn't about you."

"Oh, no? When it's my company that's going to go down the tubes, I think it is. I raised you better than that. We Coltons don't go back on our word. The three of us—me, you and Hamlin—entered into a business agreement. While it was only verbal, you gave your word. You have to marry Hamlin."

The desperation in her father's voice failed to move her. "I'm sorry, but this is going around and around in circles. I don't know how else to make you understand. But please, listen to me. I broke off the engagement. It's over. It's final. There's nothing you can say to make me change my mind."

The back door opened, and Hunter and Goose came back inside. Goose ran over to Layla, wagging her tail furiously. "There's my girl," Layla crooned. "She's such a good dog."

When she looked up, she was surprised to see an expression of distaste on her father's aristocratic face. When he noticed her looking, he lifted one shoulder in a shrug. "You know I'm not a fan of animals. That was your mother's thing."

Though she nodded, Layla's gaze slid past him to Hunter. His large size and muscular physique made the room seem smaller. And while she'd never been one to care much about things like physical beauty, something about Hunter struck her dumb. She looked at him, aware her heart shone in her eyes, glad she'd found him. Right now, she might not know for sure where this thing between them might lead, but that was okay. It made her happy, brought her passion and peace and contentment. A good start, for sure.

"Are you effing kidding me?" Fenwick snorted. "Is that what all this is about? You and K9 Cop here are having a fling?"

Layla opened her mouth, but before she could respond, her father continued.

"So what?" he sneered. "The two of you go ahead and get it out of your system. I see no reason why you can't go through with the marriage to Hamlin once you've finished. He won't care. He's already made it clear that he has no expectations of faithfulness since he has no intentions of being faithful himself."

Layla didn't know whether to laugh or to cry. "I meant what I said. I won't be marrying him. Not ever."

"But—"

Hunter stepped forward, the swift movement cutting off Fenwick midsentence. "Mr. Mayor, I think it's time for you to go." He opened the door and waited.

Fenwick spun to face him, fists raised. For one heart-stopping moment, Layla thought he meant to actually fight Hunter.

Instead he spun on his heel and left without another word.

Chapter 15

After Layla's father roared off in his expensive car, Hunter closed the door and locked the dead bolt. When he turned, he took one look at Layla's ashen face and went to her, gathering her close and simply holding her. Smoothing her hair, he breathed in the intoxicating scent of her. "It's going to be all right. I promise."

"I'm so sorry," she murmured, mouth against his chest. "I have no idea what it will take to get him to understand that I'm serious."

Hunter knew better than to say anything. He waited another moment or two and then released her. "I have an idea. How about we get cleaned up and then you can come with me to pick out a Christmas tree?"

"A Christmas tree?" She pulled back, gazing up at him, her expression perplexed. "What exactly do you mean?"

"A day or two after Thanksgiving, I always go to the big Christmas tree lot on Third and get one. Usually a Douglas fir, though I've had a few Scotch pines. I wouldn't mind some help with making my choice."

"Help?" she asked, her eyes huge. "I'm afraid I wouldn't be much good there. Not only do I have no idea what a Douglas fir or Scotch pine is, but I've never in my life picked out a Christmas tree."

Again that squeeze to his heart. Careful to keep his expression neutral, he shrugged. "All the more reason for you to go with me. You've got to learn sooner or later."

"Really? I thought most people went with artificial these days."

He made a show of clutching at his heart and staggering backward. "That would just be wrong. There's nothing like a live tree at Christmastime."

Her answering grin made his spirit sing. "From what I understand, that's a highly debated topic. Of course, I'm not in a position to take either side, since I've never actually had my own tree. My father always has a designer come in and set up an artificial one at Colton Energy."

"What about when you were a child? I'm assuming your family had something when you were growing up, right?"

The fact that she actually had to think about his question was telling. "We probably did," she finally replied. "But honestly, as long as I can remember, my father took trips during the holidays. Las Vegas or New Orleans at Christmas and New Year's, the Caribbean at Thanksgiving. He never was big on family get-togethers."

"What about your mother?" he asked, careful not to display his shock. "Surely all you kids got together and celebrated, right?"

"Maybe they did, but I was the only child of my father's first marriage. Bea and Patience were from his second, and Blake and Gemma his third. My mom belonged to a religion that didn't believe in observing any holidays, including birthdays, so we didn't, or so I was told. I don't remember much. She left when I was four."

Again, he had to struggle to keep from showing shock or, even worse, pity.

"Then I guess you've got a lot of celebrating to catch up on, don't you?" He kept his tone light. "Starting with helping me pick out a tree."

Forty-five minutes later, they were on their way to his favorite lot. He'd watched them getting set up, enjoying the sense of anticipation. Now he'd be among those who wanted first crack at finding the best tree.

As he'd known it would be, the parking area was full. He circled twice before someone backed out, tree tied to their roof. This particular task always made him feel like a little kid, but having someone special to share it with made it that much more enjoyable.

After parking, he jumped out of the SUV and hurried over to open Layla's door. Already halfway out herself, she eyed him with surprise.

"Come on," he said, taking her hand. Together, they slipped into the festive crowd of people moving among the trees. Christmas music played over loudspeakers, and a stand near the big tents sold hot cocoa and apple cider.

Layla gazed around, her expression full of wonder. "Wow."

Squeezing her fingers, he smiled. "It's impossible not to get in the holiday spirit once you've been here. Now come on, let me show you the different kind of trees and then you can help me pick one."

The next half hour was spent debating the merits of several trees. Finally, they narrowed their choice down to two. One Scotch pine, the other Douglas fir.

Of course, Hunter liked the fir while Layla preferred the pine. Since he enjoyed watching her passionate defense of her choice, he let her argue a bit before finally agreeing with her.

When he did, she actually jumped up and wrapped her arms around his neck, planting an excited kiss on his mouth.

After he signaled the attendant and paid, their tree was wrapped and tied to the top of his SUV. Once he'd started the engine and backed from his space, Layla fiddled with the radio until she found a station already playing Christmas music.

"That was so much fun," she enthused, bouncing in her seat even with the seat belt on. "I had no idea. Thank you so much for inviting me to join you."

"It wouldn't have been the same without you," he told her, his quiet answer nothing but the truth. "And the fact that you and I chose this tree together makes it that much more special."

Silent for a moment, she finally nodded. "You're right. It really does."

Back in his driveway, he carefully untied the tree and lowered it to the ground. He leaned it against the side of the garage while he went to get his saw.

After one quick round of cuts to the base, he carried it inside. Before they'd left, he'd already set up the stand in the usual place near the big front window. He got the tree settled, twisting the screws until Layla told him it was straight. A little water and he was done.

"It's beautiful," Layla mused.

Hunter joined her, putting his arm around her shoulders while he studied the pine. "Yes, it is." Turning to gaze down at her, he contemplated kissing her. But then his cell rang. Red Ridge PD. He answered immediately.

"The warrant came through!" Tim Lakely sounded positively gleeful. "The chief told me to let you know. Harrington Inc. has a skeleton staff working today, and they're still open if you want to do it now."

"Finally." Excitement surged through him. "I've just got to grab Goose, suit up and I can meet you there."

"Leaving in five."

Goose, who'd been eyeing the new Christmas tree with a mixture of disbelief and skepticism, ran to the door instantly when Hunter asked her if she wanted to go to work.

Layla, who'd perched on the edge of the couch watching while he talked on the phone, eyed him. "I thought you were off today," she commented.

"I am. But I've been waiting for this day for a long time." He grabbed her and, after hauling her up against him, gave her an enthusiastic kiss. "We finally got a search warrant for Devlin Harrington's office. Goose and I are going to go execute it."

"Oh." A smile trembled on the edge of her kissable mouth. "Well, then, have fun."

"I will." And then a thought occurred to him. If Layla had never picked out a Christmas tree, he'd bet she'd never decorated one, either. He went to his guest bedroom closet and dragged out four large plastic storage containers. "In case you feel like doing some tree decorating, lights and ornaments are in here. The lights go on first."

She eyed him as if he'd spoken in another language, which made him laugh. "You don't have to, Layla. Just if you get the urge. If not, we can do it together when I get back. I've got to change and get on the road."

It took him all of five minutes to get into his uniform. Whistling for Goose, he snapped on her leash, grabbed his car key and headed out.

Even though he made good time, when he reached Harrington Inc., Tim had beaten him and stood outside his patrol car, waiting.

"Evening," Hunter drawled. "Are you ready to rock and roll?"

Tim grinned, handing him a large envelope. "Here you go. The only way I'd enjoy this more would be if Devlin himself was here."

"He's not? I figured his fancy lawyer would have gotten him out by now."

"He would have," Tim replied. "But with the holiday, no one could get a judge to set bail. He's stuck until Monday."

With difficulty, Hunter kept his expression serious. "Actually, I think it will be a lot easier to conduct this search with him out of the way." He glanced down at Goose, who gazed intently at the building. "Let's get to work."

Inside, instead of the receptionist, a uniformed security guard manned the front desk. He looked up, stone-faced, noted their uniforms and asked how he could help them. Hunter showed him the warrant, and the guard called someone to take them up to Devlin Harrington's office.

A younger man, clearly a junior executive of some sort, arrived. He appeared frazzled but led the way. Hunter and Tim followed.

Once they'd stepped off the elevator, they found the door to Devlin's office locked. This flustered their guide, but he rummaged in Devlin's secretary's desk and located a key.

"Do you need anything else?" he asked after unlocking the door.

"I think that'll do it," Hunter answered. Once the other man had gone, he closed the door and locked it. "Get to work," he ordered Goose. His dog immediately and enthusiastically complied.

Though he and Tim would perform a methodical search in a bit, they both wanted to see what Goose found first. Both men put on their rubber gloves, just in case. No sense in risking possible contamination of evidence.

Her first signal revealed a cache of thumb drives, six of them, placed in a padded envelope and shoved into the panel underneath a desk drawer. In rapid succession, she pointed out several other stashes—CDs and even a small hard drive.

"I wonder what he's got that makes him need this much storage," Tim mused out loud.

"For starters, I'm guessing he's been collecting quite a bit of illegally obtained sports memorabilia," Hunter said. He watched as Goose performed another methodical search of the room, sniffing every nook and cranny a second and third time. Finally, she returned to Hunter's feet and sat, her all-clear signal.

"Good girl." Digging in his pocket, he located one of her favorite treats, which he tossed to her. She caught it, ate it and then he'd swear she grinned at him.

"Our turn," Hunter said, giving Goose a final pat. "I'll take left if you want right."

Tim nodded and got to work. Once they were done here, they still needed to search Devlin's home.

A thorough search revealed nothing else. Hunter bagged all the electronic data storage and snapped the leash back on Goose.

This time, Tim followed Hunter as they made the short drive to the gated community where Devlin lived. At first, the guard at the gate appeared reluctant to allow them access, but once he'd seen the search warrant, he buzzed them through.

Despite himself, Hunter couldn't help hoping no one would be home. He felt like breaking the door down would be a form of poetic justice.

But when he rang the doorbell, an older woman answered. "Can I help you?"

They explained why they were there and again showed the search warrant. Frowning, she stepped aside to allow them entrance. "Mr. Harrington is not here," he said. "He will not like you in his home when he's gone."

Hunter and Tim exchanged glances. "We're sorry, ma'am. But he doesn't actually have a choice."

Her sigh told them what she thought about that. "All right, then. But please, don't leave too big of a mess. I'm the one who will have to clean it."

"We'll do our best."

Working together, they began. Hunter took the top floor while Tim took the bottom. Hunter started with one of the guest bedrooms, planning to save the master for last, since he expected if there was anything to find, he'd locate it there.

His search turned up nothing unusual in the first three bedrooms and bathrooms. Goose even appeared bored, sniffing around but finding absolutely nothing. Hunter had one more to check, probably another elaborately decorated guest room, before moving on to the master suite. The closed door made him wonder, since all of the others had been open. And when he turned the doorknob, he found it locked.

Interesting. Since most people tended to be creatures of habit, he felt along the top of the door frame. As he'd expected, he found a spare key taped there.

Slowly, he opened the door and stepped into the room, Goose right beside him. And froze. Turning a slow circle, he stared. The entire space appeared to be some kind of shrine to Haley Patton, the K9 center dog trainer who'd been engaged to Bo Gage—the Groom Killer's first victim.

After Hunter and Goose left, Layla eyed the storage tubs and the magnificent tree, inhaling the pine scent. While she'd certainly seen enough Christmas trees to figure out how to decorate one, the idea of actually doing so seemed unusually daunting.

But then she pictured Hunter returning home to a beautiful tree, and she figured she could certainly try. After all, if she didn't like the end result, she could take everything down and put it back in the tubs and he'd be none the wiser.

Out in the garage, she located a stepladder and carried it inside. Starting with the lights, she wound them around from the top down, linking individual strands together. Once she had them all on, she plugged them in so she could double-check the placing.

Satisfied, she went for the next couple of tubs, curious to see what kind of ornaments a man like Hunter would fancy. Would he have a color scheme or a theme, like the office decorator did? How complicated would this be, anyway?

Aware she might be overthinking things, she dug down into the bubble wrap and pulled out her first ornament. A dog. Brown and white, with a red scarf and matching cap. There were several more of the same, which she set out on the coffee table.

A few minutes later, she realized Hunter did in fact have a theme. Dogs. There were dogs of every breed, police dogs, firefighter dogs and Santa dogs. He also had red and gold balls, most likely to balance out all the canines. His choice of ornaments made her grin. She should have guessed. Hunter's personality shone through here.

Taking care not to place similar dogs too close together, she began trimming the tree. In the last tub, she found a glittery gold star for the top, with the Red Ridge Police Department shield in the middle.

Once she'd emptied the tubs and gotten everything on the tree, she stepped back. Pleased, she grabbed her phone and snapped several photos. Her very first tree. She wondered now why she'd never even thought of having one in her town house. Probably because she'd had no idea what fun setting it up would be. Plus, knowing she'd be sharing the holiday with someone made it that much more special.

Hunter. Since the day he'd reentered her life, she'd

felt herself changing for the better. And not to please him, but because so many new possibilities had opened before her, bringing warm yellow sunshine to a life that had been muted tones of gray.

Eventually, she knew she'd have to return to her job at Colton Energy and hopefully mend fences with her father, but she would never go back to the woman she'd been. Resigning her position was still on the table, though a lot of that depended on Fenwick's reactions. Judging from what she'd seen so far, she didn't hold out much hope that they'd be good.

Now that she'd finished the tree, she stirred herself out of her musings and turned to the final tub, which she'd set aside. It was full of accessories to be placed around the living room, and she wondered if Hunter would mind if she put them out. Granted, she had no clue as to his usual placement, but she figured she might as well give it a shot. He could always move things around to suit him if he didn't like her efforts.

Again, the dog theme prevailed. Dog Santa statuettes, a Christmas dog pulling a sleigh—each one made her grin with delight. She loved it.

Once she had everything spread out on the coffee table, she went to work decorating the mantel. Pleased with the results, she placed the remaining accessories, which included several snow globes with holiday dogs inside, around the room.

Finished.

She went into the kitchen and made herself a cup of hot tea. Sipping it, she returning to the living room and tried to view everything she'd done with a critical eye. Satisfied with the end results, she sat down with her drink and picked up the remote. She caught herself looking around for something, trying to figure out what was missing, and realized she wanted Goose. The little dog was the best at snuggling on the couch while watching TV. How Layla had managed to live her life this long without having her own dog, she'd never understand. She hadn't even realized what she'd been missing until she'd actually experienced the joy of having a canine companion.

Or the man who came with the dog.

Goose and Hunter. Hunter and Goose. *Hers.* She belonged with them. No matter what happened with her career or her father, she knew the ties they'd forged wouldn't be easily broken.

Despite the tea, she must have dozed off. The sound of the big garage door going up caught her by surprise. She sat up, listening as Hunter pulled his vehicle in. Stretching, she checked the time. Late. No wonder her stomach was growling. She'd missed dinner.

The inner door opened, and Goose came barreling inside, running full-out for Layla. The dog jumped up on the couch, entire body wiggling, tail wagging as she showered Layla with doggy kisses.

"I guess she's glad to see you." The sound of Hunter's deep voice lit a spark inside her, as did the aroma of something delicious. She looked up, saw he carried a large pizza box from Pizza Heaven and grinned.

"How did you know exactly what I wanted?" she asked.

He set the box on the kitchen table and headed into the living room. She felt mildly self-conscious, certain her hair looked a mess, but if it was, he didn't seem to notice. He stopped short, his gaze going past her to the fully decorated tree, lights twinkling.

"Wow."

Continuing to love on Goose, Layla drank in the sight of Hunter while he studied her decorating efforts.

"That's beautiful," he said, his voice full of awe. "You really have a knack for this."

She blushed. "Thanks, but you're the one who chose the cool decorations. I had a lot of fun with them."

Right then, Goose barked, which made Hunter laugh. "She's telling me she's hungry."

"I am, too." As Goose jumped down and trotted into the kitchen, Layla pushed herself up from the blanket cocoon she'd made. "I'm so glad you brought food."

He caught her arm as she headed past him. "I really appreciate you doing all this work. And…" Blue eyes sparkling, he leaned in and planted a quick kiss on her mouth. "I have to say it's awesome coming home and having you here. I can't wait to tell you what we found at Devlin Harrington's house."

Collecting herself after that kiss, she smiled up at him. "Let's eat first—and feed Goose—and then you can tell me all about it."

He poured kibble into a bowl for Goose and then, while she scarfed down her food, he grabbed a couple of plates, some napkins and two bottles of water. "Canadian bacon and pineapple," he said with a grin. "You're the only other person I know who likes it as much as I do."

At that point she would have eaten just about any kind of pizza. As she picked up her slice, it was all Layla could do not to lay into it like Goose had with her kibble. Instead, she forced herself to take slow, moderate-size bites, chewing normally and swallowing.

Meanwhile, Hunter had already demolished two

slices and moved on to a third. He must have been as hungry as she was, because he concentrated on eating rather than talking, which enabled her to do the same. Even though she could tell he was bursting to share his news.

"Okay." Pushing his plate away, Hunter took a deep drink of water. "Three guesses what we found at Devlin Harrington's house."

She shook her head. "I'm not going to guess. Just tell me." And then she listened in disbelief as he described the shrine to Haley Patton.

"I've only met her once," Layla mused. "While working at the K9 training center. She was really quiet."

"She took it hard when her fiancé was murdered. She and Bo Gage were really tight." He waited, as if aware she'd reach the same level of understanding he had.

"And since Bo was the first groom to die at the hands of the Groom Killer, it's possible Devlin's obsession with her is his motive."

"Bingo." He grinned at her, clearly pleased. "That, along with finding a murder weapon on his property and a witness who gave a statement that Devlin was the one who paid him to say he saw Demi Colton running from the Bo Gage crime scene and that he witnessed her killing Xavier Wesley, and we've got a pretty good case."

"Pretty good? What else could you possibly need?"

"I'm not sure. As soon as our electronics team tells me what's on all the data storage Goose sniffed out hidden in Devlin's office, I'm hoping the chief will feel it's enough to go to the grand jury for an indictment."

"Wow." She leaned back in her chair. "What about Demi? Everyone seems to think she's the one who's been doing all the killing."

"Yeah. We all wish we had a way to get in touch with her, but she's gone down a rabbit hole. I wish we could let her know we're close to catching the real Groom Killer and soon it will be safe for her and her baby to come home."

"Does that mean you've taken her off the prime suspect list?" Layla asked.

"Not yet." His grim expression told her how little he liked saying that. "We'll need an actual indictment on Devlin before we can do that."

Nodding, she got up and carried the plates to the sink. "There's one slice left," she told him.

"I saw you eyeing it," he said. "Go for it."

She turned and shook her head. He'd pushed back his chair and watched her with that particularly intense look that turned her insides to mush. "I have a much better idea," she replied as she moved toward him. She sat down on top of him, took a deep breath and then straddled him, thrilled at her own bravado. Already more than a little aroused, she wrapped her arms around him and leaned in to breathe against his lips. "I think a celebration is in order, don't you?"

Chapter 16

The next morning Hunter got ready for work at super speed, trying to move quietly so as not to disturb Layla, who'd spent the entire night in his bed. First time of many, he hoped. Being with her made him happy.

Despite spending most of the night making love, when his eyes popped open at 4:00 a.m., he'd found himself unable to go back to sleep. Instead, he'd tossed and turned. With his mind whirring with all the evidence on Devlin Harrington he wanted to present to the chief, he could hardly wait to get to work. Therefore, he'd finally given up on the futile attempt to sleep and risen an hour before his normal time. He'd rushed through his shower and gotten dressed. Mood great, he breezed into the kitchen, made a cup of coffee to go and snagged the last slice of pizza from the fridge for breakfast.

After letting Goose out and feeding her, he grabbed his car keys and started for the garage but spun around and returned to his bedroom instead. Gazing down on a still-slumbering Layla, he felt like the luckiest man in the world. Unable to help himself, he leaned down and placed a gentle kiss on her forehead.

She stirred, opening her drowsy eyes and smiling up at him. "Hey."

Again that clenching in his chest at the heady shock of her bright blue eyes. He got it together enough to manage to smile back. "Hey, yourself." Hearing the husky rumble of his voice, he cleared his throat. "I didn't want to wake you, but I'm going in to work early."

"You are? On a Saturday? Why?"

"I'm off on Sunday and Tuesday, not today." He jingled his car keys. "If things work out the way I want them to, today is going to be a big day."

"Hmm." When she snuggled down into the bed, her sultry look invited him to join her instead. Though sorely tempted, he knew he'd have to resist. "Get some more sleep," he said, already moving away. "You've got at least another hour. I'll talk to you later."

"Okay." Her eyes had already begun to drift closed. "Have a great day."

"You too." One last glance, memorizing the sight of her. He knew he'd carry that image with him the rest of the day.

When he reached the police station and headed inside, he was surprised to see Lucas Gage already there.

"Morning," Lucas greeted him. "You're up early."

"Yeah, so are you." Hunter eyed the full coffeepot, slightly relieved. The standing rule was first one in had to make it. "Thanks for making coffee. I figured I'd be the one doing it." He snagged his cup from his desk and poured, drinking it down appreciatively. "Ahh. I needed this."

"I heard what you guys found yesterday," Lucas said, his serious expression matching his tone. "It sounds like I have been blaming the wrong person for killing my brother."

Cautiously, Hunter nodded. Lucas had been one of the most vocal against Demi, calling for her arrest in Bo's murder, even though they didn't have enough evidence to convict her. During this entire investigation, the team had been divided. As a general rule, Hunter had avoided those arguments, preferring to keep his head down and continue working toward finding out the truth. Things had gotten pretty heated with people taking sides—Gages against Coltons with no room for any space in between.

"I really thought it was Demi," Lucas continued, scratching the back of his neck. As a bounty hunter deputized by the RRPD, he had long been in competition with Demi—and because she was a Colton and he was a Gage, there was also family-feud tension. "There was—is—so much evidence."

"Which mostly turned out to be false," Hunter pointed out gently. "Or planted."

"Yeah, I heard. But at the time, it seemed genuine. I know some of the others felt that way, too. What's killing me is that I tried to make my colleagues—her own family members—believe in her guilt. Makes me feel like roadkill." The anguish simmering below the surface in Lucas's voice touched Hunter.

"You lost your brother." Hunter squeezed the other

man's shoulder. "In your grief, your actions were completely understandable. Plus, we really didn't know if Demi was responsible or not. Until all the pieces came together, we were bumbling around in the dark just the same. All of us. Don't beat yourself up about it."

Lucas sighed. "Tim told me you've suspected Devlin for a long time."

"I have. But until now, I didn't have enough to go on. I'm hoping now that the chief will think I do. Plus, Goose found a bunch of data storage Devlin had hidden in his office. I turned it all over to the electronics guys and asked for a rush report. I'm hoping to get that today."

"Interesting. Will you fill me in when you know?"

"Sure." Hunter checked the clock. "I hope the chief comes in early. I want to run all this by him and see if he thinks there's enough to charge Devlin with another crime. Even though it was the weekend, I'm sure he's bonded out of jail by now."

"Probably." Lucas crossed over to the coffeepot and poured himself a refill. "That was pretty damn clever, too, getting him to buy stolen baseball cards."

"Thanks." Hunter shrugged. "I really needed that search warrant. Whatever works, right?"

Lucas chuckled and raised his coffee mug in a salute.

The front door opened and a moment later, Chief Colton came in, glancing from Hunter to Lucas and back again. "What are you two doing here so early?" he asked.

"We wanted to talk to you," both men answered in unison.

The chief frowned. "Now? I come in early for a

reason. This is my quiet time to work uninterrupted in my office and catch up. You know, before people start wanting to discuss cases with me or anything else. Especially on Saturdays."

"But this is important," Hunter pressed. "It's about Devlin Harrington and the Groom Killer case."

Shaking his head, the chief fixed himself a cup of coffee. When he turned back to face them, he motioned both to follow him. Once they were seated in the two chairs across from his desk, he sat and glanced at his watch. "Ten minutes. Go."

Hunter and Lucas exchanged glances. Then, instead of rushing to state their cases, they laughed and both men pushed up out of their chairs. "We can come back later."

"No." Chief Colton motioned them to sit back down. "I want to hear you out. I really do. I just haven't had enough coffee yet." To prove his point, he drank deeply and sighed. "I've already heard what you turned up yesterday. Everyone has. News like that doesn't stay quiet for long."

"I know." Hunter leaned forward in his chair. "We caught the Groom Killer."

"Not so fast. We need more than that."

"We've got the murder weapon that was found on his property," Hunter pointed out. No prints on that, but still—the gun had been found on Devlin's property. "And I'm still waiting to hear what the guys in electronics get off the data storage devices Goose located in Devlin's office."

"That could be anything," the chief said. "Hell, we already know he was involved in purchasing stolen collector's items. Honestly, I agree with you that he's probably the Groom Killer. His obsession with Haley Patton most likely was the catalyst that made him start killing."

"Then why don't we—" Hunter began.

"But." Chief Colton held up his hand as he interrupted. "Unless we find handwritten confessions on those thumb drives, all we've got is circumstantial. We could charge him, but there's not a grand jury in this county that would indict based on this. We need more."

"What about the witness who admitted to being paid off to say he saw Demi Colton kill Xavier?" Lucas asked. "He even admitted that Devlin's voice sounded like the man who asked him to do it."

"Again, not enough. We need prints on a murder weapon or an actual eyewitness. Or, like I said, a confession."

"Which isn't likely to happen." Hunter couldn't keep the glumness from his voice.

"Unless those data storage devices turn out to be a gold mine of information, no."

Lucas swore softly under his breath. "There's got to be something we're overlooking."

"Maybe so." The chief began riffling through papers, clearly dismissing them. "Get back to work. We're so close on this. I'm confident that with the team we have, we'll find that missing puzzle piece soon."

Silent, Hunter and Lucas walked back out into the squad room. A few more officers had arrived and a second pot of coffee had already been started.

"He's right, you know," Lucas said. "Much as I hate to admit it. I wish we could find Demi and let her know we're close to catching the real Groom Killer so she and her baby can come back home."

Hunter thought about Demi Colton, forced to give birth alone, on the run with a baby, unable to reach out to her family or friends. He shook his head.

"Me too, but there's no way to get in touch. Plus, you know as well as I do that we can't take her off the prime suspect list until we have solid evidence against Devlin."

"We will." The certainty in Lucas's voice matched the resolve in his expression. "I hate that I blamed Demi all these months, so I'm going to dedicate myself to nailing that SOB. But first, I'm going to find Demi. She deserves to know what's going on. And she deserves my apology."

Lucas turned and walked away before Hunter could respond. If anyone could find Demi, highly skilled at tracking and staying hidden, another bounty hunter could. And Lucas was the best there was.

Back at his desk, Hunter turned on his computer and checked his emails. No news on the Larson family, and nothing from the electronics department on the stuff Goose had found. Even though he'd asked for a rush assessment, he'd only turned it over to them late yesterday. Most of them would just now be arriving at work, so he couldn't go down there and bug them yet.

An hour later, the chief walked out and called a team meeting. Chief Colton outlined everything they'd learned about Devlin Harrington, even though he said he knew most of them were already aware. He asked them all to be vigilant and continue to work hard to get enough evidence so the killings would stop and Demi Colton could return to Red Ridge.

When he asked if there were any questions, no one

spoke, which meant they'd all hashed everything out among themselves earlier.

"Good," Chief Colton said. "Then we're all clear on what we need to do. Find irrefutable proof that Devlin Harrington is the Groom Killer and bring him back in if he's already bonded out. If not, we'll get him charged with murder while he's in custody."

"Crystal clear," Hunter said. Several others echoed his words.

Once the chief had returned to his office, everyone went back to work. Except Lucas. Watching him from the corner of his eye, Hunter noticed he turned and left once more.

Time seemed as if it moved in slow motion. Hunter must have checked his computer ten times over the course of the next ninety minutes. Nothing.

Once again, Hunter resisted the urge to pick up the phone and bug the guys in electronics. He'd wait, even though he knew it was going to be a long, long day until he learned exactly what was on those flash drives.

His desk phone rang, startling him. The double ring let him know it was an external call rather than internal, which meant it wasn't the one he'd been waiting for. Answering, he listened for a moment, at first shocked and then realizing he wasn't after all. Hamlin Harrington was on the line. Trying to use his money and social standing to learn what he could about the charges against his son.

Hunter stuck only with the basics. "Attempting to purchase stolen collector's items. Baseball cards, to be exact."

"Which he says you stole." Hamlin's smug, pompous tone made Hunter clench his teeth. "Doesn't your crime completely negate his?"

"It doesn't work that way," Hunter replied, even though he figured Hamlin already knew that. Part of him wondered if the older man would mention Layla and the broken engagement, since he no doubt already knew she was staying with Hunter.

But he didn't. Instead, he mentioned the name of a well-known attorney from Sioux Falls. "Not only did he get Devlin's bail lowered, but he got everything pushed through on a rush basis. He's released and home, without a scratch."

Released? Hunter swore under his breath. Of course someone with the financial resources of the Harrington family would have gone through the system in record time.

"I'm confident he'll get my son off, especially considering the way you used entrapment to arrest him," Hamlin continued. "And rest assured, once he does, we'll be filing charges, both against you personally and the entire Red Ridge Police Department. I intend to have your badge."

And with that, Hamlin ended the call.

After Hunter left early for work, Layla allowed herself to doze, luxuriating in the pleasant way her body ached after a night spent making passionate love. After eyeing the nightstand clock a few times, she knew she had to get up, even if what she really wanted might be to stay in bed all day. She finally rose and showered, trying to decide whether she'd go volunteer at the K9 training center as she'd originally planned or stop in at Colton Energy.

Though she'd honestly intended on taking a true vacation from her job, she'd never been the type to put aside her responsibilities. And since she'd rejected her father's plan to marry her off so the company could obtain a cash infusion, she felt compelled to at least try to come up with another, more workable plan.

And with it, her father would have to own up to his own part in the problem and promise to act more responsibly.

Luckily, she knew Fenwick would still be out of town. Though to be honest, even if he wasn't, he never worked on Saturdays, so there'd be absolutely no danger of her running into him.

While she knew she'd have to deal with him eventually, she was not in the mood today. To her surprise, when she got off the elevator on the executive floor, she saw him seated behind his desk in his office.

Damn. Swearing under her breath, she had a second's futile hope of keeping her head down and making it to her own office unseen. But no, that was not to be. She'd barely taken two steps when he called out her name.

Now she really regretted the impulse that had made her come in.

"Dad?" She squinted at him, calling on her nonexistent acting ability and hoping she could pull off pretending nothing was wrong. "Why are you up here on a Saturday?"

"I can't just let this company sink. I've worked my entire life to make Colton Energy what it is. I refuse to give up."

She nodded. Now or never. Heart hammering, she took a deep breath. "You've got to stop the crazy spending. When you dip so deeply into the profits, you deplete our cash flow. Without that, all the other departments, from purchasing to payroll, can't function. When they resort to using our line of credit, our debt skyrockets. And when we can't pay the balance in full, the interest rate charges rack up."

"I know." At least he had the grace to look ashamed. He looked down, spreading his hands to indicate piles of paperwork. "I enjoy living the good life. But my credit cards are all maxed out and I can't use them. I actually came in today to see if there was any excess money I could take to live on, but there's not. At least, not if we want to make payroll."

He appeared so shell-shocked, she actually felt sorry for him.

"Would you like me to help you set up a personal budget?" she asked gently.

Rubbing the back of his neck, he finally nodded. "Sure. And I'm going to have to ask you to take over the accounting department. I want to require your signature on anything that flows out of this company. Including cash withdrawals."

"What about Dan?" she asked, shocked. The current head of accounting and her father had been friends since grade school, and Dan had worked for Colton Energy since Layla had been a small child.

"He's going to retire. I've already spoken to him."

"Retire? With what kind of severance? You know we don't have a lot to work with here."

"I do. And believe me, Dan is well aware. Especially when one of his junior accountants pointed out all the flaws in his bookkeeping. It's a mess. I need you to straighten it out."

While she loved a challenge, this sounded different. Like there might possibly have been something criminal involved. No way did she want to be any part of that, especially since she still had Mark Hatton's false charges hanging over her.

"What do you say, Layla?" her father asked, a note of pleading in his voice. "Will you take the job?"

"Before I agree to do that, I need to know a few things. Are our books up to par, or is the IRS going to come down on us with a hammer if they do an audit?"

Now Fenwick appeared positively uncomfortable. "I don't know. Dan was in charge of all that."

"But you have your suspicions," she pressed. "Tell me the truth. I deserve that much. Did you report all income or 'forget' to do that since you made a cash withdrawal?"

His shoulders sagged. "Again, I didn't check everything Dan did. But I think it's safe to say he might have forgotten to put in a few entries."

Which meant things were a big, honking mess.

"I'll need to take a look at everything," she said. "I'll block off all reservations for conference room B next week and have everything brought in there."

Hope flooded his face. "Then you'll take over the accounting department?"

"That's not what I said. I want to do an in-depth audit of the books and see how bad a mess we're in. Once I know more, I'll be able to make a decision."

Fenwick pinched the bridge of his nose while he considered her words. What he didn't know—or maybe he did—was that as executive VP of Colton Energy and daughter of its CEO, she might already be on the hook for his actions.

"I understand," he finally replied. "Are you back in your town house now?"

Though the question made her tense up inside, she took a deep breath and tried not to show it. "No. I'm still staying at Hunter's place."

"Really? Do the police still feel you're in danger?"

Because he seemed genuinely worried, she considered softening the truth. But in the end, she figured he needed to know, so she told him. "It's possible I still am. The police think the same person who got Mark Hatton to make false accusations against me is the one who's been trying to harm me." All without giving her father a name.

Fenwick's face darkened. "Do they have any idea who?"

"I'm sure they do. But without proper evidence, I think they won't be releasing any names, even to the mayor." Especially to the mayor.

"Come stay with me," he entreated. "You know you're welcome."

Genuinely surprised, she smiled at him. "Thank you for the invite, but I'm really happy right where I am."

"With Hunter Black?"

"Yes. I really like him." That was as much as she was willing to say. Especially since she and Hunter hadn't even discussed the *L* word. Who knew if they ever would.

"I have to say, you do seem different," her father mused. "You glow with happiness, from the inside out. You're much more relaxed and even more confident."

"Wow." Touched, she swallowed. "That's high praise coming from you."

A look of regret crossed his face. "I haven't always

been the father you needed, I know. I'm sorry for that. I promise to try to do better."

Not sure how to respond to that, Layla looked down. Part of her wondered a bit cynically if Fenwick was just saying what he thought she wanted to hear in order to get her to agree to take over his mess. This line of thought made her feel guilty, but then again, she knew her father.

"You know what?" he asked, his tone brusque. "Forget I said anything about the accounting department. I'm sure I can find someone qualified from within the ranks. Dan will know who's his best employee."

Again, another button pusher. Layla had always had a competitive nature and Fenwick knew it.

Refusing to react the way he no doubt wanted her to, Layla nodded instead. "So, you're saying you want me to continue to head up marketing and sales?"

"I'm saying you should do whatever makes you happy," he replied, surprising her. "If you want to leave Colton Energy and go do something else, then you have my blessing. If you want to stay, whether it's in your current position or in another, I'll be happy. But in the end, it should be your choice. I've spent way too many years asking far too much of you. I've bullied and coerced, and I'm done. You're my daughter. I never should have treated you that way. It ends now."

Tears stung the back of her eyes, and her throat closed with emotion. He had no idea how long she'd waited to hear words like that from him.

And he wasn't finished.

"For the record, I'm glad you found your young man. I know I might not always act like it, but I love you, Layla. If Hunter Black makes you happy, then that's all that matters."

Touched despite herself, she managed a nod. She couldn't actually get any words out. If she tried, she knew she'd start crying.

Instead she took a moment to collect her tattered emotions. Finally, she felt under control and raised her gaze to meet her father's. "Thank you. That means a lot to me."

He nodded awkwardly. For one moment, she thought he might come out from behind his desk and give her a hug, but he only shuffled some papers instead.

"You've given me a lot to consider." She turned and started for her office before thinking of one other question. "If I do end up taking the accounting position, who are we going to move into mine? I know a few viable candidates, but I don't want to take anyone from the sales force. We need all the sales we can get."

"I agree." Studying her, he then said words she'd never thought she'd hear coming from him. "If you do end up taking the position, I'll leave that decision up to you. You know better than anyone what's needed for that job. I have confidence you can find the best person to do it."

"Thanks." Hurrying back to her office, she went around her desk and took a seat. Clasping her hands together, she tried to collect her thoughts. This all felt surreal and completely unexpected. She'd come in today without the slightest idea if she wanted to resign and pursue a career in police K9 training or not.

Now, she saw quite clearly what she had to do. Correction. What she *wanted* to do. She'd see if Colton

Energy could be saved and then she'd make her father an offer. Either he'd agree to step down to an advisory role and let her take over, or she'd move on.

Chapter 17

Finally, just as Hunter had decided to head directly down to their tech specialist's office, his phone rang. Internal call. And yes, Katie Parsons, the tech wizard, wondered if he had a moment.

"I'll be right there," Hunter blurted, dropping the phone into its cradle and pushing back his chair. Not wanting to attract unnecessary attention, he forced himself to walk casually, at least until he left the squad room. Once he reached the long hall, he broke into a trot. All he could think was how badly he hoped something good had been on those storage devices.

"Have a seat," Katie said, motioning at Hunter to shut the door. Young and brilliant at her job, unconventional Katie had lavender-colored hair this week, tipped with black at the ends. Hunter liked it.

He dropped in the chair, leaning forward. "Tell me what you found."

"Random stuff. The first thumb drive appeared to be photos he'd taken of his sports memorabilia collection, maybe for insurance purposes. We went through all that. It was boring as hell, so I assigned it to my assistant." Katie flashed her perfect white teeth in a grin.

Struggling to hide his disappointment, Hunter nodded. "Please tell me you found something better on the rest of the stuff."

"Oh, we did. But I'm not sure it's exactly what you were hoping for. We found evidence—hard proof—that Devlin Harrington hacked Layla Colton's texts and emails. He also hired Mark Hatton to lie about Layla sexually harassing him and photoshopped a couple of pictures to make them appear sexual. He kept copies of everything. All the documentation is there, in black and white."

"I knew it." Hunter swore. "Did you see any evidence in there about Devlin hiring someone to try to kill Layla?"

"No. But there were a few emails between the two men where Devlin is encouraging Mark to take her out. He stopped just short of offering to pay him money. It seems clear Mark is acting on his own. From what I could tell from reading the emails, he despises Layla Colton and everything she represents. Devlin's not too fond of her, either, though he appears to resent her impending marriage to his father. He's not only worried about losing his inheritance, but control of their company. There's a lot of personal information in those emails. I'm sure Hamlin Harrington won't be too happy when he learns about this."

Hunter thought of Hamlin's threats and smiled.

"Tough. I'll send a team to round up Mark Hatton. Or hell, maybe I'll do it myself. What else did you find?"

Katie nodded. "The remainder of the stuff on the other storage drives was all about Haley Patton. Photos, lots of them. Most clearly were taken without her consent or knowledge. And detailed notes of conversations, texts and such. I'm thinking we need to send a team to sweep her place for cameras and listening devices. I'm positive we'll find several."

"I'll let the chief know. Is that everything?"

"Yep. I know you were hoping for something concrete, information that would prove Devlin Harrington is the Groom Killer, but I really think this is a lot."

"It is." Hunter pushed to his feet and held out his hand. "Thanks, Katie."

"You're welcome. I'll email Chief Colton a full report and I'll copy you. Let me know if you need anything else."

After stopping in the chief's office to brief him, Hunter called Haley Patton and left a message. He didn't want to alarm her, so he didn't say anything concrete, just that he needed to stop by. He'd bring a couple of the best tech guys he knew and Goose and together they'd do a thorough sweep of her place.

"Hey, Hunter." Tim grabbed his arm as he walked past. "Bad news. Devlin Harrington bonded out."

"Disappointing, but not surprising. That's okay, we'll get him."

Tim nodded. "We'll just keep building the case."

Hunter decided he'd head over to the K9 training center and tell Layla about Mark Hatton in person.

But when he arrived, he learned she hadn't been

there at all. Pushing back a niggling worry, he pulled out his phone and called her.

The call rang and went to voice mail. He left a message. Again that prickling of foreboding at the back of his neck. Now was not the time to start ignoring his instincts. He drove to his house first, but when he didn't see her car, he drove to her town house.

She wasn't there, either. Then where? On the off chance that she'd decided to head in to Colton Energy, he headed there. Bingo. Her car was one of the few in the mostly empty parking lot. Even the most dedicated workers stayed away on the four-day weekend of Thanksgiving.

Hurrying through the unlocked front doors, he frowned at the lack of a security guard manning the front desk. When he'd worked there, Fenwick Colton had been vigilant about security. At least, Hunter thought, glancing around the lobby, the security cameras were still in place. Maybe the guard had left to patrol or something.

Taking the elevator, Hunter headed to Layla's office. He felt confident she still had the same one, right next to her father's executive suite.

When he arrived, her office was empty. But her computer was still on, and he spied her purse on the credenza behind her desk. Which meant she was around here somewhere.

He went to find her. Fenwick's office was dark and the door was closed, which Hunter expected. But as he moved past, he heard a scraping sound and a bump from inside.

Once more, he felt that tingling on the back of his neck. Drawing his weapon, he tried the door.

Unlocked. That didn't seem right. Briefly, he moved away and made a quick call, requesting backup. Once that had been confirmed, he went back to Fenwick's office. While it might seem wise to wait for reinforcements, the tingling at the back of his neck had intensified, letting him know he had to act immediately. He wasn't sure how or why, but he knew Layla was in danger.

Stepping to the side, he turned the knob and pushed the door inward with a crash. "I'm coming in," he declared, keeping himself behind the wall. If he were to stand in the open doorway, with the light behind him, he'd been an easy target. "Coming in," he repeated. Then he waited.

Nothing. Not a sound.

Still not quite convinced, he reached around the corner and flipped the light switch on. "I'm coming in," he declared again. If this turned out to be nothing, good. But his gut told him otherwise.

He spotted a vase of artificial flowers on the carpeted floor. Most likely that falling over had been what he'd heard. But what had knocked it to the ground?

A muffled cry made him spin, weapon still drawn. Layla, eyes wide with terror, hands, ankles and her mouth bound with what looked like duct tape. And Mark Hatton, holding her in front of him like a shield, had a gun to her head.

"You're just in time," Mark sneered. "I'm not missing my chance to kill her this time. There's a lot of money waiting for me once I finish this job. Unless you want me to shoot her right now, you need to lower your pistol."

"No." Instead, Hunter kept his weapon trained on

the other man. The mere fact that Mark hadn't shot her immediately meant he might still be torn about committing murder. "We found evidence that Devlin Harrington has been paying you. But only to claim Layla sexually harassed you. Not to get rid of her. From the emails and texts we saw, that was all you. You won't make any money by murdering an innocent woman."

Mark narrowed his eyes. "I don't care what you claim to have. I'm tired of people who think they know everything. You don't know me."

"I do know you don't really want to kill Layla. How would her death benefit you?"

"Benefit me?" Mark laughed, a humorless sound. "Life would be a lot better without her in it, I can tell you that."

Hunter took a tiny step forward, taking care to make the movement slight and barely noticeable. "Have you ever taken another human being's life?" he asked. "It's not like watching a movie or playing a video game. It's messy—lots of blood and brains if you make a headshot."

His graphic words made Layla blanch, but he forced himself to ignore it. Right now he had one task—to convince Mark to put down his gun and let Layla go free. Unharmed.

"I'm not afraid of a little blood and guts," Mark boasted. "Though I'd rather have run her over, whatever works, right? I almost took out old man Colton, too, but he left just in the nick of time. I got no beef with him. He's a decent boss. I really only need to kill his daughter."

Eyes wide, nostrils flaring as she struggled to breathe with duct tape over her mouth, Layla continued to hold herself perfectly still, as if the slightest movement might provoke her captor to pull the trigger.

Right now, with a pistol pressed against her temple, Hunter didn't blame her.

"Yep. Layla Colton has got to die." Mark stated again. Thankfully, he didn't appear in any hurry to actually kill her.

Good. Because right now, taking him down wasn't an option. Not with his finger on the trigger and the gun right against Layla's forehead.

Where the hell was that backup?

Stalling for time, Hunter considered him. "Why? Other than Devlin Harrington wanting her gone, what has she ever done to you?"

"You want a list?" A tic worked in Mark's jaw. "I should have her job, not her. I'm better educated, better qualified and more likable. But no, daddy's girl gets whatever she wants, even at the expense of the company. And because she knew it, she dared to start to make a case fire me."

Layla straightened, her blue eyes flashing. Despite the clear danger, she appeared to be attempting to speak through the tape covering her mouth. Fortunately, all that she could manage were a series of grunts.

In the distance Hunter could hear the sound of a siren. Finally.

Mark heard it, too. He swore, muttering to himself under his breath.

"You might as well put your gun down and surrender," Hunter pointed out, praying the other man didn't panic and shoot Layla instead. Heart hammering in his chest, he moved forward again, while Mark alternated frantic looks at the window and the door.

"Hatton?" Hunter pressed. "Surrender. You're not getting out of this alive unless you do. They're almost here. You haven't got a lot of time to decide."

All the while he watched Mark closely, waiting and hoping for a chance while his attention was diverted.

There. The slightest loosening of his grip on the pistol, allowing the weapon to sag. Not enough, since Layla would still get shot.

"Hatton!" Hunter barked. The other man jumped, pivoting instinctively.

Now. Hunter launched himself forward, chopping his arm up at Mark's. The gun discharged just as Hunter's momentum carried him forward. He knocked the other man to the floor, adrenaline pumping. Since Mark had dropped the pistol, Hunter pushed it away with his foot and then got about the business of subduing the smaller man.

He'd just cuffed him when Tim and another member of the team rushed through the door.

"We heard a shot…" Quickly, Tim took in the scene.

"Here. Read him his rights." Hunter shoved Mark at them and turned to take care of Layla. The only way to get the duct tape off was to rip it, so he muttered an apology as he did exactly that. She winced but held still while he freed her hands and feet.

Finally, he gathered her into his arms and held her close. "You're safe," he told her, feeling her body begin to shake. "Probably in shock. Let's get you to the EMT—Tim, did you call them?"

Tim nodded. "We called in shots fired. The ambulance should be here any minute."

On cue, another siren sounded in the distance.

"Come on." Releasing her, Hunter caught sight of a

large amount of blood on the front of her shirt. "Layla?" he asked. "Are you hurt?"

"What?" She looked down at herself, then back at him. "No. Hunter, you are. That blood is yours."

The moment he realized she was right, he felt it. Pain radiating from his right shoulder. "We need to stop the bleeding," he began.

"How? Tell me what to do."

He opened his mouth to speak, but a wave of dizziness stopped him.

"The EMTs are here," Tim announced. "They're on their way up. Let them take care of him."

Layla helped Hunter into a chair. The pain had blossomed all over, radiating from his shoulder to his chest to his throat. He tried to look down, to see exactly how badly he'd been wounded, but even the slightest movement made his vision go gray.

"Wait here," she ordered. Then, leaning close, she spoke directly into his ear. "Don't you dare die on me, Hunter Black. I love you too much to lose you."

Two EMTs rushed into the room and took over. Layla stepped back, heart racing. She knew nothing about gunshot wounds, but she figured being shot in the shoulder was at least better than the chest or head. The sheer amount of blood worried her more than anything. At least he seemed to be in capable hands.

Still, watching the paramedics wheel Hunter away was one of the hardest things she had ever done. She tried to go after them, intending on riding with him in the ambulance to the hospital, but one of the police officers stopped her. She recognized him since he'd arrested her when Mark Hatton had made his false claims. Tim Lakely.

"I'm sorry," he said. "But we're going to need your statement first. Once we're through here, I'll drive you to the hospital myself."

Barely able to contain her anxiety, she nodded. "Let's do this quickly, then. I don't want him to go through this alone."

"He won't be alone, ma'am. Chief Colton is on his way there, as are several others from our unit. I think some of the county police will show up, too. That's one thing about working in law enforcement. We're all family. When one of us goes down, the rest rush to show support."

Touched, she managed a smile, though it felt a bit wobbly around the edges. She told him what had happened, how she'd been tidying up her desk with the intention of going home. Her father had just left when the security guard called to let her know he was ill and would be in the men's room. "He never came back."

Tim motioned the other officer over and repeated what she'd said, asking him to check the men's room. Once he'd left, Tim asked her to continue.

"I thought no one else was in the building, at least on this floor. That's why I was surprised to look up and see Mark Hatton in the doorway to my father's office." She swallowed hard and began to shake. Realizing this, she also realized she felt detached, as if she was viewing everything from a great distance.

She looked up to find Tim eyeing her with a sympathetic expression. "Sorry," she apologized. "I can't seem to help this."

"It's okay. Perfectly normal. You've just been

through a traumatic experience. You're probably in shock. Let me finish taking your statement so I can get you to the hospital. I think you should get checked out, too, just in case."

Though she nodded, she had no intention of doing anything except getting herself to Hunter's side as quickly as possible.

She told him the rest, the ugly things Mark had called her, the venom in his voice, the vitriol in his eyes. When he'd pulled a gun, she'd thought he was about to shoot her right then, but instead he'd put duct tape over her mouth, made her tie up her own ankles and forced her to kneel on the floor with her hands behind her while he bound her wrists.

"I figured he was going to execute me, right there on the carpet in my office." Her trembling intensified. "And then Hunter arrived."

Tim carefully noted everything she said and thanked her. "Come on," he told her, gently putting his arm around her shoulders and steering her toward the elevator. "Let's head up to the hospital."

When they pulled into the emergency room parking lot, she saw police cars. So many of them, her heart sank.

Something of how she felt must have shown on her face.

"It's okay," Tim said. "They're all just here to show their support. And look." He pointed, directing her attention to two news vans from Sioux Falls. "There will be reporters. You don't have to speak to them if you don't want to."

"I don't." Glad of her heavy down parka, she once again willed the trembling to stop. It wasn't just her hands—that would have been bearable—but a deeper, more wild kind of shaking, as if she trembled from the inside out. So far, she'd been able to make it subside a little, but the second she relaxed, it came back with a vengeance.

Tim parked and they both got out. The wind had picked up and carried the taste of snow. Heads down, side by side, they hurried through the hospital entrance. The triage nurse, seeing Tim's uniform, buzzed them in and directed them to the small internal waiting room.

Once there, Chief Finn Colton spotted them and pushed to his feet. He greeted Tim and pulled Layla in for a hug. "Hunter is going to be all right," he told her. "The bullet passed right through and didn't hit any major organs. He'll have a bit of muscle loss in that shoulder, but once he's healed up, he can do physical therapy."

Relief hit her, so powerful her knees went weak. If not for her cousin's support, she would have fallen. "Thank you," she managed. "He saved my life, you know."

"Are you okay?" the chief asked. "Maybe we should have you checked out, just in case."

"That's what I said," Tim interjected. "Let me go talk to one of the nurses real quick."

"No, wait." Layla stepped back. "I need to see Hunter first. Can someone show me where he is?"

"I'll show you," Chief Colton said, touching her arm. "I just left him. Come with me."

He led her down the hall, toward room nine. Another officer who sat in the chair next to the bed rose when he saw them and exited the room, stopping briefly to speak to the chief.

"I'll leave you two alone." Chief Colton lightly squeezed her shoulder before following his officer back to the waiting room.

Heart hammering in her chest, Layla entered the small room. Machines beeped and the room smelled of antiseptic. Hunter's eyes were closed and his shoulder and arm had been bandaged. He looked comfortable, which was good, and so damn handsome the sight of him made her chest ache.

She dropped into the chair next to the bed and took several deep breaths. Just being near him calmed her, steadied her unsettled nerves. Taking his hand, she simply held on, willing strength into this brave, strong man. He'd saved her, in more ways than one. His arrival in her life had shown her the importance of truly living and given her the once-in-a-lifetime experience of knowing true, deep and forever love.

Even if he didn't feel the same way.

"Layla?"

Startled, she realized he'd opened his eyes. Blue so bright it seemed to glow.

"I'm right here," she said, still holding his hand.

"Hey." Judging from his lopsided smile, he'd been given some pain medication. "Today was a good day."

Okay. She decided to go with it. "Was it?"

"Yeah. We're 99 percent certain we know the identity of the Groom Killer."

"Only 99 percent? Not one hundred?" Half teasing, half serious, she kept her tone light.

"For right now, unfortunately. But we're working on rectifying that. And we have proof Mark made up the sexual harassment charges. You'll be cleared of that soon."

"That *is* good news."

"I know, right?" He turned up the wattage in that smile, turning her insides to mush. "And best of all, now that we know Mark was the one trying to kill you, you're not in danger anymore. You can even move back home now."

Just like that, with those words, reality came crashing down. She froze, battling a sudden urge to cry. "Of course," she managed, aware she needed to thank him for all he'd done for her.

"But Layla…" The twinkle of mischief in his gaze confused her. "I'd much rather you stay."

"Seriously?" Was he teasing her? Or did he really mean he wanted to make something temporary a bit more permanent?

"Yes, seriously, you silly, beautiful, intelligent, perfect woman."

"Maybe we should have this discussion when you're not on powerful pain medications," she offered, attempting to stifle the pure joy flooding through her veins.

"I'm perfectly sober," he protested, even as his eyes drifted closed.

Just like that, he'd fallen asleep.

Heart full of love, she continued to sit with him until Tim came to remind her someone needed to go home and take care of Goose. "I'll stay with him," Tim offered. "I'm thinking they'll probably discharge him soon. They haven't said they're admitting him, so it looks like he'll get to go home."

"Then I'll wait," she replied. But then she thought of Goose, home alone, and relented. "He'd want me to let Goose out, so I'm going to run and do that. Will you call me if anything changes while I'm gone?"

"Of course."

She drove home, realizing as she pulled up in the driveway that Hunter's house had become more of a home to her than her town house had ever been.

Unlocking the door, she crouched down to greet Goose. The sweetest, smartest dog in the world welcomed her as effusively as ever—tail wagging, body wiggling, giving little doggy kisses until Layla finished ruffling her fur and got up. With Goose following her, she opened the back door to let Goose out.

While the little dog tended to business, Layla found herself wandering around Hunter's house. For whatever reason, she felt nostalgic and raw. Maybe she should go home now that it was safe to do so. After all, she couldn't continue to wear out her welcome here.

While that sounded practical and realistic, the idea brought unbearable sadness. Going home to her empty town house, only able to see Hunter and Goose when they made plans to get together, such a thing felt untenable.

Too bad Hunter hadn't been himself when he'd asked her to stay. She shook her head. *Foolish* wasn't a word she would ever use to describe herself. Time to come back down to earth and go back to her regular life. If things between her and Hunter were meant to be, everything would eventually work out in the end.

After letting Goose in, she poured some kibble in the dog's bowl and made sure there was plenty of water. That accomplished, she considered going ahead and packing her things, but she decided to wait until Hunter was home and settled in. He might need help for the first couple of days, and she wanted to be there for him the same way he'd been for her. That's what friends did.

Her phone rang. Tim, letting her know Hunter had been discharged and as soon as the paperwork was signed, Tim would bring him home. Layla promised to wait and then, once she'd ended the call, she wondered if she should try to prepare some sort of meal. She'd never been much of a cook, but she figured she could make sandwiches or something.

As she rummaged through the refrigerator, her stomach growled, reminding her that it had been a long time since her vending machine snack of mixed nuts. Since she had no idea how long it would take before the hospital processed the discharge paperwork, she made a sandwich and wolfed it down. She made a couple more, wrapped them in cellophane and put them in the fridge in case Hunter or Tim wanted one.

An hour later, as she and Goose snuggled on the couch watching TV, headlights illuminated the front window as a car swung into the driveway. Layla jumped up, Goose right behind her, and went to the front door.

With Tim beside him, Hunter walked up the sidewalk under his own power. Her breath caught, any greeting she might have wanted to say stuck in her throat. Joy flooded her and she couldn't stop smiling. She reached for him, meaning to hug him, but caught sight of his bandaged shoulder and pulled back at the last moment.

"Hey," he said, smiling at her. At his feet, Goose danced around, performing her exuberant greeting. He managed to reach down and scratch her neck before straightening back up and moving toward the sofa.

Tim hung back, close to the doorway. "He seems fine," he told her, sotto voce. "I've got to run, but you've got my number. Give me a call if you need anything."

After seeing Tim out, she returned to the living room. Goose had attached herself to Hunter's side, her doggy expression full of contentment.

"Would you like a sandwich?" she asked. "I made a couple ahead of time."

"No, thank you. Not yet." He looked at her, his gaze clear and unclouded. "I'm in a little bit of pain."

Which meant whatever they'd given him earlier had worn off. Immediately, she moved toward him. "Did they give you some meds for home? I can get you a glass of water so you can take them."

"Wait." He held up his hand. "I want to talk to you first. Will you sit with me?"

That sounded ominous, like his next sentence might begin with *It's not you, it's me.*

Gingerly, she sat. Her stomach churned and she braced herself, instinctively anticipating bad news.

"I realized something important today when I saw that maniac holding a gun to your head."

All she could do was nod encouragement.

"I can't even begin to envision a life without you in it," he said. "When I thought I might lose you, all the color leached out of the world." He swallowed hard, clearly struggling to find the right words to convey whatever he was trying to say. He moved slightly and flinched, revealing his pain. "I've never felt such agony—grief, really—in my life."

The hurt he struggled to hide made her ache. More

than anything, she wished she could somehow ease that, take it away.

"Let me get you something so you can take a pain pill," she urged.

"In a minute. It's not that bad."

She nodded and stayed put. Though she knew it would be better for him to take something and get ahead of the pain, it was also his choice.

"I'm trying to ask you something important, Layla. Without medication, so you can't say I'm not clear-headed." He took a deep breath. "We've just about for certain caught the Groom Killer. Once he's charged, this town can start having weddings again."

Whatever she'd thought he might say, that wasn't it. She forced herself to hold still and waited to hear the rest.

"I don't have a ring, but I'm asking if you'll marry me." He shifted and then grimaced at the pain the movement brought. "I can't even get down on one knee, but Layla Colton, will you do the honor of agreeing to become my wife?"

Instead of answering, she started to cry.

Clearly concerned, he made two attempts to push himself up and go to her, succeeding the second time. Though he moved awkwardly, he sat down next to her. "That's not the reaction I was hoping for," he pointed out gently. "But I get it. You just got out of one engagement and you need some space and time to—"

"Hush." She shushed him with a soft kiss. "Don't you be trying to put words in my mouth. I'm crying because I'm so happy. I love you with all my heart, Hunter Black. And yes, I will definitely agree to become your wife. But first, let me get you some water so you can take a pain pill. We'll talk about this more once you've had some rest."

He laughed. "Does that mean we're engaged?"

Though she'd already pushed to her feet and headed toward the kitchen, she pivoted back and kissed him again. "As long as you promise to let Goose be in our wedding, yes. We are engaged."

Goose perked up at the sound of her name and whined.

Hunter ruffled her fur and smiled at Layla. "Now I know I definitely picked the right woman," he said.

"Was there ever any doubt?" And Layla went to get him his water. There'd be plenty of time to make plans. Right now, Hunter needed to heal. And she'd do her best to help him do exactly that.

* * * * *

*Look out for
the final installment of the
Coltons of Red Ridge miniseries,
Colton's Fugitive Family
by Jennifer Morey,
available in December 2018!*

*And don't miss the previous
Coltons of Red Ridge stories,
all available now from
Harlequin Romantic Suspense!*

The Pregnant Colton Witness *by Geri Krotow*
Colton's Twin Secrets *by Justine Davis*
His Forgotten Colton Fiancée *by Bonnie Vanak*
Colton's Cinderella Bride *by Lisa Childs*
The Colton Cowboy *by Carla Cassidy*
Colton and the Single Mom *by Jane Godman*
Colton K-9 Bodyguard *by Lara Lacombe*
Colton's Deadly Engagement *by Addison Fox*
Colton Baby Rescue *by Marie Ferrarella*

She wasn't accustomed to sharing a bed with anyone.

Irritated, she flopped onto her back, trying to find a comfortable position.

"Are you going to do that all night?" Xander asked.

"Sorry. I'm not used to having company in my bed," she groused. "And you take up more than your share."

"I promise I don't have cooties."

"I know that."

He chuckled. "Then relax."

"It's not that…" She risked a glance toward him. "It's because…there's history between us."

"One time does not history make," Xander said. "Or so I'm told."

She wasn't going to argue the point. Exhaling, she deliberately closed her eyes and rolled to her side, plumping up her pillow and settling once again.

A long beat of silence followed until Xander said, "Do you really regret that much what happened between us?"

That was a loaded question—one she didn't want to answer. She regretted being messed up in the head, which made it impossible to trust, which in turn made her a nightmare to be in a relationship with. Not that she wanted anything real with Xander.

Or anyone.

Her silence seemed an answer in itself. "I guess so," Xander replied with a sigh. "That's an ego-buster."

Scarlett turned to glare at him. "Did you ever think maybe it has nothing to do with you?" she said, unable to just let him think whatever he liked. For some reason, it mattered with Xander. "Look, aside from the fact that I'm your boss…I'm just not the type to form unnecessary attachments. Trust me, it's better that way. For everyone involved."

Every time she ignored her instincts and allowed something to happen, it ended badly.

"I'm not cut out for relationships."

"Me, either."

His simple agreement coaxed a reluctant chuckle out of her. "Yeah? Two peas in a pod, I guess."

"Or two broken people with too many sharp edges to be allowed around normal people."

"Ain't that the truth," she agreed, the tension lifting a little. She turned to face him, tucking her arm under her head. "Maybe that's why we're so good at what we do… We can compartmentalize like world-class athletes without blinking an eye."

"Mental boxes for everything," Xander returned with a half grin. They were joking but only sort of. That was the sad reality that they both recognized. "I know why I'm broken, but what's your story, Rhodes?"

This was around the time she usually shut down. But that feeling of safety had returned and she found herself sharing, even when she didn't want to.

Don't miss
Soldier for Hire *by Kimberly Van Meter,*
available December 2018 wherever
Harlequin® Romantic Suspense books
and ebooks are sold.

www.Harlequin.com

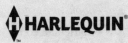

Love Harlequin romance?

DISCOVER.

Be the first to find out about promotions,
news and exclusive content!

Facebook.com/HarlequinBooks

Twitter.com/HarlequinBooks

Instagram.com/HarlequinBooks

Pinterest.com/HarlequinBooks

ReaderService.com

EXPLORE.

Sign up for the Harlequin e-newsletter and
download a free book from any series at
TryHarlequin.com.

CONNECT.

Join our Harlequin community to share
your thoughts and connect with other
romance readers!
Facebook.com/groups/HarlequinConnection

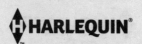

HARLEQUIN®

**ROMANCE WHEN
YOU NEED IT**

HSOCIAL2018